Dying
To Date

**Love, betrayal, murder—
a great first date**

Sharmyn McGraw

THE DYING SERIES | BOOK ONE

Dying To Date, The Dying Series, Book One
by Sharmyn McGraw

Book Design: Nick Zelinger, NZ Graphics
Editing: Lillian Nader, M.Ed.

Published by

www.sharmynmcgraw.com

ISBN: 978-1-7326721-1-6 (Print)
ISBN: 978-1-7326721-2-3 (E-Book)
Library of Congress Control Number: 2020919353

First Edition

Printed in USA

I dedicate this book to my heroes who helped get my health back and my life back as well. "Pituitary Tumors—The Best Kept Secret in Medicine." Studies show pituitary tumors and related hormonal disorders affect 1 in 5 adults. For more information on brain, pituitary and skull base tumors: Daniel F. Kelly, MD President & CEO, Pacific Neuroscience Institute Foundation Pejman Cohan, MD Specialized Endocrine Care Center

Working with my editor, Lillian Nader, has been a joy. I value her patience and expertise. Lillian, thank you for all you do.

Every writer should be so lucky to have a proper British friend like Adam Barak. He's kind, supportive, and a brilliant comedian. "You've written a great murder mystery, and you haven't murdered the English language."

CHAPTER ONE

*F*ocus. *You're not naked, Kristina.* It's not like she'd ever gone in public without clothes on—well, with one exception: underwear—but who hasn't left a boyfriend's house with their sexy lace panties strategically tucked under his pillow at least once? Kristina took a deep inhale through her nose and then a cleansing exhale through her mouth. Calmer now, she secured her battery pack to the back of her waistband, clipped the portable headset behind her ear, and adjusted the microphone alongside her cheek.

She tucked her well-pressed blouse into her buttery soft, black leather skirt. Listening for her musical cue, Kristina waited outside of the conference room while her event manager hyped the crowd.

Kristina closed her eyes to visualize the room filled with loving friends. A rush of adrenalin pulsed through her veins. *Relax. Stay focused. Don't go there.* A news headline from the past flashed before her eyes in giant black letters: "Scorned Lover Releases Sex Videos with Relationship Guru, Kristina Truly." The brazen image dangled in Kristina's head. *Breathe in through my nose; hold it … Breathe out through my mouth.*

Two years ago, she had stopped seeing her therapist and started "seeing" her therapist, Randolph Joxhel, PsyD.

Unbeknownst to Kristina, her new boyfriend must have videotaped their fiery sexcapades in his office with a hidden video camera. During her fourth therapy session, they took their client-therapist relationship to a sexual relationship. However, their six-week romance ended after the sexy shrink turned dangerous. He paid Kristina an uninvited visit late one night, through her downstairs window. Asleep upstairs in her bedroom, she woke to noises moving up her creaky staircase. She scrambled for her Taser gun in the nightstand next to her bed. Heavy footsteps slapped down the hallway toward her bedroom. Aimed and loaded, she waited with a steady trigger finger. A tall, thin figure entered the doorway. The prowler flipped the light switch on the wall near the door and yelled, "Surprise." That was an understatement. Utter fear morphed into fucking furious when she recognized who the intruder was. Dressed in some kinky bondage garb, Randolph stood there wearing a corseted, black leather bustier and a gold metal chastity belt with his penis locked in a cage. Through a clenched jaw, and a myriad of choice words, Kristina made it clear they were through. Wanting to spare him public humiliation, she agreed not to involve the police. Randolph returned the favor by hacking her social media.

The next morning, her phone blew up with text messages and phone calls from friends and the news media. Randolph posted their sex videos on Instagram, Facebook, and Twitter but protected his own identity by not showing his face attached to the male body entangled with hers. Shining at all angles, Kristina was the star of the show. In less than twenty-four hours, the sex tapes went viral across the Internet. The Feds froze his assets and opened an investigation, which led to finding out a lot more about the sick doctor. Having his medical license revoked was the least of his problems. But with the unpredictable magic of social media, Kristina's popularity skyrocketed. Until the videos hit the net, she was an unknown life coach and facilitated small motivational workshops in a makeshift banquet room at the local YMCA. It was a slow time for celebrity breakups and political scandals, so all news outlets had a heyday with her story.

Overnight, she'd become a relationship sensation and shocked everyone who knew her, herself included. In the past forty-two years, Kristina never picked the right man. Yet now, in the era of trendy social apps and fake news, she'd become a highly sought-after relationship expert. Kristina admitted the newfound fame and the large cash settlement her ex-boyfriend paid out lessened the sting of her highly publicized humiliation. Her attorney acted fast to get the videos off the World Wide Web, but as everyone knows, nothing is ever off the Internet.

However, with her *Finding True Love* relationship self-help books on the *New York Times* bestseller list and her work-shops selling out months in advance, she'd tried putting all that chaos behind her to focus on her booming career. But every time Kristina took the stage, like today, a wave of embarrassment heated up her spine. The fact was, like it or not, most of the audience had seen her naked, having sex on a couch with Dr. Sicko in the middle of the day in High Definition.

Kristina pulled herself together and continued through her mental checklist. *Damn. Where are the workbooks?* She said out loud to no one. Doing a quick about-face, she speed-walked to the hotel's foyer.

"Angel. Angel." In a loud whisper, Kristina beckoned her business partner/assistant/best friend. Without acknowledgment, Angel continued talking on her cell phone.

"I'll be home around seven-thirty tonight, and you better not be asleep in that recliner with the television babysitting your children. I mean it, Jermaine."

Kristina hushed her voice, "Angel, please. I need your help." She hiked her skirt up and bent down on her hands and knees to have a look under the eight-foot-long registration table. She needed to find the participant workbooks on *Committing to a Healthier, Loving Relationship* that was part of her motivational symposium. She crawled under the table.

"Baby, put Daddy back on the phone. Jermaine, I gotta get back to work. You heard what I said." Angel hit the disconnect button on her cell phone four times with her index finger as if hitting it harder each time got her point across that much better.

With a sharp tone, Angel informed Kristina, "I was having an important discussion with my husband about his parenting responsibilities."

"Discussion . . . argument . . . sounded the same to me." Kristina slid a heavy box out from under the table.

Angel snatched the box from the floor, slamming it down on top of the table above Kristina's already pounding head.

"Well, you're not married. You don't know what it takes to make a living, raise three kids, and hope you don't kill their father when he leaves the milk carton on the damn kitchen counter overnight to get sour."

Focused on finding what she needed, Kristina shouted from under the table, "Are these my workbooks?"

Angel rolled her eyes and shook her head, irritated. "No. Kristina, stop. The people from the conference next door asked to store their boxes while they get their table set up." Angel dropped another box on the tabletop.

"Ouch. Angel, it feels like you're slamming the boxes on my head." Kristina climbed out from under the table. She yanked her skirt back down over her thighs and took a deep breath. "Where are my workbooks? We need them. Pronto." Kristina snapped her fingers toward Angel. In the same nanosecond, she regretted it. Since the second grade, Angel and Kristina had been best friends, and Angel had zero patience when Kristina barked orders like a prima donna.

Wide-eyed, Angel stared at Kristina, who stood there with a very, *Oh Shit, I'm so sorry,* look on her face. With no urgency, Angel placed her cell phone in the side pouch of her purse. She faced Kristina with pitched eyebrows. "Yesterday, I stuffed two hundred of your *Happy Relationships, Happy Life* workbooks into the new swag tote bags we spent a bloody fortune on to have printed for this conference. Everyone got a bag at check-in." Angel doubled down with two quick snaps of her fingers. "KT, what the hell's going on with you lately? The past few days, you've really lost your focus. We talked about this. It'll save time on large conferences if everyone gets their workshop materials when they check in at registration instead of passing them out during the first breakout session. Girl, get your diva ass on stage. As always, I've taken care of everything." Angel pretended to clear her throat. She swiped her thumb across Kristina's cheek. Her tone softened, "You smeared your make-up, crawling under that stupid table."

Kristina tapped herself on the forehead with her palm, "Holy shit, shit, shit." She took a deep breath and smoothed her hands across the front of her skirt. "Sorry Angel, I forgot about the new swag and the workbooks. My head isn't on straight. I can't stop thinking about my dad. Aunt Mimi says he's only got a few days left. I'm having a hard time wrapping my head around him being gone. I mean, gone-gone, dead, gone, forever. I know it won't change anything; he's unable to talk." Kristina babbled on, "He will never say he's sorry, and even if he did, what good would it do now? He's had thirty-five years, right? Why would lying on his deathbed change anything? But whatever; we'll see. I'm not sure if I'll go see him in the hospital or not." She tried to sort out the betrayal issues she had with her dad over the past three decades. This was all a moot point. He'd be dead soon.

Angel understood Kristina better than anyone else. Angel grew up in a stable home with a devoted father, unlike Kristina. "You're a hell of a person, girlfriend. I'd let his sorry-ass rot—" Angel stopped herself. She didn't need to finish what she started to say. They both knew how Angel felt about Kristina's father, and he deserved it. Angel smiled, putting both hands on Kristina's shoulders, pointing her toward the long corridor. "Go. Before the first break, I'll have the merch table set up and a table ready for your book signing. Oh wait, Jaclyn Renzo volunteered to help today and hasn't shown up yet. If she doesn't show, we'll be short-staffed. This is the second time Jaclyn's pulled a no show. Don't worry. I'll ask one of our regulars to step in. Get going. Knock 'em dead, KT."

Hoofing it down the hall, Kristina looked back over her shoulder toward Angel. "Jaclyn Renzo?" Kristina halted abruptly. "She's missing. This morning someone put a flier on my car window with her picture on it. Shit, I knew her name sounded familiar. I think she lives in my neighborhood. Wait—wasn't it Jaclyn whose ex-husband or boyfriend showed up at a workshop, and she gave him the slip out a back door?"

Angel glanced at her watch, "Yeah, that was Jaclyn. What the hell? She's missing? It was her ex-husband who showed up." Angel pointed her finger toward the conference room doors. "You need to get on stage—now. I'll make a call to the police station and let them know what we saw in case it helps find her."

"Thank you, Angel. Love you, girlfriend." Kristina puckered her mouth with a kiss in the air and hurried down the hall to the conference room. She waited behind the double doors. The tempo of the music climaxed, and she listened for her event manager's introduction.

"Let's welcome internationally best-selling author and world-renowned relationship expert, the beautiful, articulate, charismatic, and always in fashion, Ms. Kristina Truly."

Pushing the double doors wide open, she entered the room. The crowd stood to cheer. Smiling and waving like a pageant queen, Kristina took the stage.

The audience, after almost endless applause, finally silenced. With the enthusiasm of a high school cheerleader, Kristina addressed the group, "Ladies and gentlemen, thank you all for being here at my, *Perfect Relationships are For Perfect People—They Don't Exist,* workshop." The crowd cheered again for a moment, then allowed Kristina to continue. "I'm really excited to be here to help all of you learn to (Kristina put her hand to her ear, waiting for them to say it with her) 'Turn Your Pain into Passion—One Relationship at a Time.'"

"If you're dying to have a better relationship with your partner or meet the right mate, you will leave this workshop feeling self-empowered and ready to commit to a healthier, loving relationship with Mr. or Ms. Right—Not Mr. or Ms. Perfect."

Kristina heard loud chuckles coming from the audience, reassuring her that people liked what she had to say. "I'm confident what you learn here today will give you the tools to have the relationships of your dreams. I believe there is a Mr. or Ms. Right at the end of a very long rope of Mr. or Ms. Wrongs. But most of us have had to suffer a few rope burns along the way in our past relationships. So, let's commit to not only finding the one but to finding the right one because the knot at the end of the rope may be the one you tie with Mr. or Ms. 'I Do Love You.'"

The audience roared in agreement again, and Kristina graciously waited until the clapping stopped and then dug into the full-day marathon she'd created. She based the hours of material covered in her workshops and bestselling books on her years in college to earn her Bachelor of Arts degree in psychology, but what her students liked best was her teaching by example. Kristina shared openly about her fucked-up ability to pick the right men. She connected with her audience because she shared the ugly side of unhealthy relationships. She preached the mantra, *I Own My Shit; What Part Do I Play in My Messed-Up Life?* Kristina shared the hard lessons learned through her failures over the years while searching for her own healthier, loving relationships.

Helping hundreds of people find "the One—the Right One, felt to Kristina like getting to snuggle up with George Clooney while enjoying a frozen ice-cream Snickers bar after hours of heart pumping, tongue tangling, slippery sweat-dripping sex. It left her completely exhausted but wanting more.

CHAPTER TWO

"Chugga, chugga, woo, woo." Jolted awake by a whistling steam trumpet and a train's wheels clamoring down the tracks, Kristina's cellphone bellowed. The noise continued to blare while she patted down the top of the nightstand with one eye closed, searching for her phone.

"Damn it, Poodles." With a raspy morning voice, Kristina cursed her closest male friend of twenty-five years, FBI agent, Peter Esposito, aka, Poodles. "Ugh. Stop messing with my ringtones." She squinted to see the blue numbers on her bedside digital clock illuminating 5:32 a.m.

Kristina saw her aunt's name flash on her phone's screen. Her stomach knotted, suspecting the call could only be grave news at this unusual hour. "Hey, Aunt Mimi. Everything okay? What's going on?"

"Sweetheart, sorry to call so early. It's your dad. He's opened his eyes, and he's more coherent. He's not able to talk, but I thought you could go to the hospital and see him before his wife and kids show up this morning. The doctors say he probably won't make it through another day. KT, please do this for me. I think you'll regret it if you don't. God knows you don't owe him anything, but he's my only brother, and I love him even with all his faults. KT, you know how much I love you and Timmy." Aunt Mimi's voice cracked, holding back her grief. "All I've ever wanted was to see your dad make it up to you two for leaving, but sweetheart, now all I can hope for is that you'll find some way to forgive him and move on with your life. Please, hon, go see your dad."

Tears puddled in Kristina's eyes. "I love you. Thanks for letting me know about Dad. You're probably right. I should go. I'm having a hard time justifying forgiveness, Aunt Mimi. He walked out on us like we didn't even exist." Her throat tightened.

"I know, honey. He doesn't deserve even an ounce of your time, but forgiveness, or closure, whatever you want to call it, is for you, sweetheart, not him. I'll send you his room number at the hospital. If you don't go, I'll understand. I love you."

Snuggled deep beneath the down comforter, Kristina closed her eyes. Her tears rolled down the back of her neck, wetting her pillowcase. The sweet fragrance of night-blooming jasmine seeping through the slightly opened bedroom window usually lifted her mood but not this morning. Her thoughts were dark and bitter. Curled under the covers, a white ball of fluff, Ms. Prissy purred a calming melody. She took a long stretch, sprung her claws, and kneaded Kristina's shoulder like a loaf of unbaked bread dough.

"Ow, ow, ouch." Kristina slipped her hands around Prissy's paws. "All right. I'll go to the hospital. Please stop torturing me with your evil nails." Kristina threw the covers off and forced herself to get a move on. Nervous about seeing her father, she felt lightheaded. Slipping into her UGG slippers, she grasped the edge of the nightstand to steady herself. Ms. Prissy lay on her back, paws limp, unbothered. "You relax, my sweet missy-girl, while I try not to get sick to my stomach over this mess going on in my life." Kristina headed downstairs to the kitchen for a protein breakfast bar and an ice-cold sparkling Perrier with a splash of raspberry bitters to settle her stomach.

~~~~

The sun glistened over the distant hills as Kristina arrived at the hospital. Thoughts of seeing her father sank in, and her nerves started getting the best of her. *I'll stay long enough to say farewell, and that's it. I can do this.* Kristina headed to the nearest parking spots reserved for valet service near the entrance of the hospital. The attendant hurried to set up his wooden podium and broad yellow canvas umbrella to start the day. The lanky young man slipped into a red vest a few sizes too large. He motioned Kristina to pull her car forward, stopping her in front of the sign stating: Valet–$15.00 All Day. She powered down her car window.

"Hi, Ms., we open at seven. In about fifteen minutes." He glanced at his cellphone for the time. "Parking's free in the garage behind the ER, but you can leave your car right here. I'll park it in a few minutes." The valet tore off a claim stub from his pad and handed it to Kristina.

"I will only be a second. I'm saying hi to my fath—to someone. I mean, I won't be long." She heard her heart pounding in her ears and wondered if the young man heard it too.

"That's fine. I'll park your car right there. Take your time. I'll comp your parking; there's no hurry." The valet pointed to a parking spot directly in front of the hospital and opened her car door.

The car's right in front of the hospital, you can leave anytime. If seeing Dad is too painful, you can get in the car and drive away. You're fine. She stood next to her car with unsteady legs. Hesitating a minute, she took a deep breath and handed her keys to the parking attendant. "Thank you, that's very sweet of you. I promise I'll only be a few minutes."

~~~~

A text came through Kristina's phone from Aunt Mimi, "ICU room 305, bed A, next to the window." Now wasn't the time for justifying anger toward her father. She'd lose her nerve and head straight back home if she allowed Krissy, her broken-hearted eight-year-old inner child, to dictate her decision. *Stop thinking, get this over with, you need to see him for the last time, on your terms.* She jumped in the first open elevator and hit the third-floor button.

The early mornings were somber for most of the hospital. Other than the night shift nurses briefing the morning shift, there wasn't much action, but the Intensive Care Unit had a flow, unlike the other floors in the hospital. An abundance of critically ill patients had the ICU staff rushing to keep up. Wall plaques with room numbers and arrows pointed her down a corridor past a nurses' station. The faster the pace of everyone around her, the slower Kristina walked. She felt her cheeks warming, and her stomach triple knotting the closer she got to her father's room. Looking through the open door, Kristina vaguely recognized the emaciated, cancer-ridden man lying in the bed. The bald patches on her father's head made her throat tighten. Most of his hair had fallen out from the chemo treatments, but no one bothered to shave the few scraggly strands sticking out of his head. *A loving daughter would have cut your hair. Shame on all of you for not taking better care of him. I would have done that for you, Daddy.* She stood in the doorway, half in and half out.

Swooshing sounds from the respirator reminded her of when she and her father watched ships in the harbor. For a moment, she could taste the salty air of the ocean. Kristina heard the seagulls' cries along with the pump of his blood pressure cuff. Watching her father's chest expand in and out, she imagined the tide rushing in over their feet as her daddy scooped her up tightly in his arms to keep her dry. The nurse walked past Kristina, focused only on her patient, and perhaps the end of her twelve-hour shift.

"Mr. Truly, can you hear me?" The nurse projected her voice. "Mr. Truly, I'm going to change your bandages." She gripped his toes through the bedding to rouse his attention. His eyes fluttered but didn't open. Kristina walked closer. She stood inches away from her father, well hidden by the curtain pulled halfway for privacy. Kristina peeked at her father through a gap next to the wall. Right by his side, inches from her father, she wiped her nose with the cuff of her sweatshirt. Struggling not to gasp out loud, she cried in silence.

The nurse drew back the curtain, startling Kristina. "Oh,

Hello." The nurse waved her hand to get her attention. "Ms., are you here to see Mr. Truly?" Kristina stood there, speechless, with her mouth gaped. The nurse shrugged her shoulders and kept moving, checking her patient's vitals, and tucking his bed linens.

Kristina stared at her father, hooked up to tubes connected to clear plastic bags filled with medication fed by machines. This person wasn't the man imbedded in her memory that she'd held on to all those years.

The nurse glanced at Kristina while she typed notes on the portable computer. "Miss, you okay?"

With no expression, Kristina continued staring at the man in the bed. Her heart pleaded for one last moment with her hero, the father she remembered. But with every beat, a lifetime of painful memories sliced deeper as she looked at a frail old stranger.

Loud voices echoed from the doorway as a woman and two men entered the room. Not sure what to do, Kristina backed against the wall, disappearing behind the bunched curtain as her dad's other family trampled past her.

A slender woman of medium height, dressed in tight jeans with bedazzled pink rhinestone hearts on the back pockets, whipped back the curtain with authority. "Daddy, rise and shine. It's Mommy. Smells like he crapped the bed. Goddamn. It stinks in here. Nurse, clean him or something, for Chrissakes." She clicked her long red patent leather high heels across the vinyl floors like a prancing pony. Her tight, low-cut floral print blouse accented her firm, buxom breast implants. Her two sons in their mid-thirties, were almost as round as they were tall. The close resemblance to one another made it unclear who was older, although they were born a year apart.

Kristina waited until they were well inside the room, huddled around her father's bedside before she put her head down and slipped out of the room like the invisible man. She darted in the room across the hall, allowing a perfect view of the shit show going on in his room. A patient in the bed next to Kristina looked worse than her father, so she felt no need to apologize for intruding. By now, she needed to leave the hospital or throw up, or both, but the bathroom in the patient's room had an orange caution cone propping the door open. The cleaning person had wandered off talking on their cell phone, leaving the mop and cleaning supplies in the middle of the floor. The elderly male patient, breathing on a respirator, woke up, staring wide-eyed at Kristina. She rubbed the man's hand, sliding the curtain around his bed. "Great to see you, Mr. Um? Well, I hope you feel better soon. Bye, bye." Kristina headed out the door.

"Shit," Kristina did an about-face and darted back in the other patient's doorway. She recognized the woman walking into her father's room, Taryn Kennedy. Taryn attended Kristina's workshops several times. Angel pointed out how much Taryn looked like Kristina, and their mannerisms were undeniably similar to one another. Neither Angel nor Kristina would admit they knew Taryn was Kristina's half-sister. Aunt Mimi never shared many of the details about her brother's other family. Deedee Marie, Kristina's mother, only allowed mention of her ex in the house when she ranted about the rotten sonofabitch. Through the years, there'd been stories that slipped out. Kristina had heard enough to know that the two men visiting her father were his sons, and the obnoxious woman was the fucking home wrecker. Kennedy must have been Taryn's married last name. Kristina never imagined the last time she'd see her father would be in a hospital watching his damn family standing at Daddy Dearest's deathbed.

The situation was surreal. Yet, Kristina didn't stop watching the circus going on in her father's room. She had spent her entire life resenting his other family, but she mostly blamed her half-sister, the firstborn of his new family, who was the same age as Kristina's brother, Timmy. At eight years old, Kristina had only one explanation for her daddy choosing another family over theirs: *Daddy must love his new little girl more than me. I'm not lovable.* Standing in the doorway, fifteen feet away from the family she despised, Kristina's emotional wounds spread wide open with toxic memories of growing up without a father.

Shouts echoed from inside her father's room. One brother raised his fist toward Taryn; the other brother blocked him from striking her. Taryn didn't flinch, and with her petite frame, she gave him a hell of a shove, landing his ass in the chair against the wall. The wicked bitch-mother pointed her finger toward the door, yelling at Taryn to get the hell out. Taryn left the room, wiped her tears with her sleeve, took several deep breaths, and then stopped for a minute to straighten her skirt and secure her purse on her shoulder. Well composed, she headed for the nurses' station.

"Please, someone, go in there." Taryn pointed toward her father's closed door. "I think my father's dead. I'm sure my brother killed him with Dad's morphine pump." Taryn jerked at her purse's zipper, digging in the pouch for a tissue to wipe her nose.

"Don't worry, Ms. The pump won't distribute more than a standard dose every hour, no matter how many times they pushed the button," the nurse sounded reassuring, but his face looked concerned as he hurried into the room.

Taryn took the elevator going down. She never looked back.

CODE BLUE, CODE BLUE, sounded over the intercom, and a team of medical staff rushed into Kristina's father's room. She waited outside his doorway as the doctor pronounced his time of death: 8:33 a.m.

Dire thoughts about her childhood made Kristina's skin crawl. She hurried down the hospital stairs to help clear her head. Old feelings of rejection by her dad bubbled inside. A full-blown panic attack was brewing, and she was about to explode. *Compartmentalize, fast, Kristina.* With each step down, she took a deep breath and put her emotions in check.

The time for an actual tear-jerking breakdown would come later once she crawled into bed, with her always reliable home support team: Ms. Prissy, a Snicker's bar, a box of tissues, and most likely a glass of wine or two.

CHAPTER THREE

A jackhammer pounded in Kristina's head after she left the hospital. Normally she self-medicated with a pair of new shoes, but she didn't have time for shopping. She settled for her other favorite pain reliever—gooey, crunchy, chocolates. In a few hours, she needed to deliver a keynote speech at a women's luncheon for the organization, Women at the Top. It was too late to cancel. So as always, she pulled herself together and studied the note cards she'd made for her lecture, "Why Traditionally Committed Relationships Are Turning Out to Be Just a Fad."

On her drive to the venue, she turned up the radio when she heard the disc jockey say, "Kristina Truly, an Internet dating relationship expert, will join us on Monday to talk about her latest book, *Dying to Date the One—the Right One.* She's also promised to share some internet dating tips. Be sure to tune in Monday to hear from the gorgeous relationship expert and dating dynamo, Kristina Truly."

"Damn it, Booker. You need to knock this stuff off." Kristina lowered the volume. Her anxiety level was a solid ten. She wasn't in any mood to deal with Booker, her publicist/third cousin, without her refill on Xanax. Booker was an attractive, Hollywood A-lister's publicist, who conducted her business and personal life on speeds of immediately if not sooner. She was a millennial hotshot who closed all her high-powered client deals straight from her smartphone.

Before making the call, Kristina took a cleansing breath to calm down. "Booker, I heard on the radio—"

"Oh, hey Cuz, before I forget, I've booked you on several radio shows to talk about the new book."

"Booker, you absolutely have to check with Angel before you book a gig. Last week I had less than twenty minutes between book signings. By the time I found parking at the book store in North Hollywood, the lesbian clairvoyant on that new daytime talk show had already started signing her books. I signed three books in two hours."

"Dope, KT. Good job. It's hard to compete with a gay celebrity author in Hollywood. Psychic mediums are uber-trendy right now. Were her people there? Did you ask about getting on her show?"

"Booker, that's your job; you ask her people. But check with Angel first."

"It's all on your Instagram and Twitter. Angel needs to check your social media. Love you." Booker disconnected their call.

~~~~

For years, Kristina swore off Internet dating. She argued fate is the science that brings people together, not algorithms. But with her reputation growing as a relationship expert, online dating was an essential part of her research. Internet dating allowed anomalous access to complicated, sexually diverse cultures, but she wasn't there to judge. Kristina needed insight into modern-day dating to help a wide audience. So, she joined nearly all the online dating sites. She wanted to unravel what made people tick nowadays and help them successfully navigate their intimate relationships.

Staying in the know with social media trends was a daily task and one that neither Kristina nor Angel enjoyed. They studied the science of micro expressions through online psychology courses, and Peter supplied them with FBI training manuals on criminal behavior. Everything about dating with social media has changed from the days before smartphones. No matter the angle, with the Internet, having sex without commitment is as simple as a mutual swipe right or swipe left. Whichever way people swipe, they can do it with complete strangers.

They spent hours analyzing dating profiles, chatting with people online, and learning as much as they could from the people that attended their workshops. The research gave them invaluable insight into the person behind the electronic masquerade. Even the shyest, most seemingly awkward guy and the most buttoned-up woman could have a hidden persona when meeting a stranger online. Kristina and Angel figured out fast that what you see is rarely what you get when hooking up with someone you meet on the Internet.

CHAPTER FOUR

"Incoming call from Angel. Answer or ignore?" Kristina's Bluetooth earpiece sounded in her ear. Mentally wiped out, Kristina fumbled with her house keys before unlocking the front door. Inside, a high pitched beeping sound continued until she pushed the last button on her security keypad, disarming her home security alarm.

"Answer or ignore?" The artificial woman's voice repeated in her ear, "Answer." She checked the pocket of her jacket for her cellphone. Next, she checked the pockets of her pants, and then between her cleavage. That's where she often stuck the phone when she needed both hands, but no luck.

"Ignoring call."

"Come on ... Seriously?" Frustrated with everything about her day, she swallowed hard against her dry throat as she bent down to give Ms. Prissy a quick head scratch. "How's my sweet, Prissy girl? Girly-girl, remind me to call your auntie Angel back in a few minutes."

Ms. Prissy curled up on the tan overstuffed chair in the living room. Kristina plopped her butt on the sofa. She pried off her red and white polka dot heels that stuck to her feet like suction cups. Her pinky toes were numb. She dug her thumbs into the balls of her feet to get the circulation flowing. "Ow, my poor feet. Why do the cutest shoes hurt the worst?" Her swollen feet felt like warm marshmallows when she slid them into her furry slippers. She stretched her legs out across the ottoman and closed her eyes. The fragrance of two large lavender and Eucalyptus scented candles filled the room.

"Incoming call from Angel. Answer or ignore?" Kristina's earpiece sounded again.

"Answer, Answer, Answer, you stup—"

"Answering call."

"Hey, Angel. What's up?" Kristina fiddled with the volume on her earpiece.

Angel wasted no time getting to the point, "KT, where are you?"

Kristina lowered her stiff legs and sore feet to the floor and pushed herself up off the sofa, "I'm about to walk out to the car. I left my phone in there. I've got my earpiece in. What's going on?"

A whiff of the neighbor's fresh-cut grass breezed by when she opened the front door. "Angel, please remind me to look for a new gardener tomorrow. My yard looks like crap." Most of her neighbors' houses were clones of one another—all with a flawless emerald green grass and a variety of award-winning roses vining through their shiny white fences. The weeds had taken over Kristina's yard. Her fence needed painting, and her roses were not exactly winning any awards. It was time to fire the old gardener and hire someone to work some magic.

A car key dangled from a silver ring around Kristina's middle finger. She headed toward her car parked in front of the garage. A shadow of someone or something caught her eye. She stopped. Whatever, or whoever it was, triggered her car alarm.

"Kristina, what's that chirping noise?"

Kristina whispered into the microphone on her earpiece, "Someone triggered my car alarm. I think it's my crazy neighbor. The one who thinks she's the trashcan police." Kristina ducked from sight against the tall bushes beside the house. She'd forgotten to take in the empty garbage bins again this morning, but she was in no mood for a lecture. The side wall of the garage blocked Kristina's view of the driveway until she rounded the corner of the concrete walk. She poked her head around the corner of the garage. *Oh good—not the nutty neighbor.* Kristina smiled, watching an orange-haired cat use the hood of her SUV like a springboard to land gracefully on the roof of the house.

A youthful man ran down the street in pursuit of his brindle haired bulldog. The bruiser flew across the pavement with his stout sausage legs barely touching the ground. "Barney, no. Sit. Barney, sit." The dog skidded to a stop on Kristina's driveway. "Barney, stay." The young man latched a leash to the barking dog's collar. Barney spun in circles, baffled by the whereabouts of the nimble tabby.

"What's happening, KT?"

The alarm silenced when Kristina unlocked the car door.

"The neighbor's cat jumped on the hood of my car, that's all." Kristina sat behind the steering wheel and took her phone off the charger.

A stranger in a silver Lexus screeched to a stop in her neighbor's driveway, parallel to hers. Tinted windows hid the driver's face. "What the hell?" Wide-eyed, Kristina watched the man shift the car in reverse. He punched the gas pedal. Kristina could tell from the stranger's profile it was neither Jim nor Lois, her elderly neighbors that lived in the house.

He made a sharp turn from the street straight into Kristina's driveway toward the rear of her SUV. His Lexus skidded to a stop inches from her bumper.

"Shi ... t." Kristina gripped the steering wheel to brace for impact, but it seemed he teased for her attention, and he got it. Her eyes fixated on the rearview mirror. The man sported a tightly groomed black beard with gold-framed aviator sunglasses covering most of his face. With the speed of a Formula One driver, he backed out to the street. A FedEx truck skidded to a stop to keep from plowing off the tail end of the Lexus. Smoke burned from the rubber tires of the stranger's car rounding the street corner out of the housing tract.

Angel spoke up, "Girlfriend. What the hell's going on? What's all that noise?"

"Nothing, a neighbor's dog got loose." Kristina tried to wrap her head around the bizarre scene that took place. Explaining it to Angel would have led to a police officer at Kristina's house filing a report for the next two hours, so she gave Angel a synopsis instead. A shot of cortisol sped through Kristina's veins. She grabbed her cellphone, locked her car door, and hurried her ass back in the house.

"Listen, Kristina; I want you to be careful. You got a threatening email from one of your online crazies. I don't want to freak you out, but I'm concerned." Angel cleared her throat. "This is the email they wrote: *Ms. Truly, you are a relationship fraud. You know nothing about having a healthy, loving relationship with a man, especially with a Jewish man. You need to stop dating Jewish men, stupid Shiksa. End your membership on GoodJewishDating.com, or I will have you taken care of.*" Angel paused only to catch her breath, then continued, "KT, I called the Newport Beach police. I asked them to put extra patrol officers in your neighborhood. Keep your Taser gun in your pocket." Angel stopped long enough for Kristina to butt in.

"Angel, listen, I'm sure it's nothing."

Kristina glanced toward the living room, looking for Ms. Prissy. She wasn't grooming herself on the sofa, so Kristina headed to the kitchen. "Ah, holy crap, Prissy." Kristina jumped backward, knocking over a plant stand. The automated Bluetooth sounded, *low battery.*

"Now, what's wrong Kristina, can you please stop for two minutes and talk to me?" Angel snapped.

Kristina took a deep breath, put the phone on speaker, and placed the earpiece on the charger.

"Yes, yes, sorry, Ms. Prissy jumped off the top of her scratch tower and scared the bejesus out of me." Kristina changed the topic, "You called Newport Police Department? Angel, you're too funny. I'm sure they're still laughing. Besides, I know who wrote the email. Remember, I told you about the Jewish Mother Mafia on the Jewish dating website. The other day, I may have pissed one of them off. I'd been corresponding with a guy named Erwin. He asked me to meet him for a glass of wine. Before I could respond, I got an email from his mother telling me to stay away from her son, or else. So, I wrote back, *too late, I had sex with Erwin, and we're in love.* But I think it's safe to say she didn't find the humor in it like I did."

"I thought you were kidding when you told me about the Jewish Mother Mafia."

"Nope, from what I've read on the chat boards on the dating website, the JMM is a real group of Jewish mothers that have formed an alliance. They all have fake profiles to go online to find their kids a nice Jewish partner. They have full access to their grown children's online dating accounts. They can see who they are talking with, and if they don't like you, well, you get the verbal kibosh beat out of you. Don't worry, Angel. I'll have Peter contact the FBI's Internet narc squad and have the JMM put in their place. I'm sure they're harmless. Peter sent me a text, and he's coming by with Italian for dinner and Cabernet. Also, I didn't have time to tell you earlier; I saw my dad this morning. He passed shortly after I got there. I'm not even sure where to start with everything that happened. I'm glad I went, I think. Oh, hell. I don't know. Going to see him may have messed me up more, but let's chat about it tomorrow. The entire thing has me wiped out."

There were high-pitched screams in the background at Angel's house. It was bedtime for her kids. Kristina imagined

Jermaine was doing his best to help with the three little hellions, but he didn't have his wife's stern parenting skills.

"I'm sorry your dad passed before he admitted to being a terrible father, and you deserved better. It seems he took the coward's way out, again. First thing in the morning, tell me everything. I've got to get the monsters in bed. We'll talk about it when you get to the office. And KT, do me a favor, put your Taser gun in your pocket. Love you, have a good night."

"Love you too, Angel. Kiss Jermaine and the kids for me."

Some Cabernet promised to brighten Kristina's mood. She poured a full glass for herself and got one ready for Peter. Dark-haired, Mensa smart, dates women and lots of them, but schedules a mani-pedi once a week, gaining him the nickname, Poodles.

Kristina didn't want any drama from Angel so she couldn't let on, but something felt off. The stranger in the Lexus wanted her attention, and thinking back, he looked familiar. Her gut told her something wasn't right. She picked up the phone and dialed her next-door neighbor's cell number.

"Hey Lois, it's KT. How's Hawaii?"

"Aloha, KT. It's so good to hear your voice. Are you calling to tell us you will join us after all?"

"Aw, Lois, I wish I could, but that's not why I'm calling. I saw a man in a silver Lexus backing out of your driveway earlier, and I wondered if it was a Lyft or Uber driver dropping you back home. I thought maybe you came home early." Kristina took a big sip of wine.

"No, we're still in Maui, having a marvelous time. The

weather's been wonderful. Jim's finally learning to play golf, and I'm kicking his butt. Did the man leave a note? Think there's a problem?"

Lois switched to the speaker on the cell phone, and Kristina heard Jim in the background. "You should fly out and meet us, KT. We'd love for you to join us. There are a lot of nice-looking single men on the island."

"Lois, I'm sure everything is fine. I'll walk over and check if he left a note. I'm just a busybody. Besides, it gave me an excuse to call and say hi. Jim, next time I will join you, I promise. You two have fun. I'll see you next week."

Jim finished the call, "Love you, Sergeant Truly. Thanks for policing the house while we're gone."

The driver hadn't gotten out of his car to leave a note. Kristina took another gulp of wine and double-checked the lock on the sliding glass doors in the kitchen and pulled down the blinds.

Feeling jumpy, Kristina hurried to open the front door to wait for Poodles when she heard his car pull up outside. Peter wiped the bottoms of his perfectly polished loafers on the welcome mat before coming inside. He gripped a plastic bag in each hand filled with white Styrofoam containers.

Kristina held Ms. Prissy close to her chest and shut the door. "I just remembered the man in the Lexus. He was parked next to my car when I left the hospital. That's bizarre." Kristina scratched Prissy's ear.

Poodles walked past her with a bottle of wine tucked under each arm and the aroma of oregano, basil, parmesan cheese, and sweet garlic. "What Lexus? Who are you talking about?"

"It's nothing. My imagination running wild again. Yum. Smells scrumptious, I'm starving."

Peter set the table for dinner. Kristina secured the deadbolt.

CHAPTER FIVE

Juggling the mail, along with her car keys, and a venti half-caf almond milk latte, Kristina pushed the office door open with her foot.

"You need some help?" Angel lowered the volume on the radio and took the mail out of Kristina's hand. "Good to see the Jewish Mafia Mommies haven't taken you out this morning. Did you tell Peter about the email?"

"Yep, he's looking into it. Don't worry, girlfriend. It will take more than a crazy Jewish mother to take me out. You know my mother—right."

. Angel belted out, "Amen." She waved her hand in front of her chest in the shape of the cross. "A fleet of helicopter mothers have nothing on Irish Catholic Deedee Marie."

"Wait till you hear what happened at the hospital yesterday." Kristina sounded self-assured. She wasn't. Her stomach turned, thinking about her father's straggly hair sticking out of his bald head and the crazy family by his side.

Angel read a text and then silenced her phone. "I'm all ears. What the hell convinced you to go see him?"

"Aunt Mimi. She thought it would help me forgive him or move on, or whatever. Honestly, I only went because it was so important to my aunt." It hurt to look Angel in the eyes. They both knew Kristina went to see her father because she still had deep abandonment issues.

"Did he know you were there?" Angel asked. Deep down, she hoped that Kristina's deadbeat dad would at least acknowledge she was there. She'd given up hope a long time ago that the jerk would ever tell Kristina and Timmy that he loved them, he was sorry, and beg for their forgiveness. Through the years, it was obvious to Angel that most of Kristina's poor choices in men reflected Kristina blaming herself for her father leaving. Growing up, it broke Angel's heart to listen to her best friend making excuses for her father not being around.

"No. I didn't speak to him. He passed away before—" Kristina started choking up.

Angel hurried to Kristina's side and wrapped her arms around her. "I'm sorry, KT. You deserved better than that poor excuse of a man." Angel handed Kristina a tissue, knowing she usually wiped her eyes or her nose with her sleeve or another convenient part of clothing.

"Angel, like we thought. That fucking Taryn Kennedy is my half-sister. I still can't believe she has the nerve to attend my workshops." The situation enraged Kristina with feelings running amuck in her head. She felt ashamed for wanting to blame this mess on Taryn, but until she got her emotions sorted out, it felt best to stay pissed off at the whole fucking family. Her heart softened when she thought about the scene at the hospital when Taryn's brother nearly hit her. Kristina wiped her nose and took a few deep breaths.

"I never doubted Taryn was your sister. Either that or a much younger doppelgänger." Angel grinned, hoping to lighten the mood.

"Slightly younger would do, thank you very much." Kristina glanced at Angel with a stink eye and smirky grin.

"My point is, I agree it's strange that she'd attend your workshops. It seemed to me, she needed you, or what you teach. I've worked with Taryn at the workshops, and she seems very sweet. Remember, we saw her with bruises on her face and arms that she tried to cover with make-up. I suspect she's had a rough life. The mess your dad made was all on him. Neither of you deserved it."

"She looked really upset yesterday at the hospital, and it seemed they were all yelling at her. Who knows? I'm not sure I'm buying her sweet little innocent act. All of this is weird." Kristina looked at her computer screen, trying desperately to compartmentalize all the thoughts racing around her head the past couple of days. *One foot in front of the other, one task at a time.* This craziness would take time to get over, so for now, Kristina focused on the one thing she could control: work.

"Un-fucking-believable. I got an email from Chuck Truly, my half-brother. He's asking me to pay for Dad's funeral. He says if I don't, they'll abandon his body to the county coroner's office because they won't pay to bury him." Kristina stared at her computer screen, speechless, unable to wrap her head around the craziness from the family that she despised.

"Are you frigging kidding me?" Angel jumped to her feet

to see the email for herself. "No—way. You tell him to go to *hell*. No, don't even respond. What an ass." Angel sat back at her desk, fuming. She waited for Kristina to go off on the entire damn clan of nutcases.

Angel saw her friend had a look of uncertainty on her face. "You're *not* going to pay for your father's burial. Please tell me, KT, you aren't considering it?"

"No, not even, I'd never. I'm in shock over the balls they have asking me to pay for his funeral when he never gave my mom one dime of child support after he walked out on us." Kristina took a deep breath, blowing out slowly through her mouth.

"My dad's dead; one of his sons tried to overdose him on morphine, and my half-sister attends my workshops. It's too much to think about. So, anyway." Kristina cleared her throat. "I need to get on with work." Kristina acted like this was life as usual, but Angel knew too well how her best friend often gave attention to those that didn't deserve it.

"Girlfriend, I hate to say it, but there's more grave news. Peter sent me a text." Angel stared wide-eyed at her phone. "They found Jaclyn Renzo. She's dead. Looks like murder. It's an ongoing investigation, not for public knowledge as yet. That's all he said."

Startled, Kristina dropped her stapler on the floor. "Oh, my God. I had a bad feeling her missing person's case would not turn out well. Any time someone's missing for more than a few hours, it's never good. I can't believe this. I've only briefly spoken with Jaclyn. I thanked her for volunteering for us, but not much else. What a nightmare for her family. I'm betting it was her ex." Kristina wiped her tears with the cuff of her jacket sleeve.

"Jaclyn and I chatted a little. We spoke mostly about what days she wanted to help with the workshops. She showed up late a lot, but she always worked hard and got along well with the others at the meetings. I agree her ex probably did it. Let's send flowers or make a donation if her family would prefer. This is shocking." Angel poured herself a Diet Coke and called her mom to check on the kids.

Frigid air seeped from an open window near Kristina's desk, but that wasn't the only thing making Kristina shiver. The stranger in the Lexus, a warning email note from someone online, she's expected to pay for her father's funeral, and now a woman—killed. All of it had Kristina desperate to refill her prescription of Xanax. Murder wasn't something she could compartmentalize.

CHAPTER SIX

"Angel, this afternoon, I think we should update my profile photos on GoodJewishDating.com. I don't want the Jewish Mother Mafia to think they got away with intimidating me." Kristina felt a stabbing, pulsating pain in her head. Her bottle of Xanax had been empty for months, and her doctor refused to refill it but suggested Kristina take up yoga and meditation. She usually found the brighter sides of life, but today wasn't one of those days. "I think I'll take Larry's yoga class at 6:30 tonight. I need to find some Zen." Kristina stretched her back, twisted at the waist, and rolled her neck side to side.

Breathe in through my nose, hold it, let it out. Kristina felt a panic attack brewing inside. She quickly found a distraction by posting inspirational quotes about love and peace on her Kristina Truly, Finding the One—the Right One Facebook page.

"I'm not posting pictures of you, KT. I deleted your profile this morning. We don't know for sure that the JMM wrote the note. Whoever it is could be real trouble. There's no need to push your luck." Angel sat in front of her computer, scrolling through more of Kristina's online dating emails, sorting through hundreds of profiles, and collecting data; however,

Kristina knew Angel would also keep an eye out for a few prospects for her. Angel had given up years ago on Kristina's ability to pick the right man and took on vetting potential Angel-approved prospects for Kristina while gathering profile information to help create workshop material.

"Please, undelete it or redo it or whatever you do with that stuff. A bunch of overbearing mishegas—aren't going to bully me."

Angel drummed her nails on the top of her desk while she jiggled one leg. Visions of women's bloody bodies flashed in Angel's head. Her nervous energy had Kristina tempted to call her chiropractor's office to see if they could squeeze her and Angel in for an adjustment and massage.

"Listen, KT. It's not worth it. Dangerous people lurk on the Internet. You have no idea what that person's capable of, and the email may not be the end of it." Angel meant what she said and would not budge.

Kristina pursed her lips and swallowed hard to resist having to have the last word. This wasn't the time to cause Angel added anxiety, so without further debate, she got back to work on her next workshop.

~~~~

"Angel, I've been thinking. The problem is there are just too many toads cleverly disguised as sexy, handsome princes. We need to focus on finding a true prince. A loving and trustworthy man who is—" Angel cut Kristina off mid-sentence.

"Who is cleverly disguised as a nerdy, awkward toad, which turns into a handsome prince when he meets the right person? This isn't Hollywood, girlfriend." Angel laughed and continued to check their social media accounts.

"No, that's not it, smartass. But sometimes we overlook the right partner just because they don't fit our delusional Hollywood image of a good person. We need to stay open to meeting people who, at first, may not seem to be our type. That's what I was trying to say. I have a new topic for my next workshop. *When you least expect it, you may meet the person you least expected to fall in love with.*"

"Okay, Baby Buddha. I hope you find yourself a sweet toad soon that turns out to be a real prince and not a guy that runs from a committed relationship or that you need to take care of, like, oh, let's just say, one or two of your past relationships. One thing's for sure, Cinderella, the only shoes you don't have in your collection are a pair of glass slippers. They couldn't be any more uncomfortable than all the other shoes you wear. So now that your dad's gone, you've got no one to blame for another fucked up relationship, so it's time to find the right man, just not off the Jewish dating site." Angel sounded like she was preaching behind the pulpit when she wanted to bring her point home.

Teasing Kristina about her poor choices in men was one thing, but her popularity had grown faster than either of them could keep up with. Millions of lonely people spent much of their day checking their smartphones for flirts, heart emojis, winks, super likes, texts, the unexpected dick pic, or any other line of communication for a spicy hot rendezvous. On the Internet, potential relationships are a click away. Internet scammers prey on the naivety and desperation of those dying for a warm body next to them, even if it's only for a quickie. There has been an explosion of mismanaged relationship skills, not to mention the dangers of meeting up with a stranger from a hook-up app. However, for Kristina, there was a growing trend of people who wanted a lasting, loving relationship and seeking her expertise to help them find the "one," the right one.

"Angel, what do you think of this guy?" Kristina turned her computer screen around so Angel could see the pictures of the man who had caught her eye. It was free to join this online dating site, and Kristina didn't feel the bar was set any lower than the other dating sites with a paid membership.

"Until Peter's team has time to look into the email, I think you should take a break from any online dating. We aren't a hundred percent sure the threat came from the mob mothers." Angel walked to meet the UPS driver at the door and signed for a small package delivery.

"Don't worry, girlfriend. I'm sure the email was a gag. By now, the FBI's probably given them an official lashing of some sort. The whole thing's silly, and I'm not putting my life on hold. Besides, I get my best material for workshops and books from the men I date. Having coffee, dinner, or just a good old fashion chat on the phone with men continues to be my most reliable research. Angel, you know ninety-five percent of the dates I go on are strictly for new material. What tiny bit of entertainment I get, I totally deserve after sitting through the endless boring stories about their children. For fucksakes, I deserve a medal for the coaching I've given during coffee to the numerous bitter divorcés. Having a little fun with my job is just a bonus. What can I say, girlfriend? Dating's a whole new ball of wax since you were single," Kristina lectured with authority.

"Yes, I get it. Understanding modern dating is a huge part of our business. However, for now, I think you need to take a break." Angel took a pair of scissors out of her top desk drawer to slice open the package.

"Okay, girlfriend. Will do. What's in the UPS box?" Diverting the conversation from herself was something Kristina had become great at ever since she and Angel met.

"As usual, I assumed that you weren't going to listen to me about taking a timeout from dating the Internet lunatics, so Peter and I got you a new Taser gun." Angel unpacked a petite black handheld pistol and proceeded to read the operating manual.

"Why did you buy me another stun gun? And what is that? It looks like a real handgun." Kristina slid her chair across the hardwood floors and stopped in front of Angel's desk, reaching for the mini toy looking gun.

Like a mother confiscating a dangerous item from one of her children, Angel snatched the Taser before Kristina could touch it.

"KT, it's not a toy. This is a high-powered stun gun. It's extremely technical and powerful. It can really hurt someone, preferably not you or me. It has WIFI, GPS, and fires a few electrical darts without reloading. I need to read the manual; there are other bells and whistles that I need to research before you can touch it. It's not on the market yet. It's a test model. Peter and his FBI colleagues are testing it out for the manufacturer. Peter pulled some strings to get you one." Angel flipped through the pages of the booklet with *WARNING* written in bold red letters across the front cover.

"Great, Poodles got me a prototype stun gun. What if I need it and the damn thing doesn't work? I will jot down a quick note: 'Dear manufacturer, I regret to advise your Taser didn't work. Sincerely, the dead girl.' I guess I better carry my old clunky Taser with me for back-up." Kristina laughed at all this nonsense.

"KT, you can quit pretending. You know damn well the police confiscated your Taser when you stunned your dry cleaner over the sweater he ruined. Peter told me all about the incident when he called this morning to tell me your new stun gun would be delivered today."

"He's such a blabbermouth. He promised he wouldn't say anything. Besides, it was an accident, not an incident. When the red light flashed, I thought it meant a low battery. I figured it would be a mild zap. And in my defense, for twenty years, Uncle Ronnie's been stretching out my cashmere. I finally caught him wearing my favorite pink sweater. Uncle Ronnie's a sizeable man. He swore he'd stop wearing women's clothes. He got zapped for lying. I'd forgotten about the pacemaker."

"Agreed. Your drag queen dry cleaner uncle needs to wear his own women's clothing, and he probably deserved a proper telling off, but it's a damn good thing he's family. And lucky for you, Peter's attorney talked him out of pressing charges." Angel placed the stun gun in her palm, pointed it at the rattan wastebasket ten feet away, and zapped. The wastebasket split into pieces, sparking the paper in the trash. Kristina doused the flames with her lukewarm latte. "Whoa, it's not even charged. Full battery, this puppy will do some damage. I better keep reading before either of us hurts ourselves." Angel buried her face back into the owner's manual.

A text from Peter flashed on Kristina's phone. *KT, there's been a report of another woman missing in Newport. She fits a similar profile to Jaclyn Renzo. This is a longshot, but thought I'd ask, do you and/or Angel know Sophia Clark? Here is her picture. FYI: classified, an ongoing investigation; you know the rules, not for public knowledge as yet. XO Peter.*

Kristina stared at the screen in shock, gripping her phone tightly with both hands. "Fuck. Angel. Sophia Clark is missing. Peter sent me a text asking if we know her."

"What? She helped me with the back of the room sales at our last workshop because Jaclyn didn't show. I can't believe this." Angel picked up her phone in disbelief. Peter had sent her the same message.

"I will contact Sophia's mom to see what's going on. I dropped Sophia off at her mom's house after a workshop a few months ago, and I had a cup of tea with them. Her mom's in her late eighties with slight dementia, and Sophia stays with her a few nights a week. I'm really worried. Angel, this is not good." Kristina took a deep breath.

"KT, you can't contact her mom. Peter will have your ass. Let the FBI do their job. You know how mad Peter gets when he thinks we're crossing the line of his friendship and his work. Besides, you may upset her mom. You don't know how much the family has told her about Sophia missing. Until they release this case to the media, or Peter informs us otherwise, we have to stay out of the investigation. Let's think positive; maybe she's just gone somewhere and neglected to tell her family." Angel knew better but wanted to discourage Kristina from getting involved.

"Okay, you're right. I'll wait for Peter to fill us in with more details. I'll let him know she's one of our volunteers."

Hey P. Yes, we know Sophia. She's volunteered for us twice. I think she's recently divorced. I had tea once with Sophia and her mom after a workshop. We know her, but not that well. WTF's going on, Jaclyn, now Sophia? WTFFFFFF? Very worried. xoxo, KT.

CHAPTER SEVEN

"How much is this one?" Kristina pointed to a lustrous bronze casket while lifting the top to peek at the roomier than normal interior.

"Ah, excellent choice, Ms. Truly. You have a keen eye for exquisite detail. This is our finest casket: thirty-two-ounce, traditional bronze coating around all its spaces, including the rails. It uses bisque colored plush chenille interior with an additional six cubic inches for added comfort. An adjustable mattress comes standard along with a firm memory foam head pillow, a gold-plated engraved plaque to identify the deceased in the unfortunate event that the body has to be unearthed, full rubber gasket seal, continuous weld construction and …"

Kristina stared at the mortician's lips while he described the casket as a work of fine art. His lips were a disturbing shade of gray. Opaque. Almost white but not quite, more ash color to be exact. His eyes, dark and bug-like. He looked like a talking corpse from a scene in an old black and white horror film. *Do all morticians look so gloomy? They probably learn to do that in school.*

Only half-listening to Mr. Simm's overzealous sales pitch, Kristina's thoughts wandered in a bizarre direction even for her. She perused the ample display of caskets, caressing her hand across the tiny satin pillows while straightening a few that were slightly off tilt.

"How much does it cost?" Kristina dipped her head into the open casket to look under the half that would cover the deceased person's legs. Child-like, she poked at several of the well-padded interiors with the tip of her index finger.

"As I was saying, the Sunset Bronze model is one of our finest. It's fully insured." Mr. Simm fondled the casket's handcrafted iron hardware like he wanted to make love to it. Kristina had to interrupt him before she finished her lewd thoughts about the corpse having sex with a coffin.

"Fully insured? You put it in the ground and cover it with dirt. What part's insured?" Kristina knew she'd been harsh and condescending, but she couldn't help herself, not today. "Mr. Simm, How. Much. Is it?"

Mr. Simm stiffened his stance, puffing out his scrawny chest with confidence. "It's sixty-nine hundred dollars. We offer twelve months, no interest financing with approved credit."

Kristina stopped herself from making another sarcastic comment. "Great, thank you, Mr. Simm, but there'll be no need for financing; we'll take the casket made of recycled cardboard in the corner. You said it cost eight hundred— correct?" Kristina waved her hands underneath a dispenser of hand sanitizer mounted on the wall, lathering the foaming disinfectant from her hands to her forearms.

"Yes, correct, Ms. Truly. But that style is primarily designed for cremation or someone impoverished. What about this navy blue one? The price is exceptional for the quality. For a modest fee, you can enhance the interior from satin to velvet; it's a bit more masculine with velvet rather than the satin-poly blend, or you can upgrade to linen. Light gray linen looks quite posh with the navy blue. I might mention, we have floor models deeply discounted. Of course, some may have minor blemishes, hardly noticeable."

"No, I like the thought of him in the recycled cardboard. My father recycled our family for a different one; now it's his turn. It's perfect. Put it on my credit card and let me know how much this funeral is costing me," Kristina said as if she were talking about a poor business deal she'd just made.

Looking at her younger brother made it harder to keep up the callused, nonchalant demeanor she had going, pretending to be untouched by any of this mess. Timmy saw right through her act. He went along with burying their father, hoping it would finally put an end to the mission Kristina was on to fix broken men.

"Timmy, are you okay with this? I'm sorry I didn't ask which one you liked. What do you think? Should I get the navy blue one?" The look on his face pierced her heart. Timmy was nine months old when their father left. His only memories of their dad were the rotten ones their mother ranted about for the past thirty-five years. Thank goodness Timmy was too young to remember the night their father walked out on them to live with the homewrecker. Their dad left them for the same bitch that can't find any cash in her bank account to pay for her loving dedicated husband's funeral, not after her facelift, boob job, and tummy tuck anyway.

"Kristina, I said I would help you pay to bury Dad, but why are you doing this? We shouldn't have to take care of his funeral. We don't owe him anything." Tears filled Timmy's eyes. It concerned him to watch Kristina desperately trying to feel in control. Kristina put her arm around his shoulder. She needed to convince Timmy that his big sister could take care of everything and everyone. Somehow through their dysfunctional childhood, Timmy grew into an emotionally secure, self-confident, successful, kindhearted soul with high morals and deep compassion for people. He was a loving husband and father despite not having a solid male role model to look up to. Instead, he had Kristina, his wise, older sister, constantly drilling into his head how a real man should behave. Timmy has been her best student, and he loves everything about being a good husband and father. She kissed his cherub-like cheek. Even at thirty-five years old, Kristina felt she needed to protect him from evil things in the world.

"Timmy, don't you worry about me. Haven't I always taken care of everything? I've got this. I want to. I need to. You don't owe Dad anything, but I do. Besides, you're starting your own practice, and doctors don't make the money they used to make. You save your money for my beautiful niece and your adorable wife. I appreciate you coming here today, but it's not your responsibility, it's mine. I do owe Dad; I owe him for the first eight and a half years of my life. The diapers, the food, school shoes, birthday gifts, dance lessons, and whatever else he paid for while he played his good daddy façade. I've figured out what it cost in those days to take care of me for the few years he was there with us. And after I pay for his funeral, he and I will be square. I won't owe him anymore. But you have to promise me you will never tell Mom that I paid for Dad's funeral. She'll kill both of us." Kristina's throat tightened when she heard the words coming out of her mouth.

Memories of how deeply she'd loved her father consumed her. The muscles in her thighs weakened when she thought about the night her dad slammed the front door for the last time. Her heart never stopped aching since the night he left. Most of her childhood, she'd wake up crying from an awful dream where her father sped away in his shiny blue Buick. The sound of the screeching tires still haunted her. Taking care of others became Kristina's full-time job while growing up. Loving someone was the simple part—allowing someone to love her back, well, that's where it got complicated. She promised herself she'd work on that another day.

Mr. Simm returned with a stack of paperwork. "Ms. Truly, your total costs for everything, including your father's burial plot near the rear wall of the cemetery, not the plot near our beautiful stream and—"

Kristina interrupted, "Did you remember to exclude the cost for the other burial plot? The one I told you I'm not paying for?" Seated on the arm of an overstuffed chair with both arms folded tightly across her chest, she began to think twice about paying for anything. She stewed. Angry with herself for agreeing to foot the bill for dear old Dad's final adieu.

Her therapist's voice resounded in her head: Kristina, *by paying for your father's funeral, you're playing your last martyr card.* "If I pay for Daddy's funeral, surely he'll finally see what a good person I am and realize he made a mistake. He'll love me more than them this time." *Do you really want to go there?*

For goodness sake, my dad's dead; he'll never know I paid for his frigging funeral.

We both know he's dead, Kristina; that's my point. He's been dead since he walked out the door thirty-five years ago, but you haven't completely let go. The relationship that you continue to hold on to between you and your father is exactly why you continue to date men who can't be trusted and who don't want a long term committed relationship. Kristina, I'm right; we've been over this in numerous sessions. Kristina tried to ignore the words of her therapist screaming in her brain. Anyway, it was too late. She said she would pay the expenses to bury her father, and she always kept her word, even to a fault.

"Indeed, Ms. Truly. You're not paying for the original plots your father had previously picked out for him and your stepmother. When the time comes, she'll need to be buried elsewhere; the plot you selected is a single plot with only the cinderblock wall on one side and Sister Mary-Elizabeth on the other. He'll be alone. His wife will not be with him, as you requested." Mr. Simm's admonishing tone grated on Kristina's nerves. "The total cost is thirteen thousand, eight hundred dollars." Mr. Simm spread the papers out on his desk for her approval and her method of payment.

Kristina scribbled her signature on the last piece of paper, authorizing payment on her credit card. "Thirteen thousand, eight hundred is more than I figured I owed him. Good, now he owes me," Grumbling under her breath, Kristina tried to rationalize her need to have the last bit of control between her and her dad.

"Shall I let your stepmother know that you took care of all the details today?"

"She's *not* our stepmother." Kristina nearly snapped the pen in half, clicking it closed while shoving it back in the cheap plastic pen caddy sitting on Mr. Simm's meticulously organized desk. Tears pooled in Kristina's eyes. *Breathe in through my nose and out through my mouth.*

"Would either of you care for a cup of coffee or hot tea?" Mr. Simm said. He sat in a badly worn black tufted leather chair with his pointed nose and narrow chin tilted upward.

"No, thank you, Mr. Simm, nothing for me." Timmy squeezed his sister's shoulder in an attempt to cool her down. "I must get going soon."

"Shall I include the two of you on the memorial bulletin? The information for the bulletin will need to go to the printer fairly soon, but I'm happy to add your names to the itinerary. Will you be saying a few words along with your father's other children at the church service? After Pastor O'Malley finishes the eulogy, your siblings, excuse me, I mean, your father's family will pay their respects with some personal stories. Will you be doing the same?"

"No. My brother and I will *not* be attending his memorial services." With death rays beaming from her eyes, Kristina sent Mr. Simm a hateful stare as if it were his fault they were estranged from their father for all these years. Mobilized by so many uncomfortable feelings, Kristina paced between the desk and two chairs. *Breathe in. Let it out.* She relaxed her clenched fists and collected herself.

"Mr. Simm, I apologize for my unkind behavior; none of this mess is your fault. I'm sorry for being harsh. You've been more than helpful. It's just that my father walked out on my brother and me when we were young. We received twelve Christmas cards from him over the past thirty-five years. That's it, nothing else. *Merry Christmas, Dad.* Yet, his family contacted me to pay for his funeral. Otherwise, they would abandon his body. He'd become a ward of the county coroner's office. The coroner's office would have to pick up the bill to cremate his body, and they'd dispose of his remains. I assume they'd toss him alongside other unclaimed ashes. I'm a public figure. I don't need the negative publicity. How would it look allowing my father a pauper's funeral? Besides, I love my Aunt Mimi, my dad's sister, and I don't want to burden her with all of this mess. Thank you for your service, Mr. Simm." Kristina gathered copies of her paperwork and crammed them in her purse. Her reserved demeanor didn't match the turmoil going on inside. The devastation she felt over her father's death didn't match the bitterness she felt for him leaving Timmy. She would have been fine growing up without a dad; this is what she told herself anyway, but her brother deserved better.

"No need to apologize, Ms. Truly. I'm rarely privy to the family's dynamics. It's a shame to hear you're burdened with your father's expenditures. You've done a good deed. I will see that your father's church service, burial, and lunch reception are honorable. My deepest sympathy for your unfortunate circumstances." Mr. Simm gracefully retreated to another room, politely excusing himself while Timmy and Kristina said their good-byes.

"Kristina, one day, you'll have to stop taking care of everyone. Find a nice guy, Krissy, and get married. You deserve to have a loving husband and family of your own. You deserve to be happy. Dad missed out; you're an incredible person, and one day, some incredibly lucky man will be wise enough to marry you, if you'll let him. No one's perfect, Krissy—no one. Not even your brother." Timmy gave his sister an endearing grin and a kiss on the cheek. "I love you, Auntie, Krissy. Your niece is starting to walk. Please, come by to see her. She misses you." Timmy checked his watch for the time.

With the back of her hand, Kristina dabbed the tears from the corners of her eyes. "Never worry about me, baby brother. Don't forget who your big sister is; I'm a relationship expert." Kristina let out a pathetic little laugh in an attempt to fool no one about the shambles of her love life. "You need to take off. You'll hit a lot of traffic if you don't hurry. Thank you again for coming here. I'm going out the other door; my car's parked in the back lot. I love you too, and stop calling me Krissy." She smiled like a Cheshire cat because they both knew she loved it when he called her by her childhood nickname. With a hurried hug, she pushed him out the door.

Kristina stared out the mud-splattered glass window at the poorly groomed cemetery, "I should have cremated him."

CHAPTER EIGHT

*W*hat the hell did I do, paying for Dad's funeral? I have *lost my mind.* Kristina rubbed her temples with her thumbs for relief from the pounding in her head.

Crucifixes of all sizes with red price tags attached hung over the faded floral wallpaper of the funeral parlor. A lifelike statue of the Virgin Mary stood next to a metal rack with Jewish prayer shawls draped over it and a sign that read: "Sale: 30% Off," while water trickled from a lotus flower at the feet of a plastic Buddha. Kristina's heart tightened with remorse. *Maybe even Dad deserves better than this.*

She hadn't felt lovable since her father walked out thirty-five years ago. Her dear old dad, the one person she blamed whenever she fucked-up in life, was dead, but this mess between the two of them wasn't over. Not yet.

Kristina walked down the hall toward the back offices. "Excuse me, Mr. Simm. I've changed my mind. I'd like a few minutes alone with my father, please."

By a marginal rise of one eyebrow, Mr. Simm showed a hint of surprise but didn't say a word as they went down the stairs to the basement of the mortuary where they had her father's body.

"Mr. Simm, umm … I'd like to change my father's casket. I'd like the navy blue one with white velvet interior. When I was a kid, he drove a blue car with white leather seats. Please put the additional cost on my credit card."

"Certainly, Ms. Truly. The blue one is a lovely choice. I'll email you a copy of the revised paperwork and your credit card receipt. Please take as much time as you'd like. There's a door at the end of the hall; it leads to the parking lot." Mr. Simm tucked the toe tag under the sheet covering her father's body on his way out.

Kristina glanced around the room at the specimen beakers and medical instruments, wondering if burying her dad in the blue casket would finally bury the nightmares of her father speeding away in the shiny blue Buick. Given her current state of mind, that was the best logic she had to justify the insanity of paying for his funeral.

The musty odor of the gray cinder block walls overpowered the subtle fragrance of the tiny room deodorizer plugged in the outlet next to boxes of embalming fluid. Droplets of water hit the tin sink basin, vibrating in Kristina's eardrums. "What the hell; this place is a nightmare." Kristina tried turning the spigot—it didn't budge. With both arms crossing her chest, Kristina rubbed her chilled forearms at the sight of the wall stacked ten deep with bodies lying in narrow drawers, two high and ten across. Most doors had the metal latch draping half off.

Kristina gripped her purse tighter against her breast under her crossed arms. "Let's hope none of you wake up or get undead." She needed to get on with settling the score and get the hell out of there.

"Hi, Daddy, remember me? It's your pretty little princess." Not comfortable speaking directly to a dead man in a chilled basement of a mortuary, she stood back, near the door.

"Well, I suppose we're even. I don't owe you anything anymore. You sort of owe me now, but we'll call it square." Kristina trudged across the room toward the man she no longer knew. Standing next to his chilled, lifeless body, more memories of their lives together flooded in. Daddy's pretty little princess, the one who keeps all twelve Christmas cards tucked away in the top drawer of the nightstand beside her bed. Her body shivered from the cold refrigerated room or maybe from nerves.

"I guess it's a little late to ask, but after all these years, I still can't understand why you left us. How could you be so cruel and act like we were worthless to you? Well, we didn't need you either, so again, we're even."

Glancing around the room, Kristina avoided looking at her dead father. She watched the second-hand jerk as it ticked around the face of the wall clock. Her stomach muscles twitched at the realization of her inability to fix their relationship. Since her father left, she'd felt like a piece of shattered glass, and if she didn't let people get too close to her, no one would notice how broken she was. Now, the biggest broken piece of her was gone. Kristina had no more excuses, she had to fix herself, and it scared the hell out of her.

Krissy, the eight-year-old little girl who had disappointed her daddy stood there scared to death to start living her own life. All she'd ever wished was to fall in love with a man she trusted not to leave her. She wanted to believe honorable men still existed, but so far, she'd only mastered pushing the good ones away while believing if she tried hard enough, she could fix the bad ones.

Years of feeling betrayed by her father tightened in her throat. "I deserve to know why you stopped loving me. I'm a sweet girl, Daddy." Kristina felt her voice getting stronger and her temper too. "How dare you raise that bitch's daughter and not me? You sonofabitch. Were you proud of yourself, getting two women pregnant at the same time? Why them and not us? Well, Daddy, I'm the fucking princess that paid for your goddamn funeral," Kristina screamed, causing her to cough.

Tears flowed. Taking a deep gasp of air, she lowered her voice. "What sort of man forgets about his children? Your sweet baby boy was only nine months old. Timmy deserved a good father in his life. It wasn't my job to help raise *your kid*." Snatching the last couple of tissues out of the Kleenex box on the cabinet, she flung the empty box across the room, mostly by accident, but it felt good. Kristina wiped her tears, and she took a deep breath. Nothing she'd said to the dead man would reverse the past. As her therapist repeatedly reiterated in their sessions, He has his own demons. *You can't fix what you didn't break, no matter how hard you try. Kristina, stop dating men who don't want a serious relationship. You can't change them either.*

Kristina's big strong superhero crushed her faith in love and affirmed her distrust in men. It was time for her to start working on healing both issues, or she'd continue to pay the price through more failed relationships.

She had to stop blaming herself for him leaving. Now, only a cold stainless-steel tray held her dad's broken soul. Krissy took his hand. The innocent little girl needed to feel close to her daddy one last time. The voices sang in her head of kids laughing as her Daddy held her hand and walked her to the school bus in the mornings before he went to work. She remembered the warm breeze of the summer evening air. She thought about the times her dad swung her in circles until they both landed on the grass with the sky spinning above them. His gentle fingers tickled her tummy, making her laugh so hard her sides hurt. She felt the peacefulness of falling asleep in her dad's arms, knowing that he loved her, believing he'd take care of her forever.

Her father's handsome face, once full of smiles and butterfly kisses, now lay weathered and empty. She closed her eyes and cuddled her face next to his. She heard his voice softly singing as he tucked her in bed: *Goodnight my princess, and dream sweet dreams. Sleep tight my sweet girl and may you always know, Daddy loves you so.* Her tears sprinkled his face as she kissed his cheek.

"Goodbye, Daddy." Kristina closed the door behind her.

Chapter Nine

Downward dog and standing on one foot in yoga class helped to balance Kristina's chi, but her creative juices had tanked. Booker and Kristina's publisher prepared for a big media push when they launched her new book, *Dating for the Clueless: Kristina Truly's How-to Guide to Modern Day Dating.* The media had already started booking interviews on local news channels and radio stations. The heat was on with the nonstop talk about book sales from the publisher's marketing team, and Kristina needed a break from the pressure. Spending time in nature would do a hell of a lot for her psyche.

There was still no word on Sophia Clark's disappearance, and the possibilities of her being found alive grew grim. Kristina couldn't let go of the fact that Sophia wouldn't go somewhere, leaving her elderly mother alone. The local news stations released Sophia's photos in a missing person's story with no mention of a connection to Jaclyn Renzo. Peter assured Angel and Kristina the FBI had no hard evidence that the two knew each other. The only connection the two women had at this point was they both attended Kristina's workshops *along with hundreds of other people. Yes, an outdoor adventure is exactly what I need to get my spark back for work. I need a few laughs and a nice outing, that'll help me refocus.*

Looking through her messages from the men online, Kristina deleted the standard: "Hi there, I like your pictures." But one message from Sam Brutarea, a handsome, brown-haired, green-eyed forest ranger at Angeles National Park, piqued her interest. They exchanged some getting to know you back-and-forth banter before Sam asked Kristina if she'd like to meet him for a day hike on Sunday afternoon. And since her online dating profile said she liked to hike, she thought: *Well, I'd pictured more of a hike from the car to the bar on the beach in Malibu, but we'll be outdoors, and it's as good a time as any to start actually hiking,* so she responded to Sam's message. "Would love to hike with you on Sunday."

~~~~

The Angeles National Park was located an hour or so from Kristina, who lived south of Los Angeles in Orange County. The park was a popular treasure for hikers that wanted a break from the hustle of the city. The two agreed to meet Sunday around lunchtime in the parking lot inside the main entrance.

Kristina woke to the bright early morning sun shining through her window. Excited to enjoy some California sunshine, she hopped out of bed and into a warm shower, made coffee, then thought twice about going hiking in a forest with a stranger. That's the mistake everyone made on the *Detective Murder Mystery* series Kristina watched obsessively, contributing to her already vivid imagination. She'd only spoken to Sam through a few texts. He could be another internet fraud. Kristina started thinking about the men she'd met over the years on the Internet. Most were odd in some way or another, but none of them had done anything to give her serious concern. But now, with Jaclyn found murdered and Sophia missing, she had serious trepidation about meeting a stranger alone.

Deedee accused Kristina of having poor judgment when picking men ever since she went to her high school prom with Joey Nuccio. Joey arrived at Kristina's house in his father's chauffeur-driven black sedan with tinted windows, rumored to be bulletproof. The driver waited outside the high school gymnasium until the dance was over. He took them for ice cream before dropping Kristina off at home. Deedee met Kristina at the front door, "Did you know Joey's dad is an Italian mob boss? Mrs. Peewits heard from her sister that Mr. Nuccio had someone whacked for welching on a hundred-dollar bet."

"Mom, relax. Joey will not hurt us. He made out with Lynnie Cowper at the dance. His dad's driver took me home after he dropped Joey off at the bowling alley to meet his friends. He didn't even say goodbye to me." Thinking about it now, Joey might have been the start of Kristina's poor relationship choices. Before Joey graduated from high school, he went to a maximum-security federal prison for stabbing a neighborhood kid thirty times for stealing his skateboard. Ended up, Joey's mom had put the skateboard in the garage when she found it on the front lawn. Joey pleaded self-defense. The courts tried him as a juvenile, but the judge gave him thirty years. Joey asked Kristina to visit him in the clink. Her fascination with true crime stories and whodunit murder mysteries started at a young age with Nancy Drew. So, Kristina went to see Joey, equipped with a new spiral notepad and a box of ball-point pens, ready for the full confession about the Nuccio family business. *Crime Novelist, Kristina Truly, Tells All.* She had the title of the book, and she was excited to write her first story. Joey had other plans for the two of them, such as conjugal visits. He wanted booty; she wanted scoop. She cut all ties. In Joey's last collect call, he let Kristina know he planned on taking care of her when he got out, and by the temper in his voice, not in a good way. The judge who sentenced Joey turned up in the Newport bay wearing a pair of concrete booties. With good behavior, Joey was due to be released anytime.

The notion of Kristina dating men she'd met over any electronic device drove Deedee to start nagging. Deedee's graveled voice sounded like alarm bells in her ears, "Kristina, it wouldn't hurt to date in groups. In my day, my girlfriends and I hung out together, and we'd meet with our dates in a group. We had a lot of fun; you should do that too, it's safer."

Kristina decided to invite her girlfriend, Susie. Not for protection. Susie's the size of a minute, and definitely not a bodyguard. Susie was, however, quite the outdoors person; she'd hiked Angeles National Park's trails a hundred times.

Sipping her coffee, Kristina pictured Sam showing up for their date, looking like the animated Smokey Bear. "Suz, good morning. Hey girl, how about going on a hike with me this afternoon?"

"A hike? KT, you've never gone on an actual hike. What's up?" Susie knew Kristina too well.

Kristina kept her fingers crossed, "I've got a date with this guy. He read my profile and thinks I like to hike. And maybe I will enjoy hiking; we'll soon find out. I thought it would be fun if you came with us. We'll get formally introduced at the parking lot where I agreed to meet him. I'll tell him I made a picnic lunch for all of us, and after lunch, we'll see how it's going. We also have a Plan B. If we're not up for a hike after lunch, we'll tell Sam you have to get back home for a niece's birthday dinner or something. Either way, it'll be fun. We'll get fresh air, and possibly meet a nice guy." She waited for Susie to buy in, or she'd cancel the date.

"Sounds like fun, let's do it. You'll love it. I'll pick you up; I don't mind driving. I know exactly where he said to meet."

CHAPTER TEN

In a previous life, Susie was probably a tree. She loved everything about the outdoors. That's why Susie and Sam, with his master's degree in forestry, immediately showed signs of old soul cosmic connections. Kristina, on the other hand, hadn't broken in her new, peony pink suede hiking boots. The leather was stiff, the laces too snug, her socks too thick, and her feet were swollen a half size larger from the bucket of popcorn she'd eaten while watching a movie the night before. None of it made for an enjoyable hike.

Susie took in a deep breath and closed her eyes. "This is perfect weather to get outside today." She opened her arms out wide, tilting her face toward the sky.

"Yes. Excellent weather for January, seventy-three degrees, clear skies, a pleasant breeze, absolutely splendid." Sam made the same gestures as Susie, soaking in the sunshine. He looked like a model in an outdoorsman catalog, down to the proper socks and boots. His short-sleeve T-shirt had safety reflectors on the back and front. His pewter colored backpack reflected the heat and had a tube that fed into a water bag inside. His lightweight orange jacket tied around his waist had solar-powered LED lights across the front and back.

The hiking trails were less than a mile from the parking lot, and Kristina didn't dare confess she felt a painful blister on her right heel. One thing was for certain, Kristina's designer hiking boots, although incredibly cute, would not get much use today. Her feet in those boots would never make it past the first picnic bench.

Blue skies and warm sunshine brought out the weekend hikers by the groves. People passed Kristina on the trail while she limped along with her eyes peeled for a spot to sit and rest her feet. Sam and Susie were plowing up the hills like two Energizer Bunnies, yakking like old pals. Both of them were plant nerds and started calling out the scientific names of every shrub, plant, tree, and weed on the path.

Susie enunciated perfectly, "Cystopteridaceae,"

Sam looked at Susie like a sixteen-year-old with a crush on his new BFF. "And the Cystopteridaceae are surrounded by lovely bryophytes mosses and liverworts." It was all Kristina could take while the two of them giggled like school kids.

At a fork in the road, Susie and Sam discussed which trail to take. A good distance behind the two of them, Kristina trudged her way up the trail using a crooked tree branch as a cane.

Susie glanced back to see how Kristina was doing. "Are you okay, KT? Do you want to sit down, or you wanna go back to the car? Your boots are cute but not great for hiking, are your feet hurting?" Susie's concern sounded sincere, and her suggestion for returning to the car was the perfect solution to the throbbing pain in both of Kristina's feet. But before Kristina could get a word out of her mouth, the human Smokey Bear chimed in.

"KT, there's a nice flat rock over there in the shade, why don't you relax for a while, have some lunch, and Susie and I will pick you up on our way back down. We won't be long. The sun will set in a few hours."

Kristina said, albeit sarcastically, "Yes, perfect. Sounds good to me." She flashed them two thumbs up, but she had a blatant look on her face that strongly hinted; let's get our asses back to the damn car. It all went right over Susie's head, and without hesitation, the happy couple headed off together, yapping and laughing. "You two go on, enjoy yourselves. I'll be right here, alone," Kristina muttered under her breath. "I'll be here eating the lunch I made for the three of us," her voice trailed off. She scouted for a place to rest and get off her feet.

Gathering dried pine needles, she veered off the dirt path toward the thick of the forest. She placed the pine needles down for some cushion on a large flat rock hidden from the noisy chatter of the hikers on the trails. High above the congestion of the city, Kristina soaked in the view of lush green pine trees towering as far as she could see. The breeze on her face relaxed her tight jaw and shoulders. *Aw, this is actually nice and just what I need, a bit of tranquility all to myself.* Kristina spread out her blanket and settled on the rock to enjoy the lunch she packed. Comfortable with her back perched against a tree, she propped her oozing blistered foot on an old hollowed out dead tree trunk. The wide tree trunks shadowed the sun, and the shade of dense branches cooled the air. Kristina zipped her jacket and covered her head with a wool beanie she had tucked in her backpack. The crisp scent of pine reminded her of the freshly cut Noble Fir tree she bought with Peter last month for Christmas. The sliced turkey on freshly baked lemon rosemary bread hit the spot. Kristina relaxed for the first time in weeks. She turned up the volume on her earbuds plugged into her iPhone to listen to her audiobook. The narrator's soothing voice put her right to sleep.

"Oh, shit. I'm covered with red fire fucking ants." Up off the rock, Kristina flew. How the hell those ants got down the back of her skintight jeans to bite her ass was a mystery, but she could light the Olympic torch with the flames coming from her tooshie. Kristina itched in places she couldn't access in public.

The sun had set, and the breeze felt much cooler now. Kristina looked around at the towering pine trees. She listened but heard only silence. When she'd sat down to rest earlier, the trails were hopping with hikers, and now there wasn't the slightest sound of voices in the distance. She was alone. "Susie, Sam, Susie, yoo-hoo, anyone …," Kristina yelled over and over; she heard nothing. Towering trees swayed in the chilly breeze, and their spindly branches cast long crooked finger-like shadows on the deserted trails. It looked like a perfect spot for the Zodiac Killer or a crazy homeless man to stash her body in a shallow grave. The hair on Kristina's arms stood up as she looked around, not sure which direction to go.

Cellphone service in a forest was spotty, but Kristina couldn't get a signal at all. Running wasn't an option; the blister throbbed with a pulse up her calf. With every step, her sock rubbed like sandpaper against her raw flesh. Her heart raced as though she'd just done crack cocaine. Kristina thought about pushing through the pain and start running, but she was positive she would have a heart attack or end-up tumbling down the hill if she attempted to break into a sprint. Time ticked on, so she picked a direction and headed down-hill, fingers crossed. Plodding along the path, she stumbled on every damn rock and twig. The moon hid behind treetops. She shuffled her feet with her arms stretched out in front of her. She looked like Frankenstein but felt like Helen Keller while she fought to see anything in the dark. The dim flashlight on her phone had barely enough juice to highlight her pink, now brown, hiking boots covered in dirt as she pointed the light towards the ground.

Something rustled in the bushes. Kristina heard branches snap nearby. The heat of something or someone brushed beside her body. *No one's there, just keep walking,* she tried to convince herself. Just the same, Kristina picked up the pace.

Caw, caw, caw. "What's that?" Some kind of creature screeched, and so did Kristina. Something from above breezed her head. In the blackness, her automatic reflex took over. She ducked her head, shielding her face with her arm. A huge crow swooped over her head, catching a clump of her hair with its claws as it flew away. Caw, caw, caw. It swooped again, but this time toward something or someone beside her.

"Mudder fuckin' bird. I'll kill ya. You cock sucker."

Kristina froze mid-step. The crow had pissed someone off, too.

"Hey, pretty girl. Wanna fuck?" Kristina caught a shadow of a hefty man followed by a strong stench. Kristina cupped both hands over her nose and mouth to keep from gagging.

"Need help, pretty girl. Bitch. Ruff, ruff, ruff, aw-ooh, aw-ooh." The man, probably a drug-induced schizophrenic, barked and howled at the moon as he pissed into the breeze, spraying a urine mist at Kristina, all the while heaving pinecones at her back.

Snap. She tripped on a fallen tree branch in the middle of the trail. "Ouch. Fuck." Kristina quickly hushed her voice as she slid on both hands and knees, trying to break her fall. She sprung to her feet like a ninja. Shocked as shit at her nimble moves, she didn't even drop her cellphone or lose her backpack. Blister or not, Kristina blazed that trail toward somewhere, but no idea where.

CHAPTER ELEVEN

Too much time had elapsed with no parking lot in sight. She had taken a wrong turn and had no idea which way to continue walking. *Breathe in through my nose; breathe out through my mouth,* Kristina chanted to keep from a full-blown panic attack. A grave situation got worse when she came upon three forks in the path. "I'll go right. The trail looks like it goes downhill. Wait, left feels instinctively the way I should go, or straight ahead? Damn it. I've lost my sense of direction since I started driving with a GPS. Ugh, which way do I go?" She was spinning in circles, and her chest felt tight. "Fuck me— I'm so lost. Breathe in through my nose and out through my mouth," Kristina chanted, but it didn't help. "Oh shit, oh shit, what do I do?" Her eyes darted back and forth in the darkness. Her heart thumped harder.

Off in the distance, she saw something flicker, and then again. Two flashlights beamed farther down the path.

"Help. Please, God: please be someone here to help me."

"Ms. Truly?" A faint voice echoed.

"Yes, yes, it's me. I'm straight ahead."

"Security, Ms. Truly. Your friends sent us to find you. They're very worried. You should not hike alone. It's very dangerous out here at night." Two young men in their early twenties dressed in brown jackets with the park's logo embroidered on the front chest pocket, green cargo pants, and hiking boots approached Kristina. She didn't need the lecture but wanted to kiss both of them.

"Oh my God. I'm so happy to see you two. I have a blister, and I'm not sure I can walk much farther."

"The parking lot is about a half-mile, can you walk, or do you need us to carry you?"

"No, I'll make it, but thank you."

"We'll take it slow." They took Kristina's arms, one on each side, and led her down the trail, shining their flashlights to keep them moving in the right direction.

Twenty minutes later, they reached the trail's opening where Kristina could make out two silhouettes sitting in Susie's front seat. Barely able to walk, she thanked the two rangers, giving each a grateful hug. Susie and Sam jumped out of the car when they saw her.

"KT, where were you? We came back for you, and I yelled your name until I was hoarse. I've been worried sick." Susie wrapped her arms around Kristina's neck.

Kristina didn't fess up; she wasn't where they'd left her and didn't want to mention falling asleep with her earbuds in either. "Let's not talk about it now. Thanks for sending help." She opened the door to the back seat. Her ass felt like hot lava, so she slithered across the seat on her stomach like a snake. "Get me out of here, please." To get relief from the itching, Kristina clawed her nails into the pant leg of her jeans.

She watched Susie make googly eyes at Park Ranger Romeo in the front seat of the car.

"KT, are you upset at me? We went back for you—we did."

"I'm not upset. In fact, I had a ball. If it weren't for the fact my ass is on fire from the fucking fire-breathing ant hill I sat on, and the blood poisoning in my foot from the dirt in my fucking blister, and the flesh wounds on my hands and knees from falling halfway down the goddamn hill—oh, and let's not forget the missing hair the crow pulled out—I would have stayed here all night."

Not hearing a word Kristina said, Susie and Sam chatted about the lovely day they had together, paying no attention to the bitch-tirade shot at them with both barrels.

"Yeah, yeah, you two, take a break, and Susie, please, drive me to the nearest drug store, I need Benadryl." Sam, the grownup Eagle Scout's ears perked up with the word, Benadryl.

"No wait, I have an organic antihistamine," Sam said like he had the cure for cancer. "I carry it with me in my Jeep for bug bites. I'll get my emergency hiking bag. Be right back." Sam leaped out of the car, hurdled over a concrete barricade, and darted in-between moving cars. He maneuvered like he was after the gold medal for the 100-meter dash on a mission to most likely kill the two of them with some kind of camping gear. That's the shit that ran through Kristina's mind.

"Hurry Suz, let's go before the human granola bar gets back and tries to kill me with some of his homemade snake oil." Kristina lay back down in the back seat and closed her eyes, waiting for Susie to start the car.

"KT, what do you mean? Sam's a very nice man. This is a perfect example of why you always pick the wrong guy. You don't know a good man when you meet one. And his name is Sam." Susie said and firmly gripped the steering wheel with hands at ten and two o'clock.

It took a lot to get Susie riled up and even more for her to raise her voice. Kristina knew she'd better button it because Susie was probably correct. No one deserved to find a nice guy more than Susie after her ex-husband cheated with her twin sister. Susie and Sam had a genuine connection. Sam and Kristina didn't have anything in common, so who was she to throw compost on the two all-natural, vegan, gluten-free, lovebirds? Sam and Susie were twin souls from another galaxy.

"Sorry, Suz. I've had a rough day. Did I mention a bushman pissed on me?" Kristina and Susie laughed; it kept Kristina from crying.

Sam came back with a large army duffle bag filled with camping supplies, including a small portable folding chair and a hefty size lantern bright enough to use as a searchlight. "Kristina, drink this." Sam handed her a paper cup of white, milky liquid. "It may not taste great, but it will stop the stinging and itching before you know it." Sam poured water from a recycled plastic bottle onto a hand towel, draping it across Kristina's forehead.

Kristina prayed, *"Please, God, don't let me end up having to have my stomach pumped after drinking some homeopathic crap a stranger gave me. As you know, God, my mother won't let me hear the end of it."*

She heard her mother's nagging voice: *I told you so, Kristina. You will get killed by some online maniac.*

Sam narrowed his eyes with intense focus, "Let me take your boot off and look at your foot."

Putting her trust in a man wasn't in Kristina's controlling nature. She wasn't falling for Sam's alluring helpfulness, just yet. But with her ass on fire and no way to scratch the itching without pulling her pants off, she needed to rethink the situation at hand.

Well, I guess if I have to go to the hospital to have my stomach pumped, I might as well have a foot amputated too. So, she closed her eyes, propped her foot up, took a deep breath, and swallowed a big swig of something poured from an unmarked glass bottle. She took one sip, then another. It didn't taste half bad.

Sam took off her boot, then gently peeled away her dirty sock from the dried crusty pus on her heel. The six-inch bloody open sore already looked infected, but Sam began working on it. Kristina recognized Sam's charming demeanor. Although their date didn't turn out quite as planned, Sam still stuck around to help her. The human granola bar was also a great man. She had been an absolute bitch judging him so harshly. "Thank you, Sam. I'm sorry I ruined the day."

"What? No. It was a wonderful day, Kristina. I'm sorry you got lost and got bit by ants, and boy, this blister has to hurt pretty badly. Next time we'll all stay together."

"Aren't you sweet," Kristina said. "I'm not sure there'll be a next time; I'm not much of a hiker." They all took the moment to lighten the mood with a laugh at the obvious.

The homeopathic antihistamine worked quickly. Kristina's ass stopped burning, and better yet, her crotch stopped itching. Sam treated her foot with a soothing creamed ointment and bandaged it like a professional.

He scooped her up in his arms, slid her into the front seat of Susie's car, and kissed her forehead. "Kristina, thank you for a wonderful day." He and Susie exchanged phone numbers with a hug goodbye. And that's when Kristina knew, once again, she'd blown it. Sam was a wonderful man. And like too many times before, she couldn't see it until someone else snagged him.

Chapter Twelve

Mozart's double concerto in D minor blasted from Peter's stereo. He drove his 718 Boxster GTS metallic night blue Porsche with the top down past two mid-rise red brick buildings. He parked on the corner, in-between the two white stripes painted on the pitted asphalt reserved for Employee 432. Plain, generic, no-frills, designed that way on purpose with nothing to let on this building was a base for agents of the Federal Bureau of Investigation.

Lost in thought, Peter imagined himself conducting a symphony of stringed and fluted instruments while his feet barely touched the ground in his routinely hurried pace. He directed a head nod toward three female agents chatting together in the lobby.

"What's up, ladies?" Peter said, flashing a sexy grin. "Brenda, you owe me ten bucks. I placed a bet at the track Thursday night on your boyfriend's damn horse, and the turtle came in dead last."

"*Please.* I heard you were in the Winner Circle all night drinking Cristal, so don't complain to me about money. Hell, you're wearing my monthly mortgage on your feet." Brenda teased. The other ladies continued to admire the view with a smile.

"What? These old thaaangs?" Peter mimicked a southern twang and gave a quick little two-step dance with his feet to show off his expensive rustic tan calfskin penny loafers without socks.

Peter stopped in front of the facial recognition camera mounted on the wall at eye level. He stood still with his eyes focused forward, waiting for clearance. The message: *Good Morning, Agent Esposito*, flashed in blue letters on the screen. Two retractable red Lucite flaps opened automatically in the center of the silver turnstile. Peter walked through the insulated ballistic double glass doors. A soft curl wound behind his ear, and a mound of hair the color of blackberries tasseled just below his crisp white shirt collar. Peter's natural light brown complexion and devilish good looks had most women dreaming about rubbing their hands over his smooth, tightly shaven square jaw and kissing his finely sculptured body from head to toe.

Growing up in Milan, Italy, with a young, single mother exposed Peter to hip fashion at a young age. Peter loved to watch his mom turn beads, pearls, rhinestones, chiffons, colorful silks, and linen fabrics into clothing for the high fashion industry. Even at forty-three years old, he sported a tweed hand-tailored suit with peg tapered pant legs as well as any GQ fashion model half his age.

"Good morning, my friend. Damn, you look good today." Joan greeted Peter at the security desk with the spirit of a Southern preacher on Sunday morning.

Steam billowed from the paper cup Joan handed Peter.

"We're out of half & half, so I made it just like me: hot, black, and only a tad sweet." Joan winked at Peter with a wide grin.

He blew on the coffee to cool it before taking a sip, "Mm, yep, perfect, just like you. How are you this morning?"

"I'm great, but honey child, you need to get yourself upstairs; the big Brass is waiting in your office. You break some rules again?" Joan let out a belly laugh, fully aware of Peter's motto. *Better to explain how you took the motherfucker down than to explain how the son of a bitch got away.*

Peter shot Joan a devilish smirk. "Ms. Joan, you know me. I'm always trying to explain myself out of something. Hope I don't need to kiss too much ass. It's a bit early for that." He made a sour facial expression. Joan led people to believe that her security clearance didn't allow her beyond the first floor, but agents knew if you needed information and you needed it fast, call Joan.

Peter sipped his coffee, waiting for the elevator, then opted for the stairs to join two colleagues chatting about their fantasy football picks.

~~~~

Deputy Assistant Director, Cheryl Ways, sat in one of the two blue Tartan plaid chairs in front of Peter's desk. Seated next to her was Detective Richard Jakes from the FBI's Special Crimes Unit. They both stood to greet Peter when he entered his office.

Agent Ways got right to the point. "Glad you're here early, Peter. Sorry to take over your office like this, but another pipe burst. My office is shit. Soaked everything, and who knows when maintenance will have it back together, but anyway, that's not why we're here. We need to talk about the missing woman, Sophia Clark." Ways had taken down some of the most sinister mobsters and drug lords in the country. No question, she earned her impressive ranking with the FBI.

"Hey Buddy, long time. How have you been?" Detective Jakes greeted Peter with a one-handed bro-grip.

Ways focused her attention on the cellphone in her hand. Text messages flashed one after another. "Great, you two know each other." Ways swiped her finger up the screen. She glanced up, distracted. "I need to take care of this." She waved her phone in the air as she walked toward the door. Without looking back, she said, "Peter, Jakes will fill you in on the case. I've got so much shit going on right now. Brief me if you have anything new." Ways carried her five-foot, three-inch, petite size two frame out of the room with the confidence of any six-foot-six male colleague.

Peter took a seat behind his desk, "Good to see you, man." He motioned for Jakes to have a seat. "It's been a while; it'll be nice to work this case together."

There wasn't time for small talk; they needed to figure out what happened to Sophia Clark and do it fast before they found another woman with her throat sliced from ear to ear, like Jaclyn Renzo.

Jakes opened a file on his lap. "Peter, tell me what you know about Kristina Truly?" He spread several candid photos of Kristina across the desk in front of Peter.

As a highly skilled operative, Peter was all business, but he didn't expect Detective Jakes to mention anything about Kristina.

"Kristina? What do you mean?" Peter asked. "What's she got to do with our case?" He thumbed through the photos, caught off guard. "Where'd you get these pictures?" Peter didn't like where the conversation was heading.

Jakes looked up from the file. "I heard she's a close acquaintance of yours." He still didn't answer Peter's question. "I want to discuss what you know about her."

Federal agents know to keep their personal feelings out of their professional life. Crossing the line between the two could wreak deadly consequences. Detective Jakes asked a question; Peter needed to give him an answer. But Peter needed answers first. If Jakes had the slightest suspicions that Kristina could somehow be involved in the murder of Jaclyn Renzo and the disappearance of Sophia Clark, then Peter needed to set him straight.

"Kristina's my best friend. I've known her since we were eighteen. She's not involved in this case, so let's cut the bullshit. Tell me what this is about."

"No, no, Peter, I don't suspect she's involved, not knowingly anyway. I read in your report Jaclyn Renzo, and the missing woman, Sophia Clark, both attended Ms. Truly's relationship workshops, and both live within a few miles' radius of her home. From what we can determine, those are powerful links between the two women. They were both divorced as of the past six to ten months but had different legal representation.

They both were doing the online dating thing as well. Kristina's seminars do get a lot of publicity. My gut tells me there's a link to the workshops and the women also living in Newport Beach. I'm trying to connect the dots. You know Peter, it's what we do." Jakes closed the folder on his lap and gave Peter a straightforward look.

"Jakes, come on, spill it. Have you got any new information that leads you to think Kristina's in danger?" As if the stakes to finding the killer weren't high enough for Peter and the FBI, they went up about ten octaves if there was a link to Kristina in some respect. Peter contemplated recusing himself because of his close relationship with her. He and Kristina are like family, and he wasn't sure he could stay neutral. Peter knew very well how this investigation could end if this turned out to be a serial killer. He thought maybe he needed to be the one protecting her.

"No fresh evidence, but with Sophia Clark missing and having attended the workshops, we've assigned a team to keep eyes on Ms. Truly, just as a precaution. It's too early to tell if there's any connection to Kristina. We haven't seen anything too unusual, but it would be best if you could persuade her to stay clear of strangers from online dating for now. We don't know what's up, and we can't say for sure that Jaclyn Renzo and Sophia Clark didn't date the same man they met online, or perhaps they met someone at Kristina's seminars. I followed Kristina around for a few days, and I've watched her TED Talk on relationships. I have to say, Peter, I can see why she's your best friend. She seems like a great person. A bit crazy in a good way, klutzy in a very cute way, and it's hard to deny she's beautiful." Jakes's dimples gave him away. Peter could tell he enjoyed getting to know Kristina, even if it was from a distance.

"Jakes, I can't stress this enough. We can't let Kristina know anything about this. You missed the part about her being nosy as hell. She'll somehow, with all good intentions, end up in the center of this investigation. So please, by all means, keep laser sharp tabs on Kristina, and keep her away from the details of these cases for now."

The phone on Peter's desk rang. It was his line reserved for the few that had the number: Kristina, Angel, and Joan. "What's up? *Fuck*. Thanks, Joan." Peter hung up the phone. His throat tightened.

"The cops found a woman's body. Her throat sliced like Jaclyn Renzo. It's Sophia Clark. Same bloody writing on the wall. *Sorry, I wasn't Mr. Right. XO, Mr. Wrong.* We need a media press conference as soon as possible. We've got a serial killer on our hands," Peter told Jakes as they headed en route to the crime scene.

CHAPTER THIRTEEN

Peter rode shotgun while Jakes drove his white Chevy Tahoe as fast as the midafternoon traffic allowed. Authorities discovered Sophia Clark's body at her family's cabin in Lake Arrowhead, a small town in the local mountains. Weather permitting, Peter and Jakes would arrive at the crime scene in less than two hours. As they neared the base of the hill, the sun vanished behind pepper and ash-colored clouds. Climbing up the mountain on the narrow winding single-lane highway, pockets of gusting winds caused the tank size SUV to sway. Snowy roads would prevail in the next few weeks, but today, the roads were clear. Pulled off in designated turnouts were a few slow-moving vehicles waiting while other cars passed. Jakes kept a heavy foot on the gas pedal. His blood pumped harder each time he noticed the clock on the dashboard.

A firm slam to the breaks jerked Peter forward then snapped his seatbelt tight across his chest. Jakes pumped the brakes again, harder this time to keep from rear-ending the truck crawling around the tight S-curves.

"Fuck me." Jakes's voice escalated. "Come on, buddy. Let me pass." The roads cut into the sides of the mountain. The horseshoe-shaped gravel turnouts for slow traffic couldn't accommodate anything larger than a passenger car, leaving nowhere for the truck to pull over.

The driver of the truck waved a firm arm gesture outside the window, motioning to stay off his tail. Jakes ignored the warning, continuing to travel closer than a gnat's ass to the back of the truck. The curve of the mountain and the wide-angle of the truck caused a deadly blind spot for Jakes. On impulse, Jakes darted over to the limits of the lane to see around the tanker before attempting to overtake it. He counted the cars lined up, one behind another on the opposing lane. Jakes swerved back in his lane, closer than before to the truck's rear liftgate. A growling low-pitched horn held a long note, a second stern warning from the driver giving Jakes a heads-up to stay behind him. Do not pass. But Jakes had his own agenda. He noted each car as it headed down the mountain, "One, two, three …" As the fourth car whizzed by, Jakes gripped his fingers tight around the steering wheel, hoping his math was correct. He turned the wheel a firm left. The large tires on the Tahoe screeched. Jakes's body leaned into the driver's side door as he straightened the SUV out on the opposite lane of traffic. He downshifted the transmission and punched the accelerator.

Jakes craned his neck to look over his right shoulder, checking the distance between him and the truck's monstrous steel grill. Jakes watched in his rearview mirror. Bright head-lights flashed, and the truck driver flipped his middle finger over his steering wheel. "Yeah, life's a bitch, my friend." Jakes grinned and kept his foot on the gas. The side of the Tahoe hugged the cliff around a hairpin turn. More horns sounded from approaching cars. Jakes never batted an eyelash at the narrow escape from a head-on collision.

Peter held his breath with both feet slammed to the floorboard. "Yo, Dude. What the hell? My side goes over the cliff first." His white knuckles gripped the door handle.

"Relax, I grew up in Colorado. I'm used to driving through treacherous terrain in the dead of winter. This is a ride in the park." Jakes gave a halfhearted laugh.

Peter swallowed hard. "Good to know." His spine stayed erect against the seatback. He kept a vice grip on the door handle while checking the phone's GPS with his other hand.

Jakes ran his fingers through his course thick sandy blond hair. "I hate to say it pal, but give it two miles, and it'll be pea soup up here. The fog will be thick around the backside of the mountain. We won't see a foot in front of us." Jakes wanted to get to the body before the forensic team did too much. They needed a set of fresh eyes on this case. It was crucial to find something—anything that led them to the killer. Jakes feared there'd be another victim if they didn't find whoever murdered these women soon.

"I pray the sonofabitch fucked up and left us something to go on. We need a break in this case, full-tilt." Jakes slowed the car down to a snail's pace. The low clouds hovered along the edges of the mountain, and fog slithered across the road like a graveyard in a Hollywood film. By the time they reached 4000 feet, visibility was almost totally blocked by the dense gray mass that hung in the air. Jakes kept his eyes focused on the road and slowly drove their SUV up the hill.

Peter continued watching the GPS on his phone. "We only have a few feet to go. Turn right on Grizzly Court. It should be right here," Peter stuck his head out the passenger window to read the street sign. "This is it, turn right. Right here. *Right here.*"

Jakes made a sharp right into the dense abyss.

"Okay, good, now we need to turn left on Bent Twig Lane. We should be close. Let me out of the car. I'll feel my way." Jakes stopped the car. Peter stepped out. The slick leather souls on his loafers slid on the wet gravel. "There's got to be a street here somewhere." He lifted the collar on his suit jacket to block the wind stinging the back of his neck. He tucked his bare hand into the pocket. Peter's lightweight business attire felt like tissue paper up against the brisk mountain air.

"How we doing, Rudolf?" Jakes joked at Peter through the open window. The tires sloshed on the muddy unpaved narrow access road when Jakes inched the Tahoe along. At the corner of Bent Twig Lane, they could see the cabin. Colorful white, blue, and red flashing lights from police cars and the criminal investigation vans lit the street like a holiday parade.

Jakes shoved the SUV in park. "Let's find this sonofabitch."

CHAPTER FOURTEEN

"I'm Agent Esposito, and this is Detective Jakes of special crimes. Who discovered the vic?" They both flashed their badges at the police officer standing guard. One of the cops pointed to the local squad car parked on the street in front of the cabin.

"I heard a family member called the local precinct to have them check the cabin just in case Ms. Clark came up here and got hurt or something. Whoever called said Ms. Clark had been reported missing for a few days. They didn't think to check the cabin until today, and there's no phone or internet service. The family doesn't use this place much. Said they'd talked about getting it ready to sell. Sounds like Ms. Clark rarely came up without someone in the family with her. When the officers arrived, they noticed blood on the steps, and the side door opened slightly. That's when they found the body."

Detective Jakes had surveillance on Sophia Clark's apartment. It made sense the killer knew better than to dump the body there, but how did they know the police didn't have eyes on the cabin? This question led Jakes to wonder if the killer knew Sophia Clark intimately.

Another police officer stood at the front door. "Watch your step. There's a lot of blood. Looks like she fought like hell.

Bless her heart." The officer shook her head in disbelief of the horror inside.

Dressed in white cotton one-piece cover-ups, a member of the forensic team snapped photos of the crime scene. The others gathered fiber samples and dusted for prints. The message left on the wall in Sophia's blood mimicked the message in Jaclyn Renzo's apartment, which didn't give Jakes any more of a clue than anything else.

Sorry, I wasn't Mr. Right. XO, Mr. Wrong. Jakes combed his fingers through his hair as he repeatedly whispered the words under his breath. "I guess this is the sick bastard's fucking calling card. Evil son of a bitch." Jakes looked around the room. The cabin had a typical black bear and pine tree décor and knotted pine walls with old, worn-out furniture. Jakes felt the knot in his throat tighten. Nothing stood out, not even a bread crumb to help find the killer.

Sophia Clark's fair skin lay naked and badly battered. Deep gouges across her back and stomach from a sharp object and blue-black contusions up her ankles and legs indicated a gruesome beating. Matted strands of her chestnut-colored hair draped over her face. Her battered body lay saturated in blood on the living room rug.

Peter made a mental note: a pair of red and white polka dot stilettos sparkled like new on the vic's feet, unmarked, not a drop of blood. It looked as if the killer placed them on her feet after the murder. The shoes resembled or maybe were identical to a pair of heels Peter remembered buying for Kristina on one of their fun lunch-shopping sprees together.

A distinct smell of tin lingered in the air. Peter knew the smell of fresh blood. He mentally noted the vic died within the past twenty-four hours.

Peter and Jakes snapped latex gloves on their hands and white cloth booties to cover their shoes as they looked around.

"FBI, Agent Peter Esposito. What are we looking at? Do we have a time of death?" Peter questioned the lead medical examiner kneeling beside Sophia Clark's body.

Peter knelt next to the ME to get a closer look. "Jesus, her larynx is completely severed. They nearly decapitated her." Peter squeezed both eyes closed, wishing he could un-see it. This crime scene ranked in the top five worst Peter had seen as a homicide investigator for the FBI. His stomach churned, but he kept his focus. More disgusting than seeing a horrific crime was seeing the bastard get away with it, and Peter would be damned if he'd let up until he'd caught the murdering maniac.

"At this point, my best guess, TOD less than twelve hours ago. There's not much rigor mortis. Considering the cooling temperature in here, I estimate she's been dead ten to twelve hours max. Whoever did this used a six-to-eight-inch knife. Probably a fishing knife, jagged edge, none too sharp either. From the look of the throat, it's not a clean slice. They had to work at it. Let's say it wasn't quick. She fought back, but they bound her hands tightly behind her back with jute rope and a zip tie. The perp is a malicious motherfucker. Let's hope we get some DNA off something, but they were careful. It's a brutal physical assault, kinky shit. Take a look at this." The ME pointed to Sophia's breast. One of her nipples was attached only by a sliver of skin, and the other areola had dried droplets of blood from the open wound where her nipple was torn off. He handed Peter a clear plastic bag. The hair on Peter's arms stood up like bristles. In the bag, Peter could see a hunk of raw pink flesh next to a silver metal clamp. Shivers ran up his spine. He handed the bag back to the examiner.

"Looks like they used metal clamps to tear her nipples off. Nothing unique about the clamps; they could've bought them online or at any bondage shop. We'll give them a once-over for prints and, hopefully, some DNA. We found a leather riding crop lying next to the vic. My guess, they staged it. Left a trinket to fuck with us, the high heel shoes too. Probably staged after her death. I don't think we'll find DNA, but if there is a drop, our team will get it."

"This seems like a big job for one person." Peter tried to put some pieces together.

"Agreed, but one person could have done it. It'd have to be a hefty guy, although she's petite. I'd say if it's one person, then they've done it before; otherwise, I'd say they had help. We won't know if there was forced sexual penetration until we get the body back to the lab, but she's bruised between her thighs pretty fiercely. There's fresh bruising and slap marks on her buttocks. The markings coincide with the riding crop. But we need to confirm everything in the morgue. Take your time looking around. We'll be here a while."

~~~~

"This cabin has been vacant for months, maybe years. Smells like it's been closed up all summer and needs a lot of repairs. Why here? How'd the killer get her all the way up here? We'll need tox results. Could've drugged her." Jakes talked himself through the scenario. He ran his fingers covered in plastic gloves through his hair to help him think. He headed down the hall to the bedrooms.

Hey babe, like always, I need your help. These women didn't deserve this. Aw, Anne. Love you, baby. Since Jakes's wife died five years ago, he never went without asking her to help with a case. His eyes swelled with tears. He still missed Anne horribly, and talking to her gave him peace, even if it was only for a moment.

~~~~

"Soon as day breaks, check to see if any of the nearby cabins have security cameras. This is a secluded road off the beaten path; someone may have cameras. Check with any local businesses for security footage. Maybe we'll catch a break and see someone in a car or stopping for gas. Hell, I don't care if the video shows someone stopping to take a piss on a tree. I want to see every minute of security footage on this mountain. Also, run background checks on any local security companies and real estate agents. Someone may have lured her up here posing as—well, check it out, I don't want to speculate—but let's see what we have to work with around town. Talk with the locals. This is a small community, and someone may know something," Peter said to the uniformed police officers working the field investigation.

The ME still on his knees next to the body, motioned Peter over. "Peter, look at this." He lifted Sophia Clark's disjointed leg enough to slide a piece of torn paper out from under her.

Peter examined the piece of paper. A quarter of the sheet had been tucked between the throw rug and the victim's thigh. It was partly saturated in blood, partially legible.

Jakes peered over Peter's shoulder. "What is it, Peter? What's it say?"

Peter's eyebrows raised; his jaw clenched. "It's a page from one of Kristina's books: 'I believe there will be a Mr. or Ms. Right at the end of your very long rope of Mr. or Ms. Wrongs.' Fuck. I think Kristina's in danger."

CHAPTER FIFTEEN

After the grueling investigation at Sophia Clark's crime scene, the FBI broadened their profile of suspects. Everyone at this point was on their radar—no exceptions. The investigation team wouldn't release any details discovered at two crime scenes to the public. They kept a tight lid on what information they released to the news channels and reporters. It was a fine line between informing the community and exposing their hand to the killer or a copycat killer. The FBI prepared for a national press conference with precise information, hoping the killer would take some bait and play their hand again with overconfidence, giving the FBI something they could use to catch the sonofabitch before they killed again. There were multiple points of interest in this case, but the connection to Kristina was one aspect the FBI made a priority.

Meanwhile, they dug deep into the backgrounds of the victims' family members, exes, friends, and strangers the victims met online. The FBI sent the information from the crime scenes to Quantico's forensic and criminal psychologist. Organized, educated, attractive, and pleasant—not a profile description one would think to describe a murdering monster. It's not your average suspect. Profiling gave the investigators valuable insight. The murders were not random;

the killer is organized, clever, and has an agenda. They will need to strike again soon.

Detective Jakes and Peter chose not to inform Kristina about the page from her book found at the cabin. They needed Kristina to carry on as usual. The risk they were taking was dangerous, and the security team watching Kristina had to be secret service quality. If their hunches were right, Kristina maybe the next target. The killer at this point could be a stranger with a deranged motive who happened to fixate on Kristina, or more likely it's someone she knew, directly or indirectly. It was a mutual decision that Jakes keep eyes on Kristina at any large public event, starting with a gala that evening.

~~~~

The Uber driver dropped Kristina off at the entrance of The Saint Ritz Hotel for the National Behavioral Health Organization's fundraising dinner. Kristina sparkled in her long black fitted dress and thick blond hair down her back. Seated on a bench outside the lobby, Jakes blended in like camouflage as he peered at the newspaper fanned open in front of him. Looking like any hotel patron, he gave no reason to suspect he held a black belt in martial arts and had military special ops training. His sniper-sharp eyes scanned for anything or anyone who flagged a potential threat. To stay out of Kristina's line of sight at close range for an entire evening posed a challenge. Jakes was up for the task. Watching Kristina in her black gown, he had no complaints.

~~~~

Kristina arrived at the hotel early with plenty of time to relax and have a glass of wine before the gala started. Mattie Johnson, a licensed mental health professional and a friend of Kristina's, had invited her to attend the pricy social soiree, mainly to gain kudos from the chairing committee for doing her part to raise money. She also believed it would benefit Kristina's career to socialize with those in the mental health profession. Booker saw the gala as an opportunity for good publicity. Kristina enjoyed supporting the cause, so she didn't pay attention to either of the two's agenda for getting her out of the house this evening.

Magnificent displays of ornate tapestries in the lobby caught Kristina's eyes. Sapphire blues, fuchsias, and buttercup yellow wool yarns hung from iron rods mounted forty feet high across the eggshell silk fabric wall. A white marble staircase leading to the second floor, with the swirling banister, gleamed like a shiny gold coin. The expensive artwork and elegant details of this popular hotel made for a gorgeous photo to share on Kristina's social media. She aimed her iPhone toward the top of the staircase to capture a shot of the wall of tapestries. As she focused on taking the perfect shot, her eye caught a toddler standing alone at the top of the staircase.

"No, no, no, baby—no." Hiking up her long gown with a quick swoop of her hand, like a gazelle, Kristina leaped up the stairs in spiked heels. She managed to grip the back of a toddler's tiny shirt collar in time to keep him from tumbling down the stairs. The toddler's eyes grew the size of saucers, and his bottom lip quivered as he burst out an ear-piercing cry. It scared the crap out of both of them. Kristina held him in her arms while he settled down, and they looked for his parents.

"Hey buddy, you're okay. Let's find your parents." The toddler wrapped his arm around his teddy bear. Kristina held his hand firmly while they walked down the steep winding staircase. A frantic pregnant woman in her bathing suit ran inside from the pool toward the concierge's desk.

"Aw, I bet that's your mommy," Kristina said. The toddler's face lit up when he saw his mom.

"Is this you're little guy?" Kristina let go of his hand. He ran full speed, letting out a loud, playful squeal.

"Aki, oh my goodness, you scared Mommy. Thank you so much. He's very quick. My heart's racing, thank you."

"I'm happy I could help. Aki, you stay close to Mommy and help her. Okay? You be a good boy." Kristina tousled her fingers in Aki's straight black hair. Without a blink, he ran off, and his mother shuffled behind him, shouting, "Aki."

Leaping up the stairs with speeds of a sixteen-year-old track star caused the bandage to pull away from the blister on Kristina's heel. Her dress puddled the floor, leaving only the tips of her shoes visible from under the gown. If she walked gingerly, no one would know she was barefoot. The damn shoes were too expensive to throw away, although she debated hiding them in a bush and retrieving them later—much later.

Keeping the torture-chambers on, for now, she made a deal with her feet to buy comfort over gorgeous from now on.

With his eyeballs peeled from behind a marble column, Jakes's heart melted, watching Kristina rescue the little boy. His throat tightened. Anne's voice played in his head. *Baby, she never missed a beat. I like this one.* Kristina's beautiful face and kind heart sent a feeling through his body that he hadn't expected nor allowed himself to feel since his wife died. It reminded Jakes of the years when his son was that age. For an instant, he felt Anne's lips on his. He remembered her kiss goodbye the morning she died.

Chapter Sixteen

A tropical floral arrangement and clusters of blown glass flowers towered two stories high in the center of the main foyer of the hotel. A group of Japanese businessmen gathered to admire the lavish arrangement. Kristina offered to take a group photo for them and ended up with a handful of cellphones. She aimed the first camera dead ahead toward Jakes. His sandy blond hair, six-foot-four build, and casual T-shirt stood out like a sore thumb in the middle of the group of men with jet black hair and navy blue suits.

"Shit." Jakes dropped to his knees below the men's rear-ends.

"Smile—one, two, three." Kristina focused, snapping a shot with each phone.

"Enjoy your stay in Newport," Kristina said, handing cellphones back to the group. The travel guide hurried the men aboard a double-decker luxury bus waiting outside. Jakes sat squatted in the empty foyer distracted by a text from Peter.

"Need help?" Two sets of double-D, round, perky breasts barely covered by beaded bikini tops stared Jakes between the eyes. The two women, not a day over twenty-five, stopped to offer Jakes a hand on their way to the pool. He sprung to his feet.

"No. I'm good." Jakes cleared his throat. "Just inspecting the marble for safety." The red in his cheeks accented his dimples.

"When you're finished, Inspector, come join us for a margarita at the pool." With grins on their faces, looking back over their shoulders, giggling, they said, "See ya, later."

Jakes adjusted his gun under his shirt. He stroked his fingers through his hair watching the girls swinging their tiny asses like they were on a runway. "Hell, I couldn't handle those two in my twenties," he said with a grin and got back to business.

~~~~

The night was just getting started, and already Kristina needed to sit down. Her black peau de soie high heels, elegantly styled with accents of dazzling rhinestones, were pinching the shit out of her toes. If she'd only broken a heel on the marble stairs, she could have justified going barefoot and used the story with the toddler for sympathy and probably a little praise. Instead, she had to suck it up and get through the evening fully dressed, including her shoes.

Seated at the bar, Kristina watched the sky glisten shades of orange through the windows as the sun slivered away for the night. She settled in, reading emails on her phone, and washing down two pain relievers with a glass of Pinot Noir. The sweet smell of the freesia and tuberose filled the room from the floral arrangements throughout the hotel. Other guests were mingling in an area of the bar set-up for cocktails and hors d'oeuvres before the charity dinner. The clock on the wall confirmed Mattie was over a half-hour late.

Jakes leaned against a wall away from the crowd. He took notice of everyone nearby. A man seated at a table across the room had been staring at Kristina. Jakes watched the man walk over to speak with her.

"Is this seat taken?" the man asked her.

"It's all yours." Kristina blushed. The man had an uncanny resemblance to the actor, Hugh Jackman. With a closer look, he was older than Hugh Jackman but equally handsome.

"Thank you. My name's Doctor Drake Toucuti."

"Whew, glad you're not Hugh Jackman. I was about to ask for a selfie with you." Kristina gave a wide-eyed smile to the celebrity look alike.

"Ha-ha, yeah, I hear it a lot. Wish I had his money instead of his looks. Are you here attending the gala this evening?"

"Yes, I'm meeting a friend. My name's Kris—"

Drake cupped her hand in his. "Yes, Kristina. I'm a big fan. Nice to meet you in person."

The stranger knowing her name and taking her hand sent tingles up Kristina's spine and not the good sort of tingles. Her stomached knotted. *Please, don't tell me you've watched the sex videos.* She took her hand back, tucking it on her lap under the bar.

"I'm sorry, have we met? Kristina pushed herself back in the barstool.

"No, we've never met, but I've heard a lot about you from a few patients who attend your relationship workshops. I'm a psychiatrist and specialize in marriage therapy. Your business, I hear, is booming. It appears you're quite the marketing guru."

"Thank you, Drake. It's a pleasure to meet you." She tapped her glass with his.

Kristina's cellphone vibrated with an incoming text: *KT, can't make tonight. Sorry, my son's running a fever. Hubby feels bad too. Hope you enjoy. Let's do a wine night soon.*

"Darn it. My friend can't make it. Her son's sick. I don't know anyone else attending tonight, so I think I'm going to head home. I hope you enjoy the evening. Pleasure meeting you, Drake." Kristina finished the last sip of her wine a bit disappointed to be leaving after everything she'd done to get ready for the evening. All day, she'd looked forward to the steak and lobster that was being prepared by one of her favorite chefs on the food channel. She was all dolled up with her slim-fitting fancy dress draping open past the small of her back. Her perfectly straightened long blond hair took forty minutes with the flat iron and cost sixty dollars. Plus tip. Not to mention the arm and leg it cost to have her makeup done flawlessly. She looked stunning, but it would be awkward going alone to an event where most people were licensed mental health professionals, not a life coach with a certification from an online course.

Jakes strained to hear their conversation over the loud chatter in the bar. He moved to a seat at the bar beside a heavyset man, which blocked Kristina's view of him.

Keeping eyes on Kristina the last few weeks gave Jakes a taste of her kindness to people, her sense of humor, and her straightforward, no bullshit attitude. He found her adorable, and he had an undeniable attraction for a woman he didn't actually know. He even felt a twinge of jealousy watching her with Toucuti. It was time to knock it off, and he knew it. Keep her safe and catch a killer. That's it. But regardless of his personal feelings for Kristina, instinctually, there was something about Drake Toucuti that he did not like.

"Kristina, listen, I'll pass on the gala too. Bamboo under my fingernails would be more enjoyable than listening to my colleagues ramble on about a paper they've recently published in a journal. I'd much rather take you to dinner. You look stunning this evening. Please join me. There's a terrific restaurant next door; it sits on the ocean. What do you say?"

"No, Kristina, don't fall for his bullshit. The guy's a douchebag," Jakes mumbled, swirling the straw in his Diet Coke.

"Gosh, how sweet of you. I'd love to try the restaurant next door. I've heard it's awesome. And luckily for you, I'm slightly more enjoyable than bamboo under your fingernails. Why not. I'll stop in the ladies' room, and then let's go."

Detective Jakes followed Toucuti into the men's room while Kristina went in the opposite direction. "Hey, pal." Jakes slurred his words, pretending to be intoxicated. "Will you hold my drink? I have to take a leak." Jakes stumbled, tossing a full glass of red wine, aiming for Toucuti's expensive designer suit. Jakes's plan didn't account for Toucuti opting for a stall, latching the door shut as the wine splatted on the wall of the urinals, missing the jerk completely. Drake Toucuti struck Jakes as the kind of asshole who would cancel his dinner plans to get his suit blazer to the nearest dry cleaner if a glass of red wine were to spill on it.

"Sir, it's time to stop drinking. Are you a guest in the hotel?" A hotel security guard happened in the restroom as Jakes threw the wine. Toucuti walked out of the restroom to join Kristina, oblivious to Jakes's failed scheme.

"Sorry for the mess." Jakes handed the security guard a twenty-dollar bill and got the hell out of there to track down Kristina.

CHAPTER SEVENTEEN

The restaurant was hopping with the busy weekend crowd. "Bonjour, Michael." Drake greeted the maître d' but focused his attention on the attractive woman standing behind the hostess desk, placing a kiss on each of her cheeks.

Bonjour, my friend Drake. Follow me. I've got your table ready." Maître d' Michael, ready with menus in hand, sat the two of them at a table adorned in white linens and cut crystal water glasses with a view of the ocean. Drake should have been at the gala, yet they had a table waiting for him while other guests queued up with an hour wait for dinner. That didn't make sense. Kristina's radar peaked, but the gurgling in her hungry stomach overpowered her intuition.

Without warning, the waiter brought them a silver platter topped with Himalayan salt crystals, sprinkled over a bed of crushed ice, lined with a dozen raw oysters on the half-shell.

"Wim, we'll start with a bottle of Joseph Phelps Insignia Bordeaux, please," Drake said with an air of haughtiness. The waiter wasted no time uncorking the three hundred dollar bottle of wine. First, he filled Drake's glass with just enough to smell and taste then waited for his blessing. "Excellent, do pour." And the waiter did just that. Drake's public persona seemed a bit over-the-top and arrogant for Kristina's liking. However, she always enjoyed a nice bottle of wine.

"They know me here. I'm a bit of a regular." The look on Drake's face and tone in his voice insinuated she should be impressed with Drake's expensive indulgence, as well as his frequenting the trendy hot spot. Showboating didn't impress Kristina. She preferred more understated than overstated when it came to most things, especially a male ego.

"Cheers, Kristina. Thank you for joining me." They tapped wine glasses and took a drink.

"Um, nice wine, thank you." Kristina briskly circled the base of her glass, allowing the wine to breathe before savoring the bouquet of dark fruit cardamom and a hint of tobacco.

"Back at the hotel, I called ahead while you were in the ladies' room. I requested a table near the window and my favorite oysters." Drake picked up one of the shells between his thumb and index finger. He reached over the platter, offering to feed Kristina the mollusk delicacy.

With wide-open eyes and pursed lips, Kristina turned her face before the nasty shell touched her mouth. "Oh, no thank you, I'll pass." Nothing seemed less appetizing than little snotty looking hockey pucks on a plate.

"What? Are you sure? They drizzle a delicious mignonette sauce on top. It's the best I've ever tasted. Can't I tempt you with just one?"

"No, no, I'll pass. I had a big lunch. I'll save room for dinner," Kristina said, hoping he didn't hear the rumbling of her stomach. At this point, she wanted to eat Moby Dick, except the only seafood she liked was grilled lobster tail.

Drake placed the oyster shell close to his full lips, tilted his head back, and allowed the wet grey oyster to slide into his mouth. Although the little snot-balls disgusted Kristina, she had no problem imagining Hugh Jackman sucking down a dozen large oysters off her naked breasts.

"Nice wine. Yes, very nice wine." Kristina placed her glass to her lips to hide her smile. Ignoring Drake, she continued fantasizing Hugh Jackman's lips on her perky nipples. Looking around the restaurant at all the couples reminded Kristina it had been a long time since she'd been on a proper date and even longer since she felt attracted to anyone special. So, she decided to enjoy the burst of hormones and give this guy a chance.

They talked a little about global warming and the current White House administration. Kristina steered the conversation to less controversial topics, hoping to avoid the dreaded first date question—why have you never married?

Drake spoke fondly of his two children, who he shared fifty-fifty custody with wife number two, brushing over details of his son with wife one. She wondered when he would stop talking about himself. So far, she had little in common with this guy, and there wasn't even a lukewarm spark sexually. Periodically, she chimed in the one-sided conversation, uttering a few, "Oh, mmm, wow, interesting" contributions.

Please shut up and order food. I'm going to pass out. Disinterested in Mr. Self-absorbed boasting about his achievements, Kristina sipped her wine, holding back a yawn.

"Wim, we'd like to order. I'll have the Macadamia nut, crusted halibut. Please tell the chef not to overcook it. Steamed vegetables, no butter, or sauces. Let the cooks know it's for me; they know what I like. A Caesar salad, no croutons, light on the dressing. My date will have the mahi-mahi, vegetables—same as mine, and a salad with vinaigrette."

"Madame, the mahi is served with a lemon caper sauce on a bed of rice pilaf. Is that okay?" Wim directed his question to Kristina.

"The rice is fine, but no sauce," Drake answered for her as if they'd been seeing each other intimately. Considering they'd met two hours ago, Kristina butted in.

"Oh, thank you, but I prefer filet mignon well-done, no red. In fact, butterfly a baseball cut if you have one and cook the hell out of it. Please give me the biggest baked potato you have in the kitchen. Load it up with everything and then put more on top of that. That'll do it. Thanks, Wim."

"Well, a woman who knows what she likes. Is the salad okay?" Drake asked. He handed the menu half-handedly to the waiter without eye contact.

Kristina sensed animosity in his tone. "Yes, the salad with vinaigrette is perfect, thank you." Kristina calmly closed her menu, handing it to Wim with a smile.

Dating etiquette is one of the many topics Kristina and her mom disagreed about. Deedee Marie, a bit old school, argued that a lady should let the man order for her. Kristina agreed; a lot of women liked that from a man, especially in the 1940s. Kristina lived in the modern age of women, and she took care of herself. Deedee insisted this is one of the reasons Kristina couldn't find Mr. Right. Deedee preached, "Allow the man to be the man." Kristina argued tonight's scenario in her head. She concluded it would have been less egocentric of Drake to ask if he may order for her. *Yes, order me a fucking steak well-done with a big giant baked potato with butter, sour cream, chives, and bacon. And I want ranch dressing on my damn salad.*

And with that, Kristina made a note to self; new seminar: How to Get What You Want by Telling Your Partner What You Don't Want.

The candle on the table cast a soft glow over the wrinkles around Drake's eyes. Kristina saw the thin surgical scars behind his ears and at the top of his hairline. He'd had work done and was older than he'd admit, which Kristina added to the list of red flags.

"Kristina, may I suggest dessert?" Drake opened the small tan leather-bound menu the waiter left on the table.

"Yes, please. Whatever you'd like," Kristina said, accommodating his ego. Plus, she enjoyed anything sweet. Fortunately, Drake ordered her favorite: chocolate soufflé, baked twenty minutes, gooey melting hot out of the oven. The decadent dessert masterpiece came dripped with creamy dark chocolate, sprinkled with fresh raspberries and creamy vanilla ice cream, the good kind, with lots of scrumptious fat.

The waiter poured the last of the wine into Kristina's glass from the second bottle. "Wim, if you are trying to get me drunk, it's working. Where's the ladies' room?" Kristina excused herself. After all the wine, she felt a bit tipsy, waddling to the lavatory. Her foot caught in the hem of her long gown, causing her to stumble. Seated on a nearby barstool, Detective Jakes jumped to his feet to catch her before she hurt herself. Their eyes met for only a moment. Jakes's heart raced. At the same time, a woman also on her way to the restroom discretely slipped her arm in Kristina's arm and kept her from falling. Kristina glanced again toward Jakes, but he was gone.

"I'm such a klutz. Thank you. How embarrassing." Kristina and the woman giggled as they entered the ladies' room arm in arm.

Jakes nearly blew it. He questioned himself: *were his feelings for her getting in the way of her safety and the case?* Flat-out, he needed to nip the crush he had going on. *Kristina's the subject, not your girlfriend.* Kristina's thick blond hair, next to her light olive skin, her crooked smile with beaming white teeth and big round crystal blue eyes, made Detective Jakes's heart race, his palms sweat, and he got a rosy, cheeky grin on his face every time he saw her. Feelings like these hadn't been something Jakes allowed for himself since his wife was killed. He giggled like a kid, thinking about Kristina tripping over her own feet and liked it when their eyes locked. It was late, and this schmuck grated on Jakes's nerves. Kristina needed to wrap it up with Drake, but it seemed they were just getting started.

~~~~

Before Kristina went back to join Drake, she took a minute to contemplate if the evening had much potential for a second date with Drake. He had potential with his dapper hand-tailored suit and dashing good looks, but he pushed boring as hell to a new level. The bottles of wine and a chocolate soufflé with a date so well-dressed, educated, and handsome typically added up to the proverbial walk-of-shame in the morning. But the thought of waking up next to Drake and possibly having to hear another frat brother story, made her cringe. So, with freshly glossed lips and a squirt of minty breath spray, Kristina returned to the dinner table ready to thank Drake for a nice evening and call it a night.

CHAPTER EIGHTEEN

"Excuse me. Did you see where the gentleman sitting at this table went?" Kristina inquired of the busboy who was resetting their empty tabletop.

"Outside, Miss. He requested we move everything outside behind the fire-pit to enjoy the rest of the evening on our beach patio." The busboy set his tray filled with old dinner dishes on the stand next to the table. "Right this way. I'll show you to Mr. Toucuti." Kristina followed close behind, maneuvering through the crowded bar.

Ah, I like this. Drake pulled a smooth romantic move. He's been so damn vanilla till now. Maybe he's nervous; people talk about themselves when they're nervous. Angel says I do. Hmm, what the hell, let's see where this goes, Kristina thought as she joined him outside, hopeful she'd see a more likable side to her handsome date.

"Oh, good, you found me. Isn't it nice out on the beach tonight? I love the ocean. Please sit here next to me, Kristina." Drake motioned for her to sit on the thick rattan settee decorated with oversized pillows covered with large Hawaiian style floral fabric. Kristina sucked in her stomach and sat next to Drake.

The salty ocean breeze carried a faint fragrance of Plumeria, reminding her of the last time she was in Maui. A vague mist from the waves lightly dusted her face. Relaxed from the wine, Kristina enjoyed the fresh ocean air. The tempo of waves crashing on the jetty softened the tightness in her shoulders. A fire flamed through the rainbow of colorful chips of glass mixed with volcanic rocks filling the base of the ultra-modern fire pit, where Kristina and Drake sat secluded from the center of all the action in the bar. Outside, the fire pit's soft light and cool breeze felt like the nudge Kristina needed to ignite a flame with this guy.

The strap of her satin dress slipped off her shoulder. She left it draping seductively, and she leaned over closer to Drake. Staring into his emerald green eyes should have made her heart flitter, or at the least, flit, but the chemistry simply wasn't there. Kristina felt no romantic attraction for Drake. No harm, no foul, she decided to stay a bit longer and make the best of the evening.

Besides, she pretended to be interested in boring conversations a hundred times before with men she'd met on the Internet. Some even turned into friendships, and some turned into paying customers by attending her workshops and buying her books.

The cocktail bar was overflowing with people. She turned her ear toward Drake to hear him better. After fifteen minutes of chatting about his Penn State college days, he looked Kristina in the eyes with their faces so close she could smell the chocolate soufflé on his breath.

"Kristina, I'll be honest with you," Drake said.

Kristina could hardly hear him over the loud chatter from the crowd. She raised her voice, "Great, what's on your mind?"

"Kristina, the salt air makes me horny." Drake smiled with a cocky expression on his face. "I'm going to do dirty, nasty stuff to you—right here." He cleared his throat and sipped his wine.

Kristina edged back against the seat cushion. She glanced over her shoulder to see if anyone nearby overheard him. She'd consumed so much wine her brain lagged for a split second, but she thought: *What did he say? Wait, did I miss something? How long was I in the restroom?*

Not sure how to respond, Kristina held her tongue but let out a sarcastic laugh.

"No, you're not going to do anything—" and before she could finish her sentence, like a daytime soap opera actor, Drake flung himself back in the settee, stiffening his body.

"I'll be frank. I don't like games." Drake's emphatic enunciation of every word let her know this was no joke.

Kristina pulled her strap back over her shoulder and responded with the same intensity in her tone, "Okay, what's on your mind, Drake?" She looked around for an exit.

"Here's the thing, Kristina. I've wanted to talk to you for quite some time. It wasn't an accident I joined you at the bar. I heard from Mattie that you'd be at the gala. Lucky for me, Mattie didn't show."

Kristina stayed seated on the edge of the seat with her four-inch heels planted on the ground, ready to leave. For now, he had her full attention.

"I've got clients that lost their marriages because of you. Their spouses read your books and attended your relationship seminars, and the next thing they knew, they were in expensive divorces. Some clients feel you ruined their marriage. They blame you for their financial troubles. Most men don't enjoy giving the ex-wife half of their fucking money, nor do they like having their medical license revoked." Drake may have let that part slip, referring to Kristina's ex-boyfriend, Randolph Joxhell, losing his license, or perhaps it was part of his plan to fuck with her.

"Waiter, bring me a warmed snifter of Cognac, VSOP, and whatever she wants." Drake's manners tanked along with what little personality he had.

"Nothing for me, thank you," Kristina said as the waiter headed to the bar for Drake's drink.

"Kristina, I needed to have this conversation with you before you and I have sex. You're not a therapist."

"Correct. I'm not a therapist. And there's not a chance in hell of having sex." Kristina maintained a tight grip on the gold sequined clutch bag in her lap.

"You're treading on thin ice with me and many of my colleagues."

The waiter set down the cognac in a rush to attend to other patrons packed in the patio bar.

Kristina was well trained in psychological studies. She knew narcissists, perhaps even a sociopath in Drake's case, prey on a victim's weaknesses.

"Pardon me doc, but I've studied under some of the most renowned psychotherapists in the world, and I know the professional differences between a licensed therapist and a life coach. I never cross that line," rebuffed Kristina.

"Well, maybe so. However, we don't like you presenting yourself as a relationship expert. You're not."

"I've got my BA in psychology. Pursuing an MFT isn't my priority for now. I'm busy with my hugely successful relationship coaching career," Kristina fired back with a smug grin.

"Don't get me wrong. We appreciate the business your work creates for all of us with the distraught divorcées and the jilted brokenhearted." Drake carried on like he was having a conversation with himself. He smiled at a much younger woman seated at the bar and tipped his glass in her direction. "Cheers, sweetheart."

"It's endearing Drake, that you and your colleagues have such an opinion of me, a motivational speaker. I'm flattered. But as you said, I'm not a therapist. I'm not the competition." Kristina smirked but didn't want Drake to think he was getting to her.

"Like I said—thin ice Ms. Truly." Drake blew the woman at the bar a kiss.

It was time to leave. The comments Drake made let Kristina know her ex-boyfriend/ex-therapist had something to do with this evening. Randolph and Drake were likely friends, and this could be Randolph's way of reminding Kristina he still had connections to her, or maybe he was a patient of Drake's. It didn't matter. Either way, this evening turned into a dangerous situation. With her purse in hand, she stood up to walk out of the bar through the patio's exit gate.

"Kristina, I apologize if you find what I've said offensive. I like you. I just thought I should tell you what's being said among a few therapists in town. Remember, Kristina, some of our patients blame you for losing everything. Some even care about losing their money more than their spouse. Professionally, I consider a few of these people mentally deranged—and downright evil. I'm simply saying, watch your back." Drake tightened his upper lip. Aiming a vile stare straight at Kristina, he warmed his cognac near the flames in the fire pit.

"Thanks for the concern. I can take care of myself." Kristina glared at Drake as though she'd just had an injection of Botox. It would give him pleasure to see her riled up. There was no way she'd allow him that satisfaction. Inside, volcanic lava spewed through her veins.

"I've heard, sweetheart, you don't practice what you preach. Did I mention one of my patients knows you very well? Drake raised his voice. He was shitfaced from all the booze. Kristina ignored him, debating which path to the exit was closest.

"My client tells me you like it rough, real rough. Aw, cut the nice girl bullshit. I know you carry nipple clamps in your purse. You'll beg me to stop when I slap your ass. Giddy-up, you slutty little life coach." Drake laughed.

Drake slurred his words, but he knew exactly what he was saying. He didn't like Kristina putting him in his place; he enjoyed screwing with people, especially women.

"Dirty, nasty, kinky . . . hiccup, life coach. Oh, and there's no safeword when I'm fucking you," Drake shouted, laughing as though he'd said something hilarious. People in the bar looked to see who the loudmouth drunk was.

Nervous, Kristina dropped her purse. It slid under the concrete block with the fire pit on top. Drake sat out of eyeshot behind the fire pit. Kristina bent down to pick up her clutch and saw that Drake had unzipped his slacks. He sat relaxed with a proud grin and his rocket ready for blast off. That was the end of the line. She had had enough of this unhinged jerk.

The time had come to put this deranged pervert in his place. With one swift scoop, she filled her empty wine glass with pieces of volcanic rocks and chunks of colorful glass from the fire pit. Problem solved. She tossed the scalding decorative stones smack-dab onto Drake's fuselage.

"You might want to rethink that safeword when you fuck with me. It's just a suggestion. I'm not a licensed therapist." Kristina calmly set the wine glass down on the ledge of the concrete table.

"Fuc . . . Sonofabitch." Drake hopped around, flailing both hands at his crouch, knocking the hot rocks loose from his smoldering flesh.

A man seated at a nearby table with his wife let out a gasp, spontaneously clutching his own jewels. Drake spewed obscenities while pieces of sizzling volcanic rock burned through his lightweight gabardine slacks. The man's wife stood up, focused her aim, and tossed a glass of ice water on Drake's charred penis.

"Nice shot, girl. Enjoy your evening." Kristina laid her hand on the woman's shoulder as she walked past the table.

After prying off her heels, Kristina walked for two blocks to calm down before signaling on her phone for an Uber driver to take her home.

~~~~

Detective Jakes sat in his Tahoe with eyes on Kristina walking barefooted in her beautiful gown. He wiped the tears in both eyes with his sleeve, and his stomach muscles twitched. It had been a long time since he'd laughed that hard. He phoned Peter while he waited for her to get in the Uber. He squeaked out the story in between trying to catch his breath before breaking into laughter again.

"I'm not sure Kristina needs my protection. Seems she can hold her own." Jakes laughed with Peter for ten minutes as he rendered a blow by blow of the evening's entertainment.

Kristina's audacity turned Jakes on. He loved a woman with spice.

The next morning, a large man in a black suit representing Drake Toucuti served Kristina with a restraining order at her office. It wasn't the first.

CHAPTER NINETEEN

After the past few dating disasters, Kristina agreed that Angel knew best. It was time to focus on herself and her career. Growing up, Kristina learned about life bobbing around in an ocean alone. Her mom gave plenty of love but little guidance. Deedee often worked two jobs to keep up with the demands of a single parent.

At eight years old, Kristina helped run the household, take care of Timmy, and do her homework. She took care of others and navigated her life by trial and error. Mostly by error, she learned how to choose her weapons wisely and hide her wounds well. In her world, shit happened, and she figured out early, life had two options—sink or swim.

The majority of Kristina's successes came because she had the same relationship problems as everyone else. She didn't pretend to know exactly what made for a perfect relationship and what didn't. Instead, Kristina stuck to teaching with raw passion and uncensored brutal honesty. Things moved rapidly, and the stress level went from "this is a lot of fun" to "what the hell's happening to my life?"

Kristina's literary agent and book publisher rated the talent they represented by popularity and book sales. Kristina had both. She'd risen as an internationally recognized relationship expert with her books translated into several languages.

All of this contributed to mounting pressure for one book to outdo the other. Kristina felt like a tea kettle ready to whistle with all the hype from the media, her agent, publicist, and whoever else could grab a piece of her.

Kristina sat at her desk, posting on social media instead of sending her editor the requested changes. Agents and editors were going to wait because tonight, she planned to put her ass in a chair, a cocktail in her hand, and enjoy lots of laughs with her close girlfriends.

"Kristina, why don't you call it a day? Aren't you exhausted from all the writing you've done?" Angel teased while she straightened up the office before going home for the evening.

"Ha-ha, smartass. There's always tomorrow. I'm too stressed-out to be creative. I'm going to go for a run. That'll help, and then, mucho margaritas with the gals in the neighborhood. We all need a few good laughs. I'll finish up the changes and send the book back to my editor in the morning. Good night, Angel. See you tomorrow. Drive safely." Kristina tidied the papers on her desk and turned off her computer.

Angel gave Kristina a double-take with bulging eyes. "Beep, beep, back it up, KT. You're going for a run? You haven't gone for a run since PE class in high school. This is no time to go running alone at night." Angel planted her hand on her hip. That meant one thing—an earful coming Kristina's way.

"KT, another woman is missing in Newport. Peter said she lives on the beachfront. They aren't announcing the details to the public yet. FBI's keeping this tight-lipped. You know how the damn mayor cares less about people's safety than he cares about his tourism and safe streets campaign." Angel waited at the office door.

"Oh, no. Poodles sent me a text. I didn't read it yet. Did he tell you who she is? Please don't tell me she's been to our workshops."

"He didn't give her name. It seems everything lately is on a need to know only basis with Peter," Angel said.

"That's just his FBI badge talking, or in this case, not talking. Angel, I can't take someone else we know missing. I'll frigging snap." Kristina stretched her neck from side to side to keep her tension down.

"KT, go workout at the gym, and make sure a couple of big buffed gym rats walk you to your car when you're done." Angel gave Kristina the look—Angel meant business.

"Well, I'm waiting, KT. What possessed you to go for a run this evening? You aren't telling me everything, girlfriend," Angel interrogated again.

"Nothing possessed me. It's just an expression. You know, like I'm going for a run, or stop beating a dead horse, or you're a pain in my ass." Kristina smirked, trying to keep a straight face, knowing damn well Angel wasn't buying her bullshit.

"Kristina Melanie Truly." Angel let out a bold laugh. "You know my favorite expression. You're full of dookie. I know you're up to something. Talk, rabbit."

When Angel used her entire name, the gig was up. "Okay, okay, I'll talk. We have a new neighbor. His name is George Handy. The girls in the neighborhood call him Eye Candy

Handy. I could use the exercise, so I planned to run-walkish by his house on my way to Deb's house for cocktails. He might be outside unloading boxes. I'll casually introduce myself like any good neighbor. Maybe I'll luck out and get a peek without his shirt on. He's single and very handsome." Kristina knew damn well Angel wouldn't approve. "Oh, and he's actually somehow related to Kooky." Kristina hoped Angel would loosen up once she heard George was related to Koo Koo, who was like a sister to both of them.

"For god sakes, KT. You're on a break from meeting men. Give it a rest." Angel held no punches.

"Wait, let's clarify. I'm on a break from meeting crazy men on the Internet. Besides, this is harmless. I want to see what all the fuss is about. James from the hair salon says every divorcée in my neighborhood is hot on George's tail."

"Aw, I love James. His new BF, Mark, is adorable. Okay, stalk him from the inside of your car with all the doors locked. Let me know if the Handyman's as perfect as they say he is—no touching—eye candy only. KT, pack it up. I'll wait for you, and we'll walk out together. Another woman missing. That isn't good, girlfriend." Angel and Kristina secured the office door and headed downstairs to their cars.

CHAPTER TWENTY

By the time Kristina made her way home in the evening traffic with the long summer days gone, she thought it best to take Angel's advice. A drive-by with doors locked.

Turning into her housing tract, she spotted a large U-Haul truck outside George's house but no Eye Candy Handy in sight. A dense offshore fog rolled in. Kristina flicked her windshield wipers to clear the dew. Other than a vague, glowing light from an upstairs window, George's house lurked in darkness.

From the car radio, Kristina listened to her favorite *True Crime* podcast. In his gruff voice, an Australian narrator described the gruesome details involving murders of a mother and her two children. More unease ran through Kristina while listening to the story of decomposed bodies buried under the floorboards of an abandoned farmhouse. Tapping the screen on her car stereo, she quickly changed the station. Calming saxophones and horns blew jazzy tunes. Women dancing in colorful beaded dresses and men in tuxedos conjured in Kristina's imagination. She and Clark Gable danced the tango. Several chimneys billowed smoke from the neighboring homes. Slouched low in the driver seat, Kristina felt like a private investigator casing the joint. A large empty box lay on its side outside George's front door, but nothing else to report. Tired and ready to change into comfy clothes, Kristina punched the pedal and headed home a short block away.

Hair stood up on Kristina's arms when she thought about another missing woman. The prominent beach city where she lived didn't have much serious crime, especially in her neighborhood. Petty theft had risen just like inflation, but murder and women missing were far from the norm in Newport Beach. It scared the crap out of her.

"Damn it. I forgot to change the timer for the outside lights." She slapped the steering wheel with the palm of her hand. The city of Newport had started updating all their streetlights to LED but hadn't finished the work on her street. Without the lights on, all she could see was a dark silhouette of her house. And not a single light on at Lois and Jim's house. They were still in Hawaii, and the house screamed, "No one's home. Come on in."

Kristina felt a knot in her stomach. Angel's voice echoed in her head: Another missing woman. Kristina bought her house with a security system five years before. It was a safe neighborhood, and people rarely even locked their car doors. After her crazy ex-boyfriend, Randolph broke in, she got in the habit of setting the alarm. Occasionally, she'd forget, but after the date with psycho Drake, she'd been diligent about setting it.

"Incoming call from unknown caller. Answer or ignore?" Kristina's earpiece announced. Feeling skittish, Kristina welcomed someone to talk to. "Answer," Kristina said into her earpiece while pulling into her driveway. She pushed her garage door opener and remembered when it didn't open that it was time for new batteries.

"Answering call."

"Hello, this is Kristina." A static crackle in the phone connection sounded in her ear. She adjusted the earpiece, slung her purse over her shoulder, and grabbed the phone from the charger. A clicking sound repeated from the phone line. The caller didn't respond. "Hello, this is Kristina, we have a terrible connection. Who is this? I'll need to call you back." Kristina locked the car doors and hurried toward the front door.

She couldn't stop thinking about the missing woman. Her nerves got the best of her as she hurried to unlock the front door with the porch light off. She fumbled the grip on her keychain. The keys landed in the bushes, and her phone flipped out of her hand face down on the concrete, shattering the glass screen. "Ugh." The phone line continued a clicking noise with the caller still silent.

She dropped her purse on the welcome mat and tried swiping the screen on her phone for the flashlight. "Who ... is this?" The cracked screen scraped the tip of her finger. "Crap," Kristina said, sucking droplets of blood off her index finger. Down on her knees, she ran her hand under the shrubs to feel for her keys. "Are you still there? Who is this?" She barked into her earpiece.

"Hope you find what you're looking for, Kristina. I'd hate someone to hurt—"

"Who the hell is this? What do you mean? Who is—"

The clicking stopped. The phone line went dead.

From the muddy soil, she pulled out her keys. Shaken by the strange male caller, her heart pounded. It was too dark to see. She rubbed her hand along the door's hardware to search for the keyhole. "Where the hell's the slot?" Her hands trembled like her Great Aunt Sally's. "Calm down and unlock the frigging door," Kristina scolded herself.

A set of headlights from a large truck heading down the street gave a flash of light long enough to slip the key in the slot. She rushed inside, slamming the door behind her. Kristina locked the deadbolt and flipped the light switch on the wall. Her living room and kitchen lit up like a football stadium. The security system's chirping stopped after she disarmed the alarm with the five-digit code. After all of that, her exterior lights came on automatically. The timer to control the lights was in a box with a padlock on the side of the house. She needed to dig around the junk drawer to find the code, but that could wait until morning. She posted a note on the inside of the front door: *Find padlock code. Change the timer. Buy a battery, garage clicker. Replace phone screen.*

Without a concern in the world, Ms. Prissy groomed herself on the living room sofa, and with a long, extended stretch, she headed to the kitchen for dinner.

After feeding Ms. Prissy, Kristina sat frozen at the dining table. She clutched her chest, thinking about the caller. *Were they watching me? Is that what they meant by, "I hope you find what you are looking for?" Did they see me looking for my keys? Or could it have been one of the crazy men I've dated, insinuating, albeit sarcastically, they hoped I get what I'm looking for in a relationship?* Kristina ran scenarios in her head but didn't know what to think. What else did they start to say before the line went dead? *"I'd hate someone to hurt—"* To what? *Hurt me? What were they going to say?* They knew her personal cell number and possibly where she lived. Thoughts about the stranger pulling out of Lois and Jim's driveway flashed in her head. Could he have been the same guy parked next to her at the hospital? Or was her overactive imagination getting the best of her? Kristina stewed as Ms. Prissy finished her shrimp and cod pâté.

A phone call to her security company would tell her if someone had been around her house—she needed to know.

"Hi, this is Ms. Truly. I want to make sure my exterior security cameras are working properly. Could you please check the video footage from this evening?"

"Good evening, Ms. Truly. I'm happy to help you. Is everything okay?"

"Yes, I'm fine. I just want to see if the video shows anyone snooping around my property this evening. I'm sure it's nothing, but I have a feeling someone's been by my residence while I was out. I'd like for you to check for me."

"Certainly, Ms. Truly. Give me a moment."

Kristina picked at her cuticles as she waited for the representative to come back on the call.

"Ms. Truly, yes, unfortunately, it looks like your outside cameras weren't working for the last hour or so. The cameras you have installed don't perform efficiently under low light levels, and it's difficult to tell if someone has tampered with them. I need a technician to take a look physically, but I'm sure the dark video footage is because of the old equipment you have. We ran a test through our system. Vision of your property is much better now that your exterior lights are on. You have an ancient security system. I suggest we send someone out to install updated cameras. The newer systems are very high-tech and designed to perform well in low light areas. There's an app for your phone as well; you can watch your property, turn your lights on-off, and other security features. Would you like me to set up the installation for some time in the next couple of weeks?"

"Yes, please, the sooner, the better. What day can your technicians be here?"

"I'll get back to you tomorrow once I check with our installation department. Thank you, Ms. Truly. Have a good night."

Ping. Kristina's cell phone flashed a text message from Angel: *The missing girl's name is Rita L. Farshaw. I checked our database. She hasn't attended our workshops. I hope they find her soon, unharmed, but thank goodness, she's not another one of our attendees missing. Love you, KT, have fun with the girls tonight.*

Kristina returned Angel's text: *Thank goodness, I was starting to worry there may be a connection to our seminars. Love you too.*

A squirrelly feeling still lingered in her stomach. "Missing women and someone trying to scare the hell out of me on the phone. Something feels wrong, very wrong," Kristina whispered in Ms. Prissy's ear.

CHAPTER TWENTY-ONE

"Incoming call from Koo Koo. Answer or Ignore?"

"Thank God. Answer call." Kristina adjusted her earpiece. "Answering call."

Hesitating a moment, "Hello, Kooky?"

"KT, you ready to party? This'll be fun tonight. We haven't had drinks with the girls in weeks. I'm around the corner. I'll swing by and pick you up." Koo Koo's voice didn't douse Kristina's creative imagination. She pictured the bogeyman hiding in her backyard, waiting to break in her sliding glass door. She double-checked the lock after she unscrewed the brush head from her broom, placing the long wooden dowel in the track to prevent the sliders from opening.

"Yes, I'm ready. Can't wait. See you in a few." Click.

The strange caller left Kristina unmotivated to glam-up for her drinking buddies. Since black yoga pants had become the modern-day moo-moo, Kristina slipped into hers. She threw on a clean T-shirt and grabbed a hooded sweatshirt. Dressed in her comfy sneakers and purse in hand, she watched through her living room window for Koo Koo's car to pull up. She signaled her to keep the engine running with a double blink of the porch light. After a quick kiss on Ms.

Prissy's head, Kristina set the alarm and locked the door behind her.

"You're looking cozy tonight," Koo Koo said. She leaned over to kiss Kristina on the cheek. As always, Koo Koo looked like a million bucks in small change: makeup done to perfection, designer leggings spruced up with Kate Spade leather riding boots, and a heather blue sweater accented with a multi-color silk scarf around her neck.

"Yeah, comfy casual for me tonight." Kristina strapped her seatbelt across her chest. "I had a rough day. You look nice, though. New boots?"

"KT, are you serious? I stole these boots out of your closet last week. Damn, you have so many shoes you can't even recognize your own kicks."

"No wonder I like them. Don't forget to give them back." The caller still had Kristina distracted. Koo Koo pulled away from the curb. "Wait, I need to feed Ms. Prissy. I totally forgot. Sorry, I'll be just one minute," she lied, jumping out of the car before Koo Koo had time to comment.

Disarming her alarm, she hurried up the stairs, heading straight into her bedroom to dig through her underwear drawer and tossed her panties on top of the bed. Her Taser gun wasn't there. The drawer was empty.

"Where the heck is my stun gun?" Kristina thought for a minute. Ms. Prissy purred while kneading her claws into the pile of underwear. Koo Koo sounded the horn twice. "Shit, where's the gun?" Pulling open another drawer, she felt around the clothes. The Taser wasn't in there either.

"Damn it. I left it on the sink in the restroom back at the office. Crap," Kristina said. She cuddled Ms. Prissy and plucked the lacy panties from her claws. Quickly, she crammed her lingerie back in the drawer and ran downstairs to go have drinks with the girls. Lots of drinks.

"Ms. Prissy says thank you, Auntie Kooky."

Telling Koo Koo about the caller would ruin everyone's night, especially Kristina's. She wanted to forget about it for the evening. The margaritas would help with that.

On the quick trip down the block to their girlfriend Deb's condo, it dawned on Kristina that the Jewish Mother Mafia was probably behind the entire thing. She'd heard from other non-Jewish women on the dating site that the Jewish Mother Mafia could be relentless when they wanted to teach someone a lesson. From what Kristina heard from others, the JMM liked to intimidate but were basically harmless. Erwin's mother had access to Kristina's cell number from Erwin's emails. It was a reasonable assumption and made Kristina feel better for now. Peter's FBI colleagues promised to look into the JMM. She would remind Peter to remind the Feds to take care of this issue. First thing in the morning, Poodles was getting a phone call.

Deb and Susie were already tipsy. Koo Koo and Kristina hurried to catch up. They tossed a shot of tequila down, and the creepy caller seemed a lot less important.

"Get your glasses ready, ladies. I made a fresh batch of margaritas just for you. Cheers," Deb said. She made a damn good margarita, and the girls drank up.

"KT, have you seen George Handy yet?" Deb asked. Susie chimed in with, "You mean Eye Candy Handy? Hiccup."

"No, haven't had the pleasure of seeing our new hunky neighbor yet, but let's show some respect. After all, he's Koo Koo's kinfolk." Four women laughing in a small kitchen nook sounded more like a bunch of chickens clucking.

Koo Koo took it from there. "Whatever, you guys. We're not blood-related, just somehow related. My great aunt married his grandfather's brother or cousin or something like that. We're not that close. He called me to ask about the neighborhood before he bought the house. All I know about him now is what my cousins tell me." Koo Koo interrupted her story to take a sip of margarita.

"Growing up, he was a total geek. In high school, he was super shy. A total recluse, wore thick glasses, always had the worst hairstyles, and he was chubby. But the summer after his first year away at Michigan State, he showed up at our family reunion. No one recognized him. Basically,"—Koo Koo took another sip from her cocktail—"Forrest Gump left for college and came back home Magic Mike. I need another drink. Can I get anyone another while I'm up?" Koo Koo hurried toward the kitchen.

"Magic Mike is right. Damn, he's sexy. If I liked sex with men, for sure, I'd do him. KT, I can't believe Koo Koo has never introduced you to George." Deb made an excellent point.

"First, Deb, are you back to seeing girls again? Jeez, I can't keep up with your sexual preferences. And second, Kooky, why haven't you ever mentioned hottie Handy to me? What's the current smut on this guy?" Kristina shouted toward the kitchen.

Koo Koo sat back down at the dining room table with a full slushy margarita. "Oh, I don't know. I haven't thought about him in years. Last I heard George worked for a large international construction company as a project manager. He's gone from home for months at a time. Besides, KT, you date more the expensive suits-and-silk-tie guys." Kristina could tell Koo Koo was not telling the entire story about Distant Cousin George.

Organic Panic Susie couldn't hold her liquor like the others, and she'd hit her limit two margaritas ago. "He's more the cute-little-butt-in-jeans guy. I think he's more my type. Hiccup. That's if I didn't already have a sweet BF ... hiccup. I love my Sam. Deb, I will sleep here tonight. Goodnight, everyone. Love you, girlfriends." Susie wobbled down the hall to Deb's spare bedroom.

"Well, perhaps I need to meet this Mr. Handyman and see for myself just whose type he is," said Kristina. And with that declaration, she and Koo Koo helped clean up and headed to the car.

"Kooky, I'll drive. I only had one drink way over an hour ago." Koo Koo tossed Kristina her car keys, and they headed to her house. There were lights on at George's house. Someone, presumably George, stood in front of the large glass window, shirtless. Thank goodness he hadn't had time to put window treatments up, not even a sheet. A perfect eyeshot.

"Yikes, look at that body," Kristina said under her breath. She tried not to disturb Koo Koo, who lay back in her seat to catch a wink on their drive down the street. Even from twenty feet away, there was no mistaking—George Handy was some hot eye candy.

The news about George would spread like wildfire through the neighborhood. He was a good looking, unattached, forty-some-year-old, straight man living in Newport Beach without alimony or child support. Kristina needed to act fast.

"Kooky, wake up, we're home. Crawl in bed downstairs. The sheets are clean. Remember yours is the blue toothbrush. Poodles's is the pink one. Clean pajamas in the top drawer. And come morning, we'll figure out a plan for you to introduce me to Cousin George."

CHAPTER TWENTY-TWO

Without a doubt, Koo Koo and Kristina knew that practically everyone within a hundred blocks was planning on inviting George Handy to dinner sooner than later to set him up with their daughter, niece, goddaughter, fairy godmother, or whatever single family member they needed to pawn off to a guy at the altar, so they didn't dare go that overdone route. Instead, Koo Koo invited George over to her house for dinner to welcome him to the neighborhood, as a somehow related family would be obligated to do. After a well thought out plan between Koo Koo and Kristina, their scheme worked perfectly. Almost.

From her car parked down the street, Kristina watched Eye Candy Handy walk up to Koo Koo's front door with what looked like a bottle of wine, which could only start an evening off right.

Once George was safely inside, Koo Koo shut the door behind him. Kristina assumed her next stakeout position. Crouched behind some spider-bug infested shrubs by the sidewalk at the edge of Koo Koo's front yard, she waited. Soon the Chinese-meals-on-wheels delivery boy showed up with enough food for all three of them as planned. She plucked a few dried leaves from her ponytail and sprinted to the door to give the appearance of stopping over unexpectedly.

"Kristina, wonderful to see you. I'm so happy you stopped by. Come in. Stay for dinner. I want you to meet my twice removed cousin, George. He's new to the neighborhood. George, Kristina lives a block over from you," Koo Koo said, grinning.

As they shook hands and exchanged polite niceties, Kristina batted her long black fake lashes and flashed him her freshly bleached white teeth with her most enchanting smile. George paid no attention. Distracted by a clump of dried leaves wound with a spider-webby-leafy thing attached to Kristina's pale pink, slightly see-through sweater, George stared at her chest.

"You have a leaf, or something stuck on your sweater." George stared with a half-cocked grin.

"Gosh. What's that doing there?" Kristina looked down at her sweater. A clump of something from Koo Koo's hedges dangled from the tip of her left nipple.

"Please excuse me. I'll be just one quick minute." She headed into the powder room.

The embarrassing leafy brooch went straight into the wastebasket. Kristina took a quick spin in front of the mirror to make sure she didn't have a tarantula spinning its web from the back of her skirt or any more unwanted plant life somewhere. All intact. With a quick wash of her hands and a fresh smear of lipstick, Kristina went to get acquainted with the neighborhood's handsome new hunk. Prepared with a light-hearted quip with which to re-enter the room, "So where were—" she stopped mid-sentence. The look on Koo Koo's face let Kristina know something was up. "Where is he?"

"Sorry, sweetie. George got a call from his office concerning an emergency fire or water leak or something like that at one of the high-rise buildings he takes care of. Don't feel bad, KT. All's not lost. He left this nice bottle of Shiraz."

The girls grabbed their chopsticks, kicked off their shoes, plopped themselves on the sofa, and dug into kung-pao chicken, fried egg rolls, and crunchy noodles. George's wine was a perfect addition to the meal.

The more wine Koo Koo drank, the funnier she thought she was. "KT, you know George isn't the guy for you, right?"

Completely taken aback at Koo Koo's remark, Kristina gave her an overdramatic jaw dropped, raised eyebrow stare. "Why would you say that, Koo Koo? It's my turn, so why not Cousin George?"

Having drunk most of the wine herself, Koo Koo slurred her words while shoveling food in her mouth straight out of the white cardboard to-go container. "Because your pecker picker is broken. KT, let's face it, you're rotten at picking the right pecker." Koo Koo's comical word choice was what Kristina needed to laugh until she snorted like a little root hog.

"Kooky, I've never thought of it quite that way." Kristina squealed, letting out a high-pitched giggle. "But you might be right. I always seem to pick the wrong pecker, don't I?" Holding her side from laughter, Kristina slid down the front of the sofa onto the hardwood floor, lying flat on her back with her knees bent, giggling.

Koo Koo could barely speak, laughing so hard she was nearly out of breath but continued to pucker her Ps. "Pecker

Picker, Pecker Piperrrr, Peter's Peckerrrr ... say that ten times."

They both had to use their napkins to wipe the tears from their eyes. There's nothing like Chinese food, a bottle of vino, and a healthy belly laugh to help two women forget all about a man for a few hours. But come tomorrow, Kristina needed to plot a Plan B to snag Eye Candy Handy.

Chapter Twenty-Three

Kristina wondered if she'd made an impression on George. There had to be something there. Merely thinking about his firm handshake made her tingle. He must have felt the same. Deep down, she wanted some good old meow-scratching gossip flung around the neighborhood. Perhaps even a tabloid or two might write a juicy, sexy, smutty article about the two of them together because, for once, it would be about her and the hot guy.

Days after meeting George, Kristina couldn't shake the schoolgirl crush she felt. Her cheeks turned to cherry blossoms every time she thought about him noticing the spider-webbed leaves perched on the tip of her nipple at full salute.

Later in the week, Koo Koo let Kristina know the entire Cousin George plot had to wait. She announced it over the speakerphone while driving through the self-serve car wash. "KT, our boy left for the East Coast for a construction meeting at one of his projects. He'll likely be out of town for at least a week."

"Did you say George went to the East Coast?" It was difficult to hear Koo Koo through the car scrubbers and water rinsing.

"Yep. That's the scoop I got from our mutual cousin."

"Wow, I didn't even get to say goodbye."

Koo Koo laughed, "Say goodbye? Sweetie, you didn't even get to say hello. Oh well, KT, his loss. Move on. Like I always say, 'Next.'"

~~~~

The following Saturday night, Kristina made it a point to drive by George's house on her way home. His lights were on and his truck in the drive. A neighbor told a neighbor who told Kristina that the smut going around was that George accepted an invitation to a neighbor's barbecue. Kristina made sure this was one barbeque she didn't have a planned excuse to miss.

The smell of the burgers on the grill filled the air as Kristina walked through the gate to her neighbor's backyard party. Dressed in her snug-fitting jeans and knee-high black suede boots accented perfectly with a cashmere ecru turtleneck, she felt cute. While scanning the yard for the host, Kristina spotted another familiar face. With a wide smile and white teeth beaming, she headed across the soggy grass to chat with Eye-Candy-Handy.

"Wow, George, what a surprise, I didn't know you would be here. It's great to see you again." Kristina leaned in for a hug.

George hesitated, giving Kristina a bewildered stare before he engaged in her wide-open-arms embrace. "Uh, I'm sorry, have we met?" It was obvious by the wide-eyed look on George's face he didn't know who the hell Kristina was.

"How embarrassing, I thought you'd remember me. I'm Kristina Truly, Koo Koo's friend; we met briefly at her house last week sometime." Disappointment about George's lack of interest stung. Even with her humiliation, Kristina felt the same stupid attraction the minute she saw him.

"Forgive me, Kristina. I remember meeting someone at Koo Koo's before I had to leave. Well, nice to see you again."

"No big deal, really … don't think twice," Kristina said. "Well, I brought a bottle of Veuve if you'd like to join me for a glass of champagne." She pulled the bottle out of a bag draped over her shoulder.

"I'd love to." George took Kristina by the hand, leading her to an empty table in the middle of the yard. The air was brisk. Kristina hoped to cuddle next to George to keep warm.

Trying to look cute, carry on an intelligent conversation, and open a bottle of champagne all at the same time should come with a warning label. The cork shot out of the bottle like a Cruise missile. Smack. It hit George dab in his luscious sage green eye. Yep, that did the trick; he wouldn't forget Kristina this time. She gave him a real shiner.

With her mouth gaped open, Kristina watched George's eye turn a rainbow of okra, blue, and magenta. "Shit. I'm so sorry."

"Wow, I didn't see that coming. I'm fine. Really, please don't feel bad."

"Let me get some ice." Kristina hurried to fill a plastic baggie with ice from the bar and held it on his beautiful, swollen, almond-shaped eye.

George tried convincing her that his eye looked worse than it was. "Kristina, please, I'm fine."

"Well, I'm relieved to hear you're fine, but I nearly put your eye out, and I feel horrible." Kristina laid it on a bit thick and needed to dial it back, but she had him right where she wanted him—flat on his back. George lay on a chaise lounge while Kristina placed a Ziplock baggie filled with ice cubes over his eye. She wasn't about to let him mingle so that all the other single women could, *ooh* and *aah* over his poor little, sexy, black eye.

Despite the uncorking mishap, Kristina and George continued a pleasant conversation. George insisted on opening the second bottle of champagne himself. Kristina pleaded no contest.

The sun was setting and time to go home. "I'm sorry about the black eye. Are you walking home? My house is around the corner, a block before your street." Kristina crossed her fingers, hoping George would take the bait and offer to walk her home.

"Let's go. It's getting dark. You shouldn't walk alone at night." George led Kristina by the hand out of the neighbor's backyard. He tucked her chilled hand in his jacket pocket to keep it warm. They laughed about the cork hitting George in the eye on the quick walk to Kristina's house.

"It was a lot of fun getting to hang out with the neighborhood bully." George gave Kristina a tight, lingering hug goodbye, which was nothing like the awkward half-assed hug earlier. He waved goodbye and headed toward his house.

Confused by George's mixed signals, she expected him to ask her out or over for a glass of wine sometime. Kristina told herself, *maybe he's shy.* So, the next day she called his office to ask the receptionist for his email address. She let George know she had a delightful time seeing him at the barbecue, reiterated how horrible she felt for giving him a shiner, and invited him over for dinner to make up for it. The next day she checked her emails thirty-two times.

Finally, the next night, he emailed back, "Hey neighbor, it was nice to see you too. I've never gotten a black eye from such a sweet girl before. Ciao."

"Hey, neighbor? Oh, that's sexy. Shit. What am I going to do with this guy? No asking me out? No asking for my phone number? No accepting my apology by coming to my house for dinner? Just Ciao? He's not even Italian." Disappointed again by George's lack of response, Kristina rehashed the entire day at the barbeque. She was sure she'd gotten the, *I like you,* vibe. The problem was, as a March born Pisces, she wasn't good with simply letting go of things.

The next couple of days, she daydreamed about Eye Candy Handy with a goofy grin on her face. Kristina's entire life, she wanted to be the girl who met Mr. Wonderful and fell in love and lived happily together forever. Her fantasy was always the same, but this time she imagined George's bulging biceps wrapped around her tiny waist. He picked her up and lay her naked body next to him on a faux leopard skin blanket spread out on a white sandy beach. She had a flat stomach, smooth tan skin, perky boobs, and no cellulite. The crystal clear turquoise blue tide rippled over their bare feet and tickled their toes. A sweet scent of jasmine filled the warm, soft breeze, sweeping over them as the sun set. Beneath skies of pale rose, buttercup yellow, and tangerine orange, just her and her hunky George.

She laughed out loud, daydreaming about George's muscular body towering over her. His mouth inches from her lips as he pushed himself up into position, his forearms braced on each side of her shoulders, his strong hands tangled in her long thick blond hair and right when he was ready to ... POP! A champagne cork shot out of nowhere and smacked him in the eye.

Damn my vivid imagination. Kristina thought: *Just once in this stupid fantasy, I'd like to get popped and forget the cork.* But since she hadn't seen or heard a word from George in far too long, she needed to find a new go-to-guy. Her fantasies with George were getting stale, and she needed some fresh material. But until then, her cork popping beach scenes would have to suffice.

CHAPTER TWENTY-FOUR

After a long week of preaching to lovesick attendees at her seminar, Kristina wanted a change of pace, so she headed to the local pub with Koo Koo to watch the people watch football. They waited for two guys to pay their bill and leave two empty barstools with their names all over them, then they bellied up to the bar.

The bartender tossed two paper napkins on the counter. "The gentleman at the end of the bar bought you two a beer." He sloshed two glasses in front of Kristina and Koo Koo.

"Aw, sweet." Koo Koo lifted her beer with a smile toward the man that bought their drinks.

"Don't tell me it's the guy with the bad comb-over," Kristina said. Talking through her teeth with her plastered-on smile, she too lifted her glass toward the man.

"Yep, that would be the one." Koo Koo took a big gulp of beer.

The girls had little interest in the teams playing the football game, but it felt good to get out and possibly meet some interesting new people. As a professional relationship expert, and making a lot of money at it, Kristina's tax accountant considered socializing valuable research.

At halftime, the guy at the end of the bar stumbled in their direction. "Crap. Comb-over guy looking this way." Kristina said. "Don't look, don't look. Crap, here he comes."

The man had drunk too much and was intoxicated. On his way over to chat with the ladies, he tripped over his own feet. Like a tsunami wave, his hair flew in the air and landed on the side of his exposed bald head. A drunken, twirling back gainer landed him smack on his backside, sprawled out and knocked out on the sawdust-covered concrete floor.

"Ouch." Koo Koo shouted over the noisy bar chatter and left the mess on the floor to the bouncers.

Perched comfortably on her barstool, Kristina looked around to do some people-watching. Koo Koo did the same. The warmer winter weather had made a change, and the wind and rain had hit, bringing into the bar a packed house to watch sports.

"Wow, look who the cat drug in. Long time no see," Koo Koo said to someone standing behind Kristina. They wrapped their arms around Kristina's waist, pulling her back into their rock-hard chest. A pair of soft lips pecked three times on her cheek, and the fourth kiss lingered, sending tingles up her back. Her eyes sprung wide opened. And with her mouth full of beer, Kristina turned around. George Handy kissed her cheek again, then a light kiss on the lips.

Kristina swallowed with a loud gulp. "What a surprise. Haven't seen you in a while." Seeing George surprised the hell out of her, and his affection shocked her.

Koo Koo jumped right into the conversation. "KT and I were just going to order some burgers. Please, join us?" Then

Koo Koo gave Kristina the look. The look that meant she had an agenda, and it included getting to know George's friend better. They were staying awhile.

"We'd love to join you," George held up four fingers, motioning to the bartender for another round of beers.

"Ed, meet my friends," George said as if they'd all just spoken yesterday. "This is Koo Koo. We're related somehow, but the hell if I could tell you how." George draped his arm around Kristina's shoulders. "And this, my friend, is the prettiest blond bully that ever corked me in the eye, Ms. Kristina Truly."

The change in George from hardly knowing who she was to acting as if they were besties mystified Kristina. She still had a stupid schoolgirl spark for him, so she played along.

Koo Koo and Ed were hitting it off too; they jumped headfirst into a discussion about politics. And, at least for this evening, George and Kristina chatted without a champagne cork in sight or any other weapons of mass distraction.

George leaned his ear toward Kristina so he could hear what she was saying over the clamoring in the bar. She restrained herself from nibbling on his earlobe or tickling the inside of his ear with her wet tongue. For a quick moment, a flash of sober sanity stopped her from doing it. Burger and onion breath could be a real turnoff but given a few more beers and a breath mint, there's a good chance she would have done it.

George and Kristina reminisced about the first time they met. "I know you don't remember meeting me at Koo Koo's, but I went in the restroom to wipe off something you pointed out on my sweater, and then you left without saying goodbye. I've always wondered if you sent me in the restroom to ditch me."

Carefully wording a response, George sidestepped the question. "Oh, but you paid me back later. A shiner like the one you gave me should make up for any crime I may have committed the first time we met." The tone of George's voice, stern, yet seductive, turned Kristina on. George playfully tapped the tip of Kristina's nose and flashed her a charming smile that melted her heart.

"Popping you with the champagne cork was purely an accident." Kristina's cheeks blushed, thinking about the kisses George planted on her earlier.

"I deserved it. How could I leave without saying goodbye to such a beautiful woman? I plead insanity." George slid his fingers through hers, rubbing her palm with his thumb. "Will you forgive me?" He scooted her barstool around and stood between her legs, facing her. Kristina's heart flittered. She hoped he couldn't feel it racing through her shirt. Mesmerized by his smile, she couldn't take her eyes off him until she thought about her fantasy with the two of them naked on the beach.

"Does that adorable grin on your face mean you forgive me?" George asked. Like a cat that swallowed a goldfish, Kristina couldn't hide the grin on her face. George gently lifted her chin with his hand and moved closer. Kristina could feel the heat of his breath. Their eyes locked.

George responded with a playful laugh. "Well, well. I believe the famous Kristina Truly is blushing. Is my beautiful girlfriend embarrassed about something?" He kissed the tip of her nose and waved a sign to the bartender for a couple more beers for himself and Ed. Kristina and Koo Koo motioned they'd had enough to drink. Kristina cleared her throat with a slight cough and changed the subject.

Kristina made a note to self: *He called me his sweet girlfriend. I think he likes me.*

Perched on his barstool across the bar, Detective Jakes never took his eyes off the two of them.

CHAPTER TWENTY-FIVE

Cupid's arrow smacked Kristina right in the posterior lobe of her pituitary gland. An abundance of oxytocin raced through her body when she thought about Hunky Handy. Although she didn't know much about George, after the night spent together in the bar, the sparks were stronger than ever. *Slow it down and watch for red flags.* She needed to heed the same brilliant advice that she preached at her workshops and wrote about in her books. Otherwise, she'd be waking up with her head on George's chest after a rambunctious romp in the sack way too soon.

Getting to know George was easier than Kristina expected. He was easygoing with a pleasant sense of humor, carried on intelligent conversations, and he had a fun, playful side to him. For the next week, they met for drinks, dinner, and they saw a movie one afternoon. He was a gentleman and made Kristina feel special and was taking his time with making any sexual moves. Kristina appreciated that he took their relationship slowly. Her heart skipped a beat each time he called her, babe, or sweetheart. George gave her big time signals that they were moving toward a committed relationship. Kristina was sure of that, no doubt.

The more time Kristina spent with George, the more confident she was of mutual feelings with an electrifying attraction for one another. True, most conversations were about him. It was a minor red flag, but he was so damn good-looking that she'd overlook it for now. Getting ready for their first Saturday night date, Kristina decided it was time for George and her to talk about a committed relationship: exclusive, no dating other people.

George grilled steak and lobster tails on the barbeque. Kristina prepared the fresh green salad. *Gosh, we make a cute couple,* Kristina thought with a wide smile. Watching him sparked her silly, playful side. She slapped his tight buns with the dishtowel.

George grabbed hold of the end of the towel. "Oh, you asked for it." In one quick snatch, he yanked the towel and Kristina into his arms.

Kristina squirmed. "No, wait. Not fair. I'm too ticklish. Stop. Stop." George didn't let up. Her laugh turned to a squeal, and they both laughed harder. The evening was a perfect time for their talk. Since Kristina was the relationship expert, she decided at the right moment she'd be the one to bring it up. On the sofa, they snuggled up next to each other and sipped their glasses of merlot. The romantic moonlight twinkled through the sheer window coverings. It was the perfect time. Candle flames flickered, soft music serenaded in the background, a cool soft breeze hummed through the slightly open window, and all their time-wasting chit chat had finally ceased. Yes, she could tell, they were ready for *the talk.* But before Kristina directed the conversation to, *are we exclusive,* she leaned in—and kissed him. It was their first genuine kiss: a long, lingering, wet, sensual, heart-racing, hormone rising, spit-swapping, lip-locking embrace. George cuddled Kristina in his arms and said, "Um. What a surprise."

Surprise? What the Hell. Kristina thought while her brain circled back. She glared at him. Her mind raced with thoughts of: *For God's sake. I'm ready to hear he wants to date me and only me, and he's surprised that we kissed? Holy shit. Now we're both surprised.*

"A pleasant surprise, right?" Kristina asked, pretending not to be annoyed with his comment.

"Of course, Kristina. You're amazing. I have so much fun being with you." George gave her another long, lingering kiss. He put their wine glasses on the table next to the sofa, and they headed to his bedroom.

Shit, what am I doing? What am I doing? Think, Kristina. Yes, he's sexy, and yes, you haven't had sex in far too long, and yes, I'm sure he's amazing in bed, but, but . . . think, but, but what?

Kristina convinced herself there wasn't one good reason not to have sex with George. With the exception that she wanted to be in a committed relationship, but with raging over forty hormones and with the lights dimming on cue, she dropped her inhibitions and her panties.

~~~~

In the morning, Kristina woke to the sweet smell of bacon and its sizzling serenade in the pan. She combed her fingers through her hair and ran toothpaste across her teeth before joining George in the kitchen.

"Hey, good morning, sleeping beauty." George greeted Kristina as he tossed a hefty buckwheat pancake high above the skillet, catching it on a plate with scrambled eggs and bacon.

"Why didn't you wake me?" Kristina took a minute to admire George dressed only in sweatpants that were hanging low on his hips. Wearing only a T-shirt she found in George's drawer, Kristina wrapped her arms around his waist. She caressed her hands over his muscular stomach and thought about going lower.

"Mm, don't stop … How did you sleep?" George patted his hand on her ass while he flipped another pancake.

Kristina thought about the fantastic sex and smiled, her cheeks pink. "I slept well, thanks to you." She handed George his phone. "Your phone was vibrating on the nightstand. I think it's important. They keep calling." George leaned in for a kiss on her lips.

"Thanks, babe." George tucked the phone in his back pocket, unconcerned about the caller. He dished up breakfast and handed Kristina the newspaper.

He ignored the obnoxious phone vibrating repeatedly. Finally, after the third time, he took it out of his pocket. "Sorry, sweetheart, I better take this." George excused himself before walking down the hallway toward the bedroom.

"No problem. I understand." Kristina's stomach churned. Sex with George was a hell of a good time, but now second thoughts set in as she sat at his breakfast table alone.

"KT, I'm sorry. I've got something important I need to

take care of. This was a lot of fun. I'll call you later. Can you let yourself out? I'll hop in the shower and take off." George didn't wait for an answer. He shut the door to the bathroom. Kristina hurried to his bedroom, got dressed, loaded the dishwasher, and locked the front door behind her.

Driving back home, a short block from George's house, more confusion set in. Were they a couple, or friends with benefits, or even less than that? Kristina hadn't a clue.

It was hard to wrap her head around what just happened. *Nothing could be so important that you can't finish eating breakfast with a woman you had sex with—all night.* Then she worried it could be serious. Maybe something horrible happened to one of his family members or a close friend? Kristina had a true knack for overthinking things. Her motto: assume the worst, expect something horrible, and if it turns out to be nothing, then you know the worrying worked.

Kristina told herself George would call soon and tell her all about whatever happened. No big deal, she told herself to calm the anxiety. *I will simply wait for his call and not dwell on it. We had a fantastic night together, and he'll call.*

The surveillance team reported to Detective Jakes while they discreetly followed her back to her house. "Yeah, boss, we've had eyes on her all night. She's leaving George Handy's house after their sleepover."

"We have another vic. Peter and I got a call. They've found another woman's body. Same bloody writing on the wall, throat severed, and nipples ripped off. I'm meeting Peter at the crime scene. This is a deranged sick bastard, and we can't take any chances. Don't let Ms. Truly out of your sight for a second. She may be the next target."

CHAPTER TWENTY-SIX

"Angel, why do you think George hasn't called? What does your intuition tell you?" Kristina casually inquired.

"Don't know, KT. I assume it's because he's a player. You had some fun, so what? It's time for you to meet an honorable, committed man." Angel scribbled her pen on a piece of paper, trying to get it to work. She had little concern about another jerk Kristina liked.

"Angel, that's not helpful. I thought he and I had a wonderful connection."

With elbows perched on her desk, Kristina plopped her melancholy face in the palm of her hands.

"KT, unlike anyone else I know, you have a knack for kicking men to the curb. Wonderful men. Men with money, perfect looks, and some even have a pleasant personality. Yet, Handy Candy, or whatever you call him, I just don't get it. What do you see in him?"

It didn't surprise Kristina that Angel didn't care much for George. "Well, he's boiling hot. Naked. His body is bee-u-ti-full, and he's sweet, he's funny, he makes me laugh." Kristina didn't sound all that convincing. George was an ass for not calling, but she wasn't ready to admit he wasn't Mr. Right for Her. She called Koo Koo, hoping she'd commiserate about George not calling for the past few days.

"Kooky, it's me," Kristina said. "What are you doing? Wanna have lunch?" She hoped Koo Koo might have heard some dirt about George from one of her cousins.

"Sorry, KT, I'm on my way to get a mani-pedi. What's up? Have you heard from ooh-la-la Mr. Saturday night yet?"

"No. Not yet." Kristina shouldered the phone to her ear and dowsed her hands with lotion to keep from picking at her cuticles.

"What do you think? I drove by his house the other day, and it looks like he might be out of town. His mail was still in the mailbox, and his newspapers scattered on his driveway. And yes, I looked in his mailbox. I'm sure you've already done it too. You still feel like he will call? What's your gut say? You guys had been hot and steamy, right? You said the sex was awesome, right?"

"Yeah, that's what bothers me. The sex was great. Before the sex date, we talked every day. Things were moving along in a promising direction. It makes no sense. I sent him a text to thank him for dinner, sex, and breakfast. I've heard nada."

"So, after one sizzling hot, steamy sleepover; well—without the sleep—he dumped you? Damn, that sucks," Koo Koo put her feet in the spa chair's warm, whirlpool foot bath. "Ooh, that's nice. Go a tiny bit warmer. Perfect, thank you."

"Who got dumped after sex?" Kristina heard someone bellow from the nail salon in the background.

"Koo Koo, who said that? Don't tell them it's me," Kristina said, panicked.

"It's KT, Javi. She got dumped by my cousin, gorgeous George."

Like bees to honey, that Latino queen loved to hear juicy gossip. He loved dishing the dirt with his salon compadres.

"KT, querido, it's Javi," He yelled in his Latino accent from two spa chairs over. To Kristina's horror, she knew the entire neighborhood would soon know that hunky Handy had dumped her. Gossip traveled from the local nail salon faster than dry grass on fire.

"Koo Koo has you on speaker. Girl, what happened? You two diddled, and then he said, audios, no más? Tell me about the sex. Koo Koo said it was nasty good. Girl, how many times I have to tell you, hetero-men dump you when you joder too soon. Don't you teach this shit? Don't worry, mi amor; you can tell me everything, it's in the vault."

That was all it took. An eruption of smut-slinging broke out in the salon, echoing through Koo Koo's cellphone speaker.

"KT got caught having nasty sex in the vault at the bank? Ow, that's fun." Kristina could tell by the broken English, Thong, one of the Vietnamese manicurists, had just chimed into the conversation.

"No, her boyfriend dumped her," Javi said as if he were the ultimate authority. "But, I like your version better, Thong." The two laughed with each other.

After the fiasco with the peanut gallery at the salon, Kristina opted to corner Koo Koo later in person so she could see her squirm while apologizing for leaking the story about her humiliating sex life to the town gossips. But for now, she politely said goodbye.

"I need to get back to work. Koo Koo, we'll chat later." Before Kristina disconnected the call, the choir continued singing.

"KT, things obviously went a little too well and too fast for him, that's all. You deserve better, girl. Adios mi amor." Without missing a syllable, Javi's conversation drifted from Koo Koo's speakerphone to him announcing to everyone in the salon, "When will that pobre niña learn? This is why she's single. She's always picking the wrong—" The phone clicked off.

Kristina finished his sentence: "She always picked Mr. Wrong."

CHAPTER TWENTY-SEVEN

Several days passed, and it seemed George had vanished with no signs that he'd been back to the house after he left on Sunday morning. Reality set in remembering George, Mr. One Date Wonder, had said: "This was a lot of fun. I'll call you later." Kristina now realized that was code for, "I like random sex, but I'm not that into you."

The not-so-logical side of Kristina's brain hijacked the logical side. She often blamed herself when her relationships didn't work out. *Maybe I'm not skinny enough, or maybe he doesn't find me attractive, or he preferred more exotic looking women and much younger, or perhaps secretly he hates blondes and loves redheads or much younger brunettes? Could be he isn't a boob man, or maybe the skin tag under my right armpit grossed him out or maybe ...?* She thought of a million reasons why George dumped her, but she could not think of one damn reason why he didn't call to break it off. No returned phone calls, no text, no e-mail, zip, nothing, crickets, not a word.

Twenty years of good therapy shot to hell in five minutes over one fun roll in the hay with a jerk. Kristina decided, once again, to give herself a good talking to concerning her choices in men.

~~~~

"Angel, guess what," Kristina shouted, rushing up the steps to their office. "Angel, I figured it out," Kristina blurted out, walking through the doorway. "I figured out why George dumped me." She handed Angel the vanilla skinny latte she'd picked up at Starbucks on her way into the office.

"What is it this time? Another alien abduction?" Angel headed straight for the microwave to warm her latte.

"Nope, no aliens this time. After a sensible debate with myself, I came to the obvious conclusion: George is gay. He's too pretty, and his body's too ripped to be straight. He doesn't know how to tell me, that's all."

"And he had sex with you because he was on the fence and now knows for sure he prefers men? Great, now you don't need to go on an all kale and chocolate diet. And please don't change your hair color this time. I'm worried you'll cut your hair short again like when the guy from Brazil moved back home. Remember, the first thing you did is chop your hair off. All because the Brazilian swimsuit model on the cover of Sports Illustrated had a short tomboy haircut."

"Yeah, yeah, all excellent points, girlfriend. No need to worry. I even canceled my Botox appointment. I'm not blaming myself for this one. Well, I blame myself for the sex too soon, so I only half-blame myself."

"Whether he's gay or taken by aliens, you deserve better, KT." Angel sipped her coffee.

"You're right, Angel," Kristina agreed. "That's why I've decided rather than beat myself up I'm placing the blame exactly where it belongs: on him," Kristina said, knowing damn well she could kick herself for being a one-night stand with Mr. Eye Candy Handy. The hard facts were that George Handy wasn't Mr. Right for Kristina.

Chapter Twenty-Eight

There's one quick cure for feeling better after being rejected. Kristina knew exactly what she needed to lift her mood. She might not get to enjoy George's cute naked butt any longer, but she could certainly enjoy a new pair of strappy little sandals to tide her over for now. Oh Lord, the power of the shoe. Kristina didn't care what was going wrong in her life; a new pair of shoes would fix it. The number of shoes in her closet (465 to be exact, or 466, if you counted her snorkel flippers) gave a clue to the number of times she fixed a mess in her life.

Usually, the local shoe warehouse's sale rack would do the trick. Not this time. Kristina went straight to Jimmy Choo. She needed to pull out the big credit cards to get over the disappointment in her poor judgment of George. A lot of time waiting for him to notice her had been wasted just to figure out he wasn't the quality of man worth the effort. Now, all she needed was a cute pair of sandals, a hot new color of lipstick, maybe a fun new style of false eyelashes, and what the hell, a box of decadently priced chocolates: nuts and chews, of course.

Kristina walked out of the mall with her hands full of shopping bags, knowing George Handy would soon be a vague memory. Yes, she also knew therapy was cheaper but not nearly as effective.

~~~~

That evening, Poodles and Kristina made plans to meet at their favorite Mexican food restaurant, Caliente Consuela, for a couple of margaritas and a basket or two of yummy carbohydrate-dripping tortilla chips covered with fresh, chunky homemade salsa. Peter's ego could handle the nickname Poodles. He loved a spa chair for a mani-pedi, and proud of it. Gay men wished he'd swing their way, straight women were glad he didn't, and if you asked Kristina, the verdict was still out either way.

Peter assured Kristina on the phone that what he wanted to talk with her about couldn't wait. That got her attention. Five o'clock couldn't come soon enough to hear the juicy dirt too important to dish about on the phone.

Empty parking spots were everywhere, but Kristina's feet in her new heels would never make it across the concrete parking lot to the restaurant. Although adorable, the straps were already cutting into the sides of her feet. Five cars deep, she waited for the valet to open her car door. Slowly, she stretched her bronze-tinted legs with her sassy Jimmy Choo sandals to the curb. Precisely calculating, she showed just enough bare leg to be seductive. The valet, darling but barely legal, handed Kristina her claim ticket while staring her up and down, or so it appeared to Kristina. Feeling sexy, she fantasized the young valet wanting a piece of this sultry cougar. She felt his eyes checking her out. He began to say something. Kristina thought it best to appear mysterious, so she turned around before he could finish his sentence.

Check out my backside, you little cutie; this Swipe Right has it goin' on. Chic-a-boom, baby. Kristina swung her hips, sauntering toward the restaurant, laughing at herself with the little naughty thoughts she had going on in her head.

Then it happened. Kristina heard, "Ma'am, excuse me, Ma'am?" She turned around, giving the valet an evil glare. *Ma'am? He'd better not be talking to me. I'm not some dowdy soccer mom.* And that's when Kristina's four-inch stiletto heel caught on the corner of the thick Spanish tile. Splat. Down she went. Ass over tea kettle, there she was with her short-flared skirt flung over her backside, her ass sticking straight up, and her face straight down. *Damn it. These are the old lady panties Deedee gave me for my birthday. I should've done laundry last night.* She stared at the pavement, afraid to look up. *People think I'm drunk. I wish I were.*

The humiliation deepened when Kristina heard a familiar voice. Slowly lifting her head, she looked up to see an ex-boyfriend and his twenty-four-year-old Barbie doll on his arm with a baby in her belly. They both bent down to help Kristina up as the valet held out his hand and said, "Ma'am, you forgot to leave your keys. Your car is blocking the drive."

Her humiliation turned into pissed off when Kristina realized who the long-legged, skinny waist, boobs la roué Barbie doll was with her ex, Dick Wad. Here was the same bimbo Dick Wad swore that he had never slept with—before, that is—Kristina caught him bent over his desk the night he had to get a "project" finished and had to stay late at the office to "get it done." He was just getting it/her done right about the time Kristina walked in with a grilled chicken Caesar salad to surprise him with dinner. By the look of what the Barbie doll was wearing, or not wearing, and with a bun in the oven, Kristina could safely assume they didn't do much sleeping when they were together. So perhaps on a technicality, he didn't lie to her.

Kristina took Dick Wad's hand as he lifted her up. Hiding her embarrassment with an Oscar-winning performance, she acted as though everything was business as usual. Calmly, she pulled her skirt back down over her ass, fluffed her hair, adjusted her bra, brushed off a little blood mixed with the gravel embedded in her kneecaps, handed the valet her car keys, told Dick Wad and Barbie it was nice to see them both, and limped inside the restaurant.

Detective Jakes trailed three feet behind her.

CHAPTER TWENTY-NINE

S eated at the bar, Peter ordered two margaritas, rocks, no salt. He looked like the perfect catch. Nearly every woman seated within eyeshot gawked at Kristina when she scooted her butt on the barstool Peter held empty next to him.

"Ah, Poodles," Kristina sighed. And to be sure the women watching were completely envious of her when she planted a big smooch right on Peter's lips.

By the look on Kristina's face and Band-Aids on both knees, Peter sensed that she was in no mood for mockery.

"I won't ask." Peter motioned the bartender to pour two shots of tequila, the good stuff, off the top shelf.

"Saludo," Peter said, tapping his shot glass against Kristina's. They tossed their heads back, making sure to get every drop, sinking their teeth into sour lime wedges. In sync, they pushed their empty shot glasses toward the bartender.

"Dos mas, por favor," the two said in unison. Poodles and Kristina had been best friends for so long they often finished each other's sentences.

"So, what's so important, Poodles, that you couldn't tell me over the phone? Not that I didn't want to see you, but what's going on? Hurry, tell me. Did you finally break it off with your British princess, Beth?"

Peter looked down at his margarita and began spinning the ice cubes like a roulette wheel.

"Yep, I knew it. Something's up. What is it? Are you taking me to your granny's house again to get back on her good side?" Kristina scooted her barstool closer to Peter, waiting for the news.

Peter and Kristina were mad about each other when they first met over twenty-five years ago. The chemistry between them was something out of a romance novel, so ending up in bed with each other was completely unavoidable. The sex was great. Of course, they were eighteen—what did they know? In those days, even bad sex was good sex. Somehow, they ended up better as best friends than lovers. After all these years, he was still the most stable male relationship in her life.

Peter couldn't walk into a room without turning heads with his jaw-dropping good looks. A Gemini, who talks about his feelings, an impeccable dresser, and loves a good mani-pedi. Hence, why Kristina still believed he must be at least partly gay. Most people knew only his public persona, but Kristina knew better than to ever confuse his charming charisma and sweet demeanor with his professional side: a seasoned FBI operative, secret military shit trained, and when he pointed a gun, make no mistake, he didn't miss.

"KT, we need to talk about the Sophia Clark case," Peter said.

"Please don't tell me. Please don't tell me Sophia's dead." The tequila made a loop in Kristina's stomach.

Peter took Kristina's hands in his. "KT, this is a serious situation. A serial killer murdered Sophia Clark and Jaclyn

Renzo. Last Sunday morning, Rita Farshaw, our third vic, was found murdered as well. Same MO as Ms. Clark and Renzo, same sick bastard killed her. The strongest lead we have is the link between the three women and your workshops."

"No, Peter. Please, God, no. I can't breathe." Kristina fanned her face with her napkin. "Peter, are you sure it's a serial killer? Linked to my workshops? But Angel checked our registration data, and Rita Farshaw never attended our seminars. I can't believe this. What the fuck's going on?"

"Rita L. Farshaw is her birth name. She's an actress. Went by her middle name and shortened her last name, Lila Shaw. The crime scenes are brutal, Kristina. It's the same person or persons. At this point, we don't have a lot to go on."

"No, Peter, I know Lila. She's adorable. Please, God, make this stop. What if there's another? Is this somehow my fault with my workshops? What do I do?" Kristina wiped tears from her eyes with her sleeve.

"When's your next seminar?" Peter asked, chewing the end of a cocktail straw.

"Not for a couple of months. I have my book launch, so we're focused on that for the next few months." Kristina rubbed the top of Peter's hand. He seemed more nervous and distracted than his years of FBI training allowed.

"That's great. We need you to stop your seminars until we catch whoever killed these women."

"Of course, I'll do whatever I have to do. Peter, I can't afford to lose my career. What if the media gets a hold of this? It could ruin me. What happens if you don't find the killer?" There was no way to wrap her head around any of this nightmare.

"KT, we are going to get whoever's doing this soon. For now, you need to stop your workshops and stop communicating with any online men. It's too dangerous. We don't know how deep the connection between you and these women goes."

"I'm scared, Peter." Shivers ran up her spine.

"Yeah, me too." Peter ordered two margaritas. Rocks, no salt.

CHAPTER THIRTY

Another bombshell was about to drop. The timing wasn't great. There would never be a good time to tell Kristina that Peter was getting married.

"Let's eat dinner. I need to talk with you about something else. I know this isn't great timing after the conversation we just had, but I can't put it off any longer. Kristina, this is important to me." Peter poked at the ice with his straw. He stared down at his drink. "I don't want you to freak out." He turned toward Kristina but avoided looking her in the eyes. "Please promise me you won't cause a scene."

The thought of food after hearing a serial killer had brutally murdered three women made the knot in Kristina's stomach tighten. It was something serious if Peter asked her to promise not to cause a scene. He knew how easily she could go from: *No problem, it's my pleasure,* to *Fuck you.*

"I promise, no drama, just tell me." Kristina kept her voice soft. She gripped Peter's face in her hands and looked straight into his eyes, "What's wrong?"

Peter took a deep breath and took both of her hands in his, with a firm grip. "Well, I'll just say it. I'm getting married." He forced a smile, his teeth clenched.

The color ran from Kristina's face. "What the hell?" Kristina asked. It wasn't the conversation she'd imagined having tonight. She thought perhaps, "Hey, KT. I'm going on an African safari, and I want you to join me." But getting married? No, no, no. Kristina paused for a long moment, the words, *getting married*, rang like a fire alarm in her ears.

Kristina kept her voice down because it wasn't beneath Peter to cup his hand over her mouth and hold it there until she calmed down. Instead, she shook her head in disbelief and snarled, "*I knew it.* You lied to me. I asked you many times if you were falling in love with the British princess, and you insisted, no, you two are very different, and it would never work out long term between the two of you. So now suddenly, she's the perfect girl for you? Whatever, Peter. Go ahead, marry her. If you're asking for my blessing, then, no, she's not good enough for you." Kristina felt steamed that they were even having this conversation.

Their emotions ran high, knowing somehow connected to Kristina, someone was out there killing women. Her career was on the line and possibly her life. The timing with Peter announcing his engagement took the stress between them to another level. Before meeting Peter, Beth was fired from the London police department after her affair with her married boss made news headlines. Once the scandalous shit hit the fan, she moved to the States to pursue an acting career. Shortly after they started dating, Beth whined to Peter that the rejection as an actor was getting to her. She wanted to write screenplays and novels. So far, she'd completed neither. Peter fell for her load of neediness and asked her to move in with him. He foots all the bills while Beth pursues her dreams, which turn out to be expensive lunches with her girlfriends and spending Peter's money. Kristina could never figure out what he saw in Beth. A posh British vocabulary, perky boobs, a flat stomach, flawless porcelain skin, and big brown eyes—so what? Peter had women throwing themselves at him. He'd been with supermodels to Italian billionaires. For the sake of her friendship with Peter, Kristina stayed out of the minutiae of his intimate dating relationships. She assumed Peter would eventually see through Beth and move on. It seems she was wrong.

"KT, stop this. I won't apologize for falling in love with Beth. She's a really good person," Peter said defensively. "We're working on our relationship. She's trying extremely hard." Peter knew this would be difficult for Kristina to accept, given the history with her father. He wrapped his arm around her shoulder. "Come on, KT. You need to trust me, please. I wouldn't marry Beth if I didn't know, without a doubt, that we're perfect together."

"Stop. Don't touch me. You know damn well why I'm upset. Good people don't cheat on you. Not once and certainly not twice." Kristina felt a sharp pain in her heart. "Face it. She's ten years younger than you and desperate to secure a wealthy baby daddy. You fit the bill. Her clock's ticking, my friend, and she's on her best behavior. I thought you were smarter than to fall for her bullshit?" Tears streamed down her cheeks. Kristina knew Peter was making a mistake with Beth, but she felt like a hypocrite. She had no room to talk with all her past failed relationships, but she'd never been disloyal to anyone.

"That's not fair. Beth wasn't ready for a committed relationship when we first met. That's all." Peter stared at his margarita. He didn't sound convincing. Deep down, he wasn't sure he believed that, but he loved Beth and wanted to marry her.

Choking back more tears, Kristina felt like throwing up. She looked Peter in the eyes. "You know how badly I wanted my own family, and now it's too late for me to have kids, so I don't blame you for wanting a family, Peter. Look, after all these years, we've had plenty of tough conversations, and I'll admit, most of the time, you're the rational one, so I pray you're right about Beth."

"Don't worry, KT. You'll meet a great guy someday and get married. When you calm down, I know you'll be happy for me." Peter shifted uncomfortably in his seat. This conversation wasn't sitting well with either of them.

"Oh, fuck me. You really think this is about being jealous that you're getting married before me? Oh, my God, are you listening to yourself?" Kristina's temper flared. "Admit it, Peter, this isn't about me meeting some great guy, and then I'll be happy watching my best friend make a huge mistake." Peter's comments were a diversion, and Kristina knew all about diversions. She'd done the same thing when Peter called her out on many of her past poor choices in men. That's what hurt the most. The one man who never let her down, let her down. Kristina realized Peter wasn't the superhero she made him out to be. She'd found his Achilles heel. Like every other man, he'd let a woman manipulate him because she was young and attractive.

There was a lot of truth to what Kristina said, although too painful for Peter to admit. He thought about when he caught Beth cheating with an old boyfriend of hers. It crushed him. He forgave her, and he caught her again with another man. Peter remembered that Kristina helped him pick up the pieces, no questions asked. But it pissed him off that Kristina didn't understand. Beth had learned her lessons, and now she was fully committed to a monogamous relationship. Peter's FBI training taught him to see through bullshit. He knew Beth loved him, and he wasn't about to allow Kristina to second guess his competent decision making. His temper heated. "Whatever, Kristina. Your business card may read, 'Relationship Expert,' but when was the last time you were in a healthy relationship? Beth and I had a rocky start. I'll give you that. We're working on it, so please keep your relationship advice for your audience. They don't know you like I do." Peter's eyes narrowed, and his lips pursed tightly shut. He waved his glass at the bartender, "Another shot of Clase Azul, please." Through the years, he and Kristina butted heads, but now he wanted to shut her up, and he wasn't proud of it. Peter felt torn between the two women he loved in such different ways.

"Sorry, I shouldn't have said that." Peter felt his heart ache. Tonight, he'd never explain his way out of this disagreement. "It's complicated sometimes with Beth and me. She needs me, KT. Please, try to understand."

Kristina bent down and slipped off her strappy little over-priced sandals. She stuffed them into her Louis Vuitton purse, a birthday gift from Peter, and went to get her car.

Detective Jakes watched Kristina wipe her tears with her sleeve. It reminded him of Anne. She did that. Jakes wanted to grab Kristina in his arms and tell her she's okay, but he knew that wasn't true.

CHAPTER THIRTY-ONE

Fighting with a page jammed in the copy machine, Angel stopped when she heard slow-paced footsteps coming up the wooden staircase to the office. Kristina walked in, wearing a pair of pink yoga pants wrong-side-out. The purse swung over her forearm tilted, causing coffee to slop out of the paper cup down the front of her oversized, pale blue sweater. Her foot squashed the tissue box that fell out from under her arm as she walked to her desk.

Angel hid the grin on her face behind her hand when she noticed that Kristina wore a brown fuzzy UGG slipper on one foot and a neon-yellow Nike running shoe on the other. She wanted to laugh, but she knew it wasn't the time for humor. Angel's heart softened when she saw her best friend's beautiful blond hair drooped in a half-cocked ponytail and black mascara smeared under her eyes.

"Morning, Angel." Kristina's voice sounded faint and congested. She wiped her rosy nose with a frail piece of soggy tissue.

"Hey hon, you doing okay? I didn't expect you here this early. What time's your therapy appointment?" Angel observed her friend's emotional state with concern, but she'd seen Kristina go through a troubled relationship roller coaster for many years. This spat was not the first with Peter, nor would it be the last.

"I canceled my appointment." Kristina filled a cup with coffee from the machine still brewing, forgetting about the hot cup of Starbucks latte on her desk. Her brain felt fuzzy, like cotton candy winding around the paper stick at a carnival. She cried the entire night. The harsh words with Peter felt minor compared to the fears of a serial killer brutally murdering women who'd attended her workshops.

"You canceled your appointment? What? KT, you love therapy. Girlfriend, now I am worried. Are you going to be okay?" Angel sat down next to Kristina.

When it came to Kristina's friendship with Peter, Angel knew how hard the news of him getting married to Beth hit her. Angel wasn't fond of Beth either, and she didn't hesitate to put Beth in her place when she laid the British snootiness on too thick. The way Peter spoke to Kristina surprised Angel. It wasn't like him. She assumed what Kristina said about Beth rubbed his ego the wrong way. Regardless, it would leave a mark on Kristina emotionally—a big mark. In situations like this, Angel chose comedy versus lecture. She could usually help ease her best friend's pain with a good laugh, a little sympathy, and as always, Kristina would pull herself together.

"Don't worry about me, Angel. I'm fine with Peter and the cheating princess getting married. I love him, and I hope Beth proves me wrong. There's no need for therapy. I'll handle this one on my own." Kristina dropped another soggy tissue in a wastebasket next to her desk.

"Kristina Truly, please, tell me you are not going to buy more shoes to fix this with Peter." Angel joked, hoping to help her feel better. Angel and all their girlfriends knew any mention of shoes usually perked Kristina right up.

"Nope. I'm not going to buy shoes. Losing Peter isn't exactly a style-trumps-sorrow kind of problem. This scenario is messier than my usual boy breaks heart, life is short, buy the shoes in every color. We're talking about Poodles, my BFF, and backup guy in case I don't meet someone before I turned fifty, a double whammy. Angel, you know I'd be happy for him if I trusted Beth, but never mind Peter's engagement. I'm devastated by the beautiful women that have been murdered, let alone scared to death. My heart breaks for their families. Driving home after seeing Peter last night, I accepted the fact that I will be single the rest of my life." Kristina blew her nose and took a deep breath.

Angel gave a slight giggle with a half-smile on her face, wrapping her arms around Kristina. "You know what, girl-friend? You have a way of turning something that isn't about you into something all about you." It was true, and they both had to laugh.

"Besides, KT, I've told you a hundred times, you can have all three of my children every weekend and my husband too. Take their dirty underwear, their stinky feet, their loud voices—they're all yours."

"Angel, you know that's not true. You love the kids and Jermaine."

"Yes, I love them more than life itself, but often I don't

like them even a little bit. I'll trade you all of them for five friggin minutes of peace and quiet. Let's split them fifty-fifty." Laughing with Angel helped lift Kristina's spirits.

"Angel, I promise this time I will get a grip, muy pronto. Besides, I know what will help." She took a deep breath and let it out slowly.

Kristina figured out just what she needed to stop thinking about Poodles, his engagement, and rude comments. She also wanted to stop thinking about her career falling apart, and most of all, to stop thinking about murdered women for a few days. It had all been too much stress. Kristina needed a girls' trip to Viva Las Vegas.

~~~~

Angel made a call to Peter before booking the girls' flights and hotel reservations. Peter gave his blessing for the trip. He agreed a long weekend away would do Kristina good. Peter assured Angel the FBI would have top casino security watching Kristina and the girls' every move. He didn't let on to Angel, but this may be the break they needed. He and Jakes hoped the killer would make a foolish move to snatch Kristina, and the FBI would be right there.

Friday morning, bright and early, Koo Koo, Deb, and Susie pulled up in their Uber outside Kristina's house, packed and ready for their flight. Kristina wasted no time joining her posse, and off they went to live it up in the Sizzling Sin City.

~~~~

"Excuse me. Your bag is in my seat." Kristina's eyes widened when she looked up to see a striking six foot four, sandy-blond-haired hunk standing in the aisle of the airplane.

"I'm so sorry. Let me move it." Kristina stared at the familiar face, trying to recall how she knew him. Koo Koo discretely pinched Kristina's leg giving the signal: Handsome Hunk next to you. As if Kristina hadn't already noticed.

"I'm afraid I've overstuffed my shoe bag. It doesn't seem to fit under my seat." Kristina shoved with both feet, but no matter how hard she tried to cram the bag under the seat, it would not budge. She'd packed it with a pair of shoes for each night they were staying in Las Vegas. Plus, she threw in a couple of extra pairs just in case.

"Don't worry about it. I'll take it. There's room in the overhead bin." When Kristina boarded the plane, she strapped her soft canvas shoe bag in the empty seat, hoping no one would sit there. The man lifted the bag over his head, arranging the overhead bin to accommodate his carry-on and hers. Kristina and Koo Koo watched wide-eyed at the sight of his sculptured biceps. Once he'd settled in with his seatbelt fastened, he held out his hand. "Hi, my name's DJ. A pleasure to meet you both." Detective Jakes smiled and shook Kristina's and Koo Koo's hands.

Koo Koo gave Kristina her typical look, placing dibs on DJ the minute he sat down. They both knew he wasn't Koo Koo's type. After her second divorce, she liked slightly younger men, more of a boy toy, urban cowboy type, and this guy seemed sweet and sort of shy with a Southern California beachy vibe, sandy blond hair, five o'clock shadow. He was in his mid-forties, making him about five years too old for Koo Koo's taste.

"I'm Kristina. Friends call me KT. Nice to meet you, DJ." She couldn't take her eyes off his. "I feel like we've met. Did I see you a few weeks ago at a restaurant on the water in Newport Beach? Oh my gosh, you must think I'm a nut. It's just that you look so familiar. The man in the restaurant must be your twin. Well, never mind." Kristina felt the same instant attraction to DJ as she did in the split second their eyes met in the restaurant when she tripped on her gown and Jakes nearly blew his cover.

"No, don't be silly. I have one of those faces. I hear it all the time. Actually, I'm sorry it wasn't me. What a fun story that would make. Nice to meet you, Kristina." He turned toward her and was rewarded with a smile. Jakes felt his body heat up. He felt the same strange bond he felt when their eyes locked at the restaurant. Maybe the connection was mutual? *Ridiculous, of course.* Jakes had no time to contemplate his feelings for Kristina. Today, his only job was staying focused on keeping these women safe in a city filled with drifters, con-artists, drunks, and possibly a serial killer. Keeping his cover was crucial for now. He'd apologize for the lie later.

"Yes, nice to meet you too." She stared at his sexy dimples, and that's when she decided for sure DJ wasn't Koo Koo's type. Not this weekend.

CHAPTER THIRTY-TWO

Masses of people flooded into the Las Vegas airport, ready to get the gambling started over the Super Bowl weekend. Detective Jakes strategically offered to carry Kristina's bag, assuring they'd all stay together. The damn thing weighed a ton, so she graciously accepted. With Kristina's bag over one shoulder and his own duffle slung over the other, he playfully lectured Kristina on Las Vegas weekend shoe etiquette—one pair, not ten. He lagged far enough behind the four of them to keep a broad view. The girls chatted with excitement, keeping a hurried pace through the airport. They boarded the crowded tram that traveled swiftly to the baggage carousel. Jakes sat next to the girls, quiet and undistracted by their conversation. He watched for anyone to make an unsavory move.

Hundreds of tourists stood in lines waiting for a Taxi or a hotel shuttle. But expensive limousines were ready for the immediate, "Get the ladies to the Strip quick." Kristina hailed a stretch limo, and all the girls piled in. "Hey, DJ, come on, get in." Kristina motioned for DJ to hop in and get the party started. He was a good sport, listening to the four giggling girls talking over one another, rehashing silly stories of their past trips to Las Vegas. Sweet-mannered DJ simply grinned and nodded politely as conversations darted back and forth with the girls. Detective Jakes's biggest concern wasn't keeping everyone safe. As it turned out, he had a much bigger challenge ahead. How the hell was he going to manage the feelings he had for Kristina for the next three days and, more importantly, two nights?

~~~~

Three male agents standing outside the hotel all glanced at each other with confusion when they saw their boss, Detective Jakes, arrive in the limo with the four women they were there to keep eyes on. Jakes quickly filled the guys in on his plan for their cover. "Ladies, please let me apologize right now for my old college buddies from Los Angeles. They're a bunch of stockbrokers and complete assholes that love to harass me," Jakes explained. The limousine driver unloaded the luggage in front of the hotel while they all got acquainted.

"Not true ladies, we only harass him when he deserves it, and he just happens to deserve it a lot. Go ahead, DJ, introduce us to your friends." Detective Jakes's colleagues played right into their roles, pretending to be old frat brothers. Each held a full cocktail in his hand. Convincing the girls of their story was no problem.

"Okay, guys. Let me introduce you to these lovely ladies that I met on the plane." Jakes politely carried on with the introductions. "I'll settle up here with the driver and the bags. And ladies, if you'd be so kind as to join us for a drink, these gentlemen will escort you to the bar. Behave, you jerks, and order me a martini, straight-up, extra dry vermouth, double olives, and I'll meet you all at the bar in a minute."

"Hey, that's the way I like my martini." Kristina chalked it up to a good thing to have in common with this gorgeous potential friend for the weekend guy. She waited for Jakes while the others forged ahead without a second thought. He insisted on paying the tab for the limousine and gave the driver a hefty tip, even for Las Vegas high roller standards.

"This worked out well. We're all staying at the same hotel?" DJ tipped the bellman a little extra for handling the mountain of overnight bags the ladies brought for a long weekend.

Even though Peter didn't express concern about her and her girlfriends taking off for Las Vegas, Kristina felt safer with these four men hanging around with them for the evening. Ever since Peter told her about Lila Shaw's murder, she'd been looking over her shoulder, scared to death. For a moment, she wondered about DJ. *Ted Bundy was good looking, why trust DJ?* She barely knew him, but for some inexplicable reason, she felt safe with him next to her. However, she wasn't completely out of her mind, and she felt a lot safer after she dug her Taser gun out of her suitcase and stuck it in her pocket.

DJ seemed like an impressive guy. Kristina observed his every move. *He hasn't mentioned anything about being married, and he's not wearing a wedding ring. It would, however, behoove him to keep that bit of trivia to himself if he were a wife cheater. Don't overthink this, KT. He's innocent until proven guilty.* DJ definitely gave Kristina the vibes that, in all accounts, he was single and ready to mingle—with her.

After DJ helped the bellman push two full luggage carts into an elevator, he and Kristina headed toward the colorful blinking lights in the casino to join the others.

"Kristina, I know you're here to spend time with your girlfriends, and I'm here to spend time with my buddies. However, I'm hoping to see you again this weekend if that's okay with you?" DJ stopped Kristina in her tracts as he stepped face-to-face in front of her.

"Sure, I'd love to spend time getting to know more about you. The girls are here to party. I'm here to enjoy some personal time alone, so it's all good." She smiled, unable to look away from DJ's eyes. The stimulating jingles coming from the slot machines lightened Kristina's mood, but being with DJ made her heart race.

Without thinking, DJ took Kristina by the hand, and they hurried to catch up with the group. Keeping eyes on her, Jakes listened to her speak to people with kindness, and when he watched her laughing with a stranger she accidentally hit with her cart at the grocery store, he wanted to laugh with her. She reminded him of Anne, not in a creepy way, rather by her confidence and outlook on life. They were both special. It made no sense to him, yet for whatever reason, being with her this weekend took his feelings for her to a whole new level.

The bartender handed DJ and Kristina matching martinis. DJ hoisted his glass to make a toast: "Ladies, thank you for joining us." The gang lifted their glasses. In unison, the guys let out a hearty—Cheers! "Here's to getting to know all of you better and to having some fun." DJ tapped Kristina's glass with his. "Cheers, Kristina, here's to getting to know you."

Kristina's heart warmed watching DJ bantering with her friends and his buddies and yet, never quite took his eyes off her. *This weekend might end up being just what I need.*

~~~~

After a few martinis, everyone decided it was time they headed to their rooms to relax and spruce up before hitting the town for the night.

"Kooky, I need a Diet Coke. I'll be right behind you," Kristina said and headed in the opposite direction. A rowdy pack of drunken Super Bowl football fans headed her way, hooting, and hollering. Maneuvering through the pack, Kristina made a quick left turn. She lost her footing and bounced off a big-bellied man wearing a Texas Cowboy's jersey. Without a beat, she ricocheted off another belly and rammed face-first into a tall, round Texan. His felt cowboy hat fell forward, covering his eyes. Belly first, he landed in a pond four-feet deep, boots and all. Jakes swooped in, spinning Kristina around before the man had time to notice the colorful koi fish swimming around his head.

"What happened?" Kristina asked, surprised to see DJ.

He pointed Kristina toward the gift shop, "I could use a Diet Coke myself."

"Kristina, are you still game to spend time with an old guy like me who isn't hip enough to go clubbing in this wild city?"

DJ handed Kristina her drink. He needed to keep her close to him, and the more time they spent together, the more he liked her. But his personal feelings had to wait while he focused on the task at hand to keep everyone safe and catch the killer.

"Sure. That would be great. Here's my cell. Call me later, and we'll figure out what sounds fun." DJ and Kristina exchanged cell numbers, and they headed to their rooms.

~~~~

Strategically designed casinos kept their patrons wandering from roulette tables to craps tables, from poker to Keno, all before they found the right elevator up to their rooms. The success of a casino depended on how well they kept organized chaos going 24/7 with massive amounts of sleep-deprived, intoxicated tourists. The FBI expected if the serial killer or killers were watching Kristina, they'd follow her to Las Vegas. The hustle-bustle of the casino created a perfect environment for the killer to slip a roofie in her drink. It was not unusual in Vegas to see a man walking a stumbling woman out of the bar, ready to pass out. Less than five minutes is all it took, and Jakes would not take his eyes off her. You could bet the farm on that.

~~~~

DJ's charm, accented by his deep dimples, had Kristina in a tailspin. The chemistry between the two shocked her. She needed a bit of a distraction from everything, and what better way to have fun and laughs than with a gorgeous stockbroker in Las Vegas? Finding a way to have any kind of romantic interlude alone with DJ seemed impossible. Kristina quickly assessed the situation from another angle.

Her only choice was to call Poodles. They'd only spoken by text since their argument. She swore she wouldn't call unless he called her first, but she needed his help. The attraction between her and DJ had heated up in the bar. Most likely, it was DJ's confidence that attracted her to him. Kristina saw something different about him, something good. Well, maybe not good, more like sexy. He seemed kind, not arrogant. DJ made Kristina feel comfortable around him. She couldn't pinpoint exactly what she felt about this guy, but whatever it was, she wanted to find out more.

CHAPTER THIRTY-THREE

Peter had a lot of important connections in Las Vegas. The big casino owners found it worthwhile to help their friends at the FBI with accommodations and top security whenever necessary. Those were the connections that Kristina needed on Super Bowl weekend. This round, Kristina had the upper hand. If she played her cards right, Peter would hook her up with a hotel room of her own, and whatever was in the minibar had her name on it but paid with Peter's credit card. So, she pulled herself together, swallowed her pride, and made the call.

"Poodles, thank God you answered your phone."

"KT, I'm so glad you called. I'm sorry. I should have called you. I feel horrible." He sounded sincere, but she didn't have time for his feelings right then. "Yes, you should have called, and you should be feeling like shit, but let's not talk about that right now. I need your help."

"What is it? Where are you?" Peter knew everything but needed to keep Jakes's cover.

"I'm with the girls at the Bella Terra. Peter, with everything that's going on, I need my own room. I'm drained. Need to regroup. Work your magic, please, Poodles."

"Why didn't you think of that before you went to Las Vegas with the girls over Super Bowl weekend?" Peter lectured.

Peter had been in close contact with Jakes, and his feelings for Kristina were obvious each time he talked about her to Peter. It hadn't crossed Peter's mind before the case to introduce the two of them. Keeping business and personal relationships separated was best practice in their line of work. If their relationship didn't work out, Peter would be smack in the middle of the bad breakup triangle. But he trusted Jakes, and Peter felt he owed Kristina this one. What better way to keep Kristina safe than if she's dating a detective? Besides, Jakes could handle the spitfire, Kristina. Peter decided it was time to help push the romance along, and what better place than this weekend? But he needed to keep the cover.

"Poodles, please don't make me beg." She softened her voice. "You owe me this. Pull some strings, *please.*"

Peter had a plan up his sleeve: get Jakes and Kristina alone, and let fate do the rest. "Okay, calm down. I'll call you back."

Las Vegas in early February promised to be cooler than the ungodly temperatures from hell that hit by June. This weekend, the temps were topping at seventy-seven degrees during the day. Evenings, however, got below freezing your ass off. Kristina pulled a reclining lounge chair next to the pool to enjoy the sun and take a ten-minute power nap. Relaxed, she waited for Peter's call. No doubt, Mr. True Blue Reliable would come through with a decent room somewhere.

Twenty minutes passed before Kristina woke to her phone's buzzing in her pocket. "Poodles, whatcha got?"

"Okay, KT. It's taken care of. You can pick up the passkey at the concierge desk of The Arises Hotel. Be sure to have your driver's license with you, or they won't give you the key. Promise me, no one but you stays in the room. I pulled big strings, but I love you, and I was an ass the other night. You know how much I want you and Beth to be friends."

"Poodles, stop. Put that topic on the back burner for now. Let's not get mad all over again. Thank you for doing this for me. Love you. I'll call you when I get back in town."

"Have fun, KT. Remember, only you in the room. See you when you get back." Peter and Jakes worked out the security details at all the casinos on the Strip. Kristina and the girls had topnotch protection detail, but as far as the romance goes, Jakes needed to take it from there.

~~~~

Securing her own hotel room moved Kristina's plan in the right direction. Now she needed to figure out how to get the guy. *Hope I have a couple of nice chocolates on my pillow.* She headed to The Arises hotel to check in.

DJ seemed like a good man with real potential. She fantasized they could have something special for the next three days. Maybe, just maybe, it could be her turn to meet the wonderful guy for a change.

CHAPTER THIRTY-FOUR

In the cab ride over to The Arises, guilt started to set in about leaving the girls. *Four women, two queen beds, one bathroom, or my own room, slip into my soft jammies and relax in a large cozy bed with my cappuccino in the morning with no one talking, plus time alone with DJ.* Kristina justified her plan and decided that with a little time management, there was plenty of her for everyone. Peter hoped he'd played his cards right, and Kristina would order room service for two in the morning.

~~~~

A bellman at The Arises concierge's desk greeted Kristina by name before she handed him her identification. *Wow, they must think I'm royalty. Poodles must have sent them my photo. I hope it was a cute picture.*

Continuous high-pitched circus tunes from the poker machines perked Kristina's energy level from a negative two to a plus one. A security guard greeted, "Afternoon, Ms. Truly." He escorted her to a private elevator. Another bellman stood waiting in the open elevator. "Welcome, Ms. Truly." He waved a gold keycard in front of a small electronic plate on the wall. The elevator zoomed up thirty-five floors.

This is a bit much. Kristina's ears popped from a broad yawn in the elevator, which shimmied with rapid upward speed. Her stomach lurched when the doors opened on the penthouse floor. "What the hell?" Kristina whispered, wide-eyed.

The bellman waived his keycard again to open a set of solid black wooden hand-carved Asian-style double doors. Kristina stepped into her weekend palace. Her heart raced at the sight of the panoramic view overlooking the magic of the Las Vegas Strip and surrounding Red Rock Mountains.

Pale pewter carpet and white marble tiles covered the floors. Sunlight glistened on the plush lavender chenille and velvet-covered sofas. Fresh tuberose and gardenia seeped from towering floral arrangements with a multitude of brightly colored fresh flowers. Kristina wandered through the penthouse, admiring the delicate hand-blown glass vases filled with roses in every color, mixed with pink and white stargazer lilies. An embossed sterling silver plaque mounted on the wall next to the front doors stated: "Welcome to Paradise."

Poodles pulled some strings all right. Kristina had a private 4,000 square foot penthouse for the next three days all to herself—but hopefully not. Poodles loved over-the-top surprises, but this really took the cake.

Now part two of her plan: how to get DJ back to The Arises alone without their six BFFs?

CHAPTER THIRTY-FIVE

By the time Kristina arrived back at the Bella Terra to meet up with the others, she had talked herself out of trying to persuade DJ to join her at the other hotel. The reality had set in. She liked DJ, but emotionally she needed to slow down. She'd just paid for the burial of her father, the pressure cooker for book sales already started for her new book before it had even hit the printer, and a serial killer brutally murdered three women that attended her workshops. Her career might end if the media let out the connection between the murders. Plus, she got dumped by George without even a phone call after a wild night of sex, and her best friend/backup-guy, Poodles, announced his engagement to a woman who cheated on him—twice. The more she thought about it, the smarter it sounded to spend time alone in her room at the penthouse soaking in the giant whirlpool spa and regroup emotionally. That would be the best medicine.

~~~~

The Bella Terra casino bustled with an eclectic group of people. Kristina muddled through the crowds toward the elevator to her friends' room. Roulette wheels spun, blackjack dealers threw down cards, and slot machines chimed. Not much of a gambler, Kristina slid a ten-dollar bill in a dollar slot machine. "Baby needs new shoes." She chanted watching the bright gold coins, gold bars, and cherries spin until the wheel bounced to a stop. The colorful lights and bubbly music sped up, causing Kristina's heart to race. "Place Bet? That's it? I spent ten bucks on nothing? Crap." Kristina smirked with no intention to do that again.

A sloppy-dressed gray-haired man knocked his hip in the back of Kristina's seat. His breath oozed the odor of booze. "This place ain't built on charity, sweetheart. Load 'er up again. Have fun. It's just money." The man plopped his ass in the seat next to her before splashing his bourbon rocks on her foot. She rolled her eyes at the man and headed to see the girls.

~~~~

"Hi, Kooky. Where's everyone?" Kristina lay on the bed next to a suitcase overstuffed with enough outfits for a month.

Koo Koo stood in her bathing suit, sipping from a pink straw in a fresh cut pineapple filled with a slushy ice-cold Mai Tai. "Hey, KT, where you been? The girls are at the pool with the guys. They're fun. Seem like great guys. I'm heading back down. Are you going to join us? Where'd you and adorable DJ disappear to?"

"Aw, I'm sorry, Kooky, you know how I disappear when I'm feeling overwhelmed. I wasn't with DJ. I assumed he was with all of you. The events of the past month have caught up with me. Peter arranged a room for me at The Arises. I went to check in. Emotionally, I'm fried. I hope you understand?"

"Of course, KT. Even Super Woman needs downtime. I'll let the girls know we'll all hang out tomorrow. Get some rest. You've had a rough time lately, sweetie. I know your dad passing has been harder on you than you've let on. The murders, George just dropping off the face of the Earth, not to mention Peter. We'll meet up sometime tomorrow. Listen, KT, DJ seems like a great guy. We're over forty—time to live our lives without regrets. Don't let a good one get away. Who knows? He may turn out to be more than just your weekend guy." Koo Koo set her drink on the nightstand and gave Kristina a hug.

"Thanks, Kooky. I love you. I'll call you tomorrow." Kristina wiped her tears with the pillowcase.

Kristina headed through the casino toward the front of the hotel to catch a cab back to The Arises. A weight lifted knowing the girls were having fun, and Koo Koo saw something good in DJ too, which said a lot.

There wasn't any word from DJ. Kristina figured he'd gotten busy with something or someone, and with her luck, it was a pretty female someone. Usually, when she met an interesting guy in a bar, he'd end up with a random bimbo while she went to the ladies' room. DJ seemed different, but this was Vegas baby, and he was a wild card. Best case scenario, she'd probably meet up with DJ sometime the next day. Worse case, the good guy would get away again. At this point, she fantasized about powering up the whirlpool bath at the Penthouse suite, turning the water temperature up to melt, and sinking her naked body in the swirling jets. She could hear the spa's motor revving like music to her ears. A bottle of French champagne on Peter's tab in a bucket of ice had her name written all over it. She could already taste the bubbles. "Taxi ..."

Kristina opened the door of her yellow cab. "Kristina, hey, Kristina. Wait up." She looked around when she heard DJ's voice out of nowhere. DJ crawled in next to her. Dressed in a perfectly pressed linen shirt and khaki shorts, he looked and smelled too damn yummy to kick out of the cab. One glimpse at DJ shot her plans for the evening straight to hell.

"Wow, look at you, all dressed up. Where are you off to?" Kristina scooted across the seat.

"Where to folks?" The driver waited for one of them to answer.

"I'm hoping to tag along with you. Do you mind? Do you have plans?" DJ pushed the brim of Kristina's floppy straw sun hat away from her face to see her eyes. His tanned olive complexion made his teeth look even whiter. Sitting next to DJ made her forget that Peter said no one but her in the suite. Watching him run his masculine hands through his hair pushed her right over the edge of crazy, hot infatuation.

"I don't mind at all," Kristina said with a chipper tone and wide smile. "The Arises Hotel, please."

CHAPTER THIRTY-SIX

The cabbie made his way through the traffic down the famous highly populated Las Vegas Strip by weaving in and out of cars. "So why The Arises, Ms. Truly? Hiding from someone? Are the others going to join you?" DJ inquired, pretending not to know anything about the new plan.

"How do you know my last name? I don't remember telling you my last name." In an instant, Kristina got a knot in the middle of her stomach. It's the way he said it. His voice changed from shy guy to interrogator guy. Suddenly her radar kicked in. Something felt off. Her Pisces intuition fired at red alert. Who's this guy and what's he after? Kristina sat up straight, sliding herself closer to the door. As if she could jump from the moving car at the speeds the cabbies drive in Las Vegas. Her left hand gripped the door handle, ready just in case. She looked in the rearview mirror, trying to get the attention of the driver. But between his Mario Andretti maneuvers down the crowded Strip and acceleration onto the busy highway, his eyes never caught hers.

"I'm a foreign spy. *Mwahahaha.*" DJ said with the theatrics of a deviant villain. Kristina's body stiffened while tightening her grip around the door handle.

"Kristina, relax. I'm just trying to be funny. I read your

last name on your luggage tag when I tossed your bag full of rocks (cough, cough) I mean shoes, up in the overhead bin." DJ cupped his mouth with his hand to fake the coughs, attempting more humor. He took her hand in his.

"I'm really sorry." DJ gave her a sad puppy, pout. "I didn't mean to scare you. I'm so sorry, Ms. Truly, Truly, I am." DJ couldn't tell if his weak comedic attempts were helping the situation.

Breathe in through my nose and out through my mouth. Kristina took a deep breath. Dropping her shoulders below her ears, she relaxed her body. His dimples were like Kryptonite. They made her melt.

"You win this time, funny guy, but just so you know, your adorable dimples aren't why I trust you right now. It's because I carry a Taser, and I'm not afraid to use it." She grinned, and their bodies relaxed into one another. DJ rubbed her hand as she wrapped her fingers around his. So much of her mother's overprotective, always imagining everyone is an ax murderer, filtered into her psyche over the years. She needed to loosen up, but with a serial killer on the loose, this wasn't the weekend to start.

"My friend, Peter, is always telling me that I read too many mystery novels and watch too many crime shows on Netflix. I think he may be right."

DJ couldn't take his eyes off her. His heart hurt with the chemistry he felt next to her. "Kristina, I—" Detective Jakes started to tell Kristina the truth about why he and his agents were in Las Vegas. Kristina interrupted.

"So, to answer your question, no, the girls are not going to join me at The Arises. And no, I'm not hiding from anyone. Peter, my best friend, owed me a big favor, and he got me a room. Well, not just any room. He got me the penthouse suite," Kristina bragged, trying to sound intriguing. She hoped to keep him curious, then regretted sounding like a snob. *Dial it down, girlfriend. Just be yourself. You're an intelligent, successful woman.* Kristina had gone from zero to sixty, and she needed to pump the brakes, but she was already in full swing, head-over-heels for this guy and his fucking adorable dimples.

"And since I've had a bit of a rough month, I'm going to spend some time alone and regroup. I can't tell the girls I have the penthouse. They'd kill me." Kristina sounded like an auctioneer rambling so fast she had to take a quick gasp of air. Her stomach jumped up to her chest as her giddy school-girl attraction climbed another notch with a whiff of DJ's cologne. She slowed down long enough to flash DJ a little flirtatious smile. Hoping he picked up on the subtle hints that being alone, and regrouping included him.

"Wow, Peter must be some best friend. For God's sake, the penthouse at The Arises has its own swimming pool, Jacuzzi, theater, and a view of the entire city. Hell, the penthouse suite is famous for its rock star erotic history." Detective Jakes got caught up in the moment, or maybe with his hormones, and didn't explain that he was in Las Vegas to keep her and the other girls safe. But before things got too awkward, he needed to stop pretending to be DJ, the stockbroker, and fess up to the truth. Detective Jakes needed to explain that he was there hunting for a serial killer, and she might be the next victim so he couldn't let her out of his sight. Things were moving fast, and DJ needed to hurry the conversation. Perhaps after a few martinis at this point would be best.

DJ paid the cab driver and took Kristina's arm in his as they walked directly through the casino toward the elevators.

"Sounds like you've been here before," Kristina said. She was taken aback by DJ's in-depth knowledge of the expensive penthouse suite.

"Yes, quite a few times. Mostly for business," DJ answered nonchalantly, which struck her as odd. Now DJ played the intriguing card. He walked toward the private elevator like he owned the place. Still, Kristina knew they needed to show security her room-key and identification before they would let them anywhere near the penthouse. Or so she thought.

"Jakes, Bro. I heard you were in town. How long you staying?" The security guard grabbed Jakes's hand, going in for the bro bump hug.

Kristina stood unnoticed with her keycard and ID in hand, watching the unusual meet and greet as a couple of hefty built plain clothes security guys surrounded Jakes. She didn't have a clue what to think.

"Jakes. What's up?" A blackjack dealer shouted from his table a few feet away.

DJ gave a head nod, "Not much, Kev. Save me a seat later."

DJ reached behind and took Kristina by the hand, and without saying anything, pulled her next to him. She felt like a mouse in his side pocket, wondering, *who's this guy—the mayor?*

"You owe me a drink, asshole." A beautiful cocktail waitress built like a twenty-five-year-old ginger-haired bombshell walked by with a full tray of cocktails and a big smile directed at DJ.

"Last minute trip, Jeanne. I haven't forgotten about the drink, sweetie. We'll catch up later." DJ watched Jeanne's long legs attached to her tiny ass swing from side to side while she hurried by in a uniform with less fabric than the cocktail napkins on her tray.

Will this circus ever end? Kristina thought just as an incredibly handsome pit boss joined the reunion. "Jakes, my man. Fuck, does Kelly know you're in town? You better call her, pal. She's still pissed at you. If she hears you were here and didn't call her, you will be in deeper shit, my friend."

One person after another chimed in, greeting DJ or Jakes or whatever his name was. *Shit.* Kristina thought. *Come on, who the hell is this guy? But, more importantly, who the hell is Kelly?*

Chapter Thirty-Seven

Laughing it up, Detective Jakes's buddies continued to gather around. Until now, Jakes had not let his badge down, all eyes on Kristina's safety. His high alert vigilance had given Kristina the impression DJ had an introverted, shy side to him. But DJ's shy demeanor definitely flipped, and Jakes had quite a personality. His outgoing, self-confidence revved his sex appeal to a whole new height. It didn't appear Jakes had a shy bone in his body. Nor did it seem he had any intention of wrapping up old home week anytime soon. Kristina had a different agenda. A shower and clean clothes waited for her in the penthouse. Seizing the opportunity to politely excuse herself, she escaped into the elevator, leaving DJ to play with his fan club.

~~~~

"Wait." DJ's arm wedged between the elevator's doors, triggering the sensor to reopen. "Coming through." DJ hopped in the elevator. He slipped his keycard into a slot on the wall, which gave him access directly to the top floor.

A male's voice came across the speakers: "Jakes, howzit, homie? I heard you were in the hotel. Have a nice stay in the penthouse, and buzz if you need anything." Music resumed. DJ put his arm around Kristina with a pursed-lip grin.

"Okay, I will let you in on a little secret. I've worked security here in Las Vegas. It's a pretty tight-knit group."

"Damn, I was hoping you owned the place." Kristina stared straight ahead with her arms by her side, playing it cool. "You worked security before becoming a stockbroker?" she asked, trying not to look at his damn dimples. They clouded her sensibility. Her left frontal cortex had an 80/20 verdict in favor of: he's full of shit. She avoided staring into his baby blues, or she'd be dust.

DJ grinned at her sarcasm, letting out a laugh.

"Oh, yes. Now about that, see . . . well . . . where do I start? Let's get inside. I need to talk to you about something important." It was time to have the conversation they should've had hours ago.

"Please, after you." DJ opened the beautiful doors to the penthouse. Kristina headed inside.

"I need a cocktail and a shower, in that order. Do you know how to make a good martini?" Kristina sounded confident. She wanted DJ to know she was a strong-willed woman. DJ didn't need to know she had butterflies in her stomach looking at him.

"Can I make a good martini? Eh, no. I make great martinis." DJ pushed a couple of buttons on the wall. Soft jazz echoed throughout the suite in Dolby sound. Kristina shot him a curious look and confused head shake. *Worked security in Las Vegas, my ass.*

The hotel spared no expense with the perfect lighting, giving the entire penthouse an exquisite ambiance. In the foyer of the elegant suite, DJ stood underneath cut crystals dangling from a nine-foot chandelier hanging from the twenty-five-foot-high vaulted ceiling. His eyes sparkled like sapphires. His flawless olive skin tempted Kristina to run her hands over his rugged cheekbones.

"Two martinis coming right up," DJ said after making himself at home behind the bar. He read the gin labels as he organized the bottles of booze on the shelves to his liking.

"Hey, sexy bartender, let's get moving on the martinis." Kristina slapped his ass with her hand, then took a seat on a barstool to watch him mix the drinks. "What gins do they have stocked in this swanky joint?" Kristina pretended to be interested in the quality of booze, but the crime novels she read taught her to make sure DJ didn't slip her a mickey.

"Only the best for you, my dear. Well, not true. I used Nolet's Silver. It's only about fifty dollars a bottle. I can afford to replace that one." DJ handed Kristina a black and gold bottle from the top shelf behind the bar.

"Don't drop this one. Nolet's Reserve is usually nine hundred a bottle, but in this hotel, I'm guessing it's upwards of eleven hundred," DJ said.

"Whoa, that's out of my price range too. The cheap stuff at fifty dollars is out of my price range." Kristina carefully placed the bottle back on the counter.

"What about your friends at the Bella Terra? Do your homies know where you are?" Kristina smiled, hoping to sound hip as she got comfortable, making herself right at home in the ultra-luxurious suite designed for high rollers and apparently, her new friend, DJ.

"No homies tonight. They get me tomorrow. Tonight, I'm all yours." DJ added a few ice cubes and slowly stirred the gin with a splash of dry vermouth. He placed a sterling silver strainer on the cut-crystal pitcher, and with one quick shake, he poured the martinis into two chilled, gold-rimmed long-stemmed glasses. DJ caught the grin on Kristina's face as she watched his reflection in the mirror behind him. Tingles raised the hair on his arms when he watched Kristina's beautiful doe eyes admiring his backside and biceps.

"Ah, here you go. The perfect martini." DJ handed Kristina the drink with three olives and one onion on a slim sterling silver pick.

"I'll be the judge of that." Holding up her glass to his, they clicked the rims.

"Cheers, Kristina. Here's to being alone and regrouping."

"Cheers. Thank you." Kristina took a sip with a wide smile, fantasizing about regrouping with DJ. "Mmm. This is a good martini."

"Correction, my dear. It's great." DJ flashed his bright whites and dimples, and she felt a surge of a good little some-thin' somethin' all inside.

Kristina gripped the chilled glass with both hands and took a savoring sip with her eyes closed. Jakes bit his bottom lip, watching her mouth on the glass.

"My pleasure. Let me know when you're ready for another." DJ cleaned up the mess he had made at the bar. *Slow down, buddy. This is work, not a real date.* Detective Jakes heard the logic in his head but felt his hormones rev like a twenty-year-old when he looked at Kristina.

"I'll need another after I freshen up. I've been in these clothes all day. I'm going to take a long shower if you don't mind," Kristina said. She and her martini headed toward the bedroom, kicking off her shoes on the way down the long hall. The plush carpet felt like pillows under her feet. She felt safe even though she didn't know DJ. What could happen? Everyone in the hotel knew him unless they were all going to help bury her body. She'd worry about getting murdered by the hunky guy making her fantastic martinis after a much-needed warm shower.

"Enjoy, Kristina. The shower is amazing, with eight adjustable showerheads. The giant one overhead feels like you're in the rain forest. Set the three heads on the far wall to pulsate, with the dial to six, my favorite setting. Oh, and there's a knob to the left of the shower door if you want steam. Take your time. I'll shoot some pool and make myself comfortable." DJ's voice trailed off as Kristina closed the door to the large elegant bedroom.

Spinning her naked self around in circles with her arms stretched out in the lavish all-white marble bathroom, she felt like Elsa in Frozen, but before she belted out, "Let It Go," she heard DJ's voice coming from somewhere: "Kristina …"

"Shit." She screeched, grabbing a towel to cover herself, looking around the bathroom for DJ.

"I forgot to tell you; there's an intercom system in every room. It's on the wall next to the shower. Let me know if you need anything." DJ stopped talking. Kristina found the intercom exactly where he instructed.

"I'm good. Thanks," Kristina spoke into the speaker, and at the same time wondering, *what's the real scoop on this guy?* But it could wait until after she put the three pulsating showerheads to good use.

CHAPTER THIRTY-EIGHT

Clean, refreshed, and eager to get to know more about DJ after her shower, Kristina threw her makeup on to look like a professional job with not a wrinkle in sight and her thick black lashes glued on tight. She clipped part of her hair up on top of her head, leaving just enough blond wispies hanging down to feel sexy. Bending over slightly, she shifted her breasts with an upward tug. Each torpedo was displayed nicely in her little black scoop-neck dress. She hoped her curvaceous cleavage would keep DJ distracted from the robust fullness she had added to her derriere by self-medicating with a box of chocolates last weekend. Topping off her outfit, she slipped on black leather pumps with four-inch pencil-thin heels and fire-red leather souls. Thinking about the entire evening alone with DJ, her heart felt as though she'd tied a rock to a string and dropped it off a cliff. *But who was this guy? If he's so great, why hasn't another woman snagged him?*

Until the recent bombshell of Poodles's engagement, Kristina always called him while she got ready for a date with a new suitor that had strong potential. Poodles gave great best friend advice: "Let him be the man, don't you dare pick up the tab, be yourself, you're amazing, he'd be a fool not to fall in love with you the minute he sees you. But it's not about him liking you. It's about you—is he good enough for you?"

It did leave a sour taste when she thought about not being able to call Poodles to tell him how excited she was about meeting DJ, but she had to get used to the idea that Poodles's matrimony with Beth took priority over their friendship. She needed a distraction, and so far, DJ fit the bill nicely.

It was hard to deny that there was something special about DJ, and she was dying to find out what that something was exactly. Kristina performed one last twirl in front of the huge bathroom mirror. Poised and polished, she gave herself a spritz with her favorite perfume.

Voilà. She pictured herself exiting a beautiful marble castle to join her prince.

~~~~

"Did I hear the doorbell?" Kristina said, entering the living room. She lost her breath. Time stopped. The dark skies and bright lights of the city twinkled through the glass windows like a vibrant prism of dazzling diamonds. Millions of tiny lights sparkled as far as she could see. It felt magical, just like a beautiful dream.

"Holy-wow. Kristina, you look absolutely stunning." DJ's eyes widened. He stopped what he was doing to look at her. "Wow, okay, think . . . oh yeah, dinner. I hope you're hungry," DJ stammered. His awkwardness and sweet enthusiasm made her feel something she'd never actually felt before with a man. Lovable, very lovable.

Distracted by the view of the city and her sizzling chemistry with DJ, it took a few seconds for Kristina to notice the elegant dining table outside on the patio. Set with white china plates, crystal wine glasses, sterling silverware, and yellow rose petals sprinkled across the taupe linen tablecloth. "Wow, impressive. Did you do all of this?" A lump of emotion swelled in her throat. Struggling to remember a time a man had done anything this nice for her, she gave DJ a heartfelt smile.

The pool's tropical waterfall trickled as the music played from the speakers disguised as landscape rocks. Kristina tried to pull herself back to reality. She had just met this guy. Quickly she made a pact with herself: *No expectations for the evening. If nothing else, it's wonderful to have a romantic evening with a sweet, handsome man. Be cool, don't overthink this. Just have fun.*

"I opened a bottle of merlot from one of my favorite towns in France. Pomerol. I hope you like it." He poured vino while humming along with the music playing in the background.

Kristina watched in silence. Her heart couldn't get enough of him. Every bit of this man appeared to be having a good time taking care of her for the evening. His favorite town in France. *What's next, flaming Crepe Suzette for dessert from his favorite patisserie?*

The wine had a rich bouquet and was best enjoyed sipped and savored. Not tonight. She needed to drink up. Sitting there with an engaging mysterious man, feeling something for him she'd never felt for any man, she needed to drown out thoughts of what she preached at her workshops. *Don't be too hasty to believe everything you hear on a first date. Take your time to get to know each other. Watch for red flags.* This was no time to start taking her own damn advice. DJ seemed to have the makings of a perfect man. Mr. Perfect for right now, anyway.

The enticing design of the patio deck begged for an intimate rendezvous from the Très Chic Teak furniture, the saltwater swimming pool, to the tropical floral landscaping with a sleek design of overhead heaters for the few cooler months of the year. Every part of this penthouse screamed romance.

Watching DJ take charge of the evening with his charming finesse and attentiveness made her feel incredibly special, but his dimples drove her sexually mad.

"This evening, *ma dame*, I'm serving fresh asparagus and baby red potatoes sautéed with olive oil and fresh rosemary. For the petit filet, a butterfly cut prepared well done with a drizzle of light pepper capers cream sauce. I hope it's just the way you like it," DJ said with a white napkin draped over one wrist as he took a bow.

"Oh my gosh, this looks wonderful and smells delicious," Kristina gushed. He liked his filet mignon exactly the way she liked hers, he drank gin martinis as she did, he loved red wine and so did she. *It's fate. It has to be fate.* She tried to tell herself otherwise, but her heart believed it had to be fate because it was her turn to meet the great guy.

DJ moved his chair closer to hers. "Kristina, how's your steak?" He locked his eyes with hers. She felt her cheeks flush with a mouth full of asparagus.

"Umm, yum. Everything's delicious." Kristina took the opportunity in between bites to lean in closer to her dreamy date. They continued with small talk, but Kristina wanted to get to the good stuff. "Please tell me how is it you aren't married?" She smiled, looking DJ right in the eyes. He poured more wine.

"I had a beautiful, loving marriage—fifteen fantastic years. My wife, Anne, passed away the day after our son's third birthday. Car accident. Hit and run. Never found who killed her." He spun his steak knife around in circles as he shared the generic version of the story. He suspected mob revenge but lacked substantial proof, and he'd never stop looking. He kept that part of the story for only a select few.

"I've been doing my best, but being a single dad doesn't give me much time to socialize. My son, Richie, turned eight a few days ago. I love him so much. And he's young enough to still think I'm cool." He looked down at his wine glass, leaning back in his chair to create space between the two of them while thinking about his wife. Jakes worried about the dangers of someone else he loved getting hurt if his wife's death was some sort of revenge, and so far, he'd manage to keep his personal relationships at a distance because the bad guys he's put away don't play nice.

"My job's demanding. Between Richie's schoolwork and league sports, we stay pretty busy. So, until he's older, I'm trying to focus on him and me." DJ smiled at Kristina, letting her know talking about his personal life wasn't something he took lightly. It was time to come clean. He needed to explain everything. It was time to be honest about the case he and Peter were working on.

Kristina rubbed the top of his hand. "I love hearing about your life. Thank you for sharing with me about your wife and son. It must be tough." She wanted to kiss his cheeks but gave a sweet smile instead. Her tenderness turned Jakes's detective badge off, and his heart fired up ten degrees.

"Richie sounds like a great kid. Where is he this weekend?" Hearing DJ talk about his son reminded Kristina how much she'd loved her father when she was Richie's age.

"He's with my sister and her husband and their two kids. He loves his cousins. They're more like siblings. We spend a lot of time together. My sister's not trying to be Richie's mom, but she's great with him. However," —DJ got a big grin on his face, and he leaned in closer—" This weekend, dear old dad's got a hall pass."

He reached across the table for a bowl of fresh raspberries and placed a dollop of fluffy white whip cream on top. The arousing energy between them sent quivers to places in Kristina's body she'd forgotten about. She fiddled with her watch for a distraction as their incontestable attraction steamed up.

"What about you, Kristina? What's an intelligent, beautiful woman like you doing unattached?" DJ swished his wine around in his cut crystal wine glass.

DJ and his damn charm had Kristina fully infatuated, and he knew it. He leaned in closer, tucking a strand of hair behind her ear. He slid a moist raspberry across her lips. She teased, biting his fingers as she took the berry with her tongue.

With an endearing touch, he caressed her cheek. Her heart leaped into high gear. The chemistry with DJ was the kind she'd only fantasized about. He had her. There was no denying that Kristina felt something for this guy she'd never felt before.

The hours flitted by in seconds. Each story DJ told about his life increased her fondness for him. She tried her damnedest to find a few flaws, but this amazing man swept her off her feet. Confident, caring, funny, a single dad. For the life of her, she couldn't find anything not to love about him. It may have been the wine talking, but this guy felt like the type of man she wanted to share her life with, not fix him.

While DJ excused himself to the restroom, Kristina seized the opportunity to relocate from the dining table to an oversized chaise lounge, the perfect size for both of them to cuddle. She leaned back, staring out at Sin City, waiting for DJ to snuggle up next to her. She couldn't imagine this night getting any better.

CHAPTER THIRTY-NINE

DJ's tall frame towered over the chaise, where Kristina sat smiling with fresh lipstick. "Darn, that's the seat I wanted. How are you at sharing?" He said, scooting next to Kristina with her tanned smooth-shaven legs crossed below the hem of her short black dress. Sexy black pumps still on her feet, accented her shapely calves.

"Is this what you do with all the men you meet on an airplane? Let me guess. You lure them into an exotic penthouse, then come out looking sexy as hell in a little black dress." He cuddled her in his arms. "You cast your spell with an enchanting smile and contagious laugh." DJ kissed her cheek. "And, right when he thinks he could walk away at any time, realizes he'd be a fool not to stay with you forever?" He held her tighter.

Giggling, she played along. "Yes, I've lured hundreds of the weaker sex back to random penthouses across the country. I spin my tangled web and torture them with all my crazy insecurities until they fall in love with me, and then one of their good friends or a family member has their head examined and committed to an institution."

"Well, it worked. I see the men in white coats coming for me now." His lips softly kissed her forehead.

DJ got to his feet. "Dance with me." He reached for her hand. Taking Kristina in his arms, he hummed to the saxophone playing on the stereo, "When I Met You, All My Dreams Came True." They swayed to the rhythm.

"This must be the best view in Las Vegas," Kristina said with her arms around DJ's neck. His hands rested on her waist.

"*You're* the best view in this city." He pulled her hips closer to his.

"Millions and millions of lights in this unique city. Every light represents someone's life, their story, but not tonight. Tonight, it's you and me." DJ sang in perfect baritone pitch: "When I met you, all my dreams came true. Sweet dreams, sweet dreams of you. And in your dreams, whenever they be, I pray you dream a sweet dream of me." He had stepped over the line. This wasn't just his job. He'd fallen for Kristina.

Nothing mattered as much as being in each other's arms at that moment. The beat of their hearts pounded together like a ticking clock. DJ kissed her nose and then her cheek. Kissing her neck, he continued his soft lips down to her chest.

"Oh … Umm …" Kristina couldn't speak. Passion lit her body. For once, she stopped talking, leaving less opportunity for her to say something stupid by overthinking.

"Kristina, are you okay? Is this good with you?" With a firm thrust, her hips dug deep into his. Her hand groped his tight ass. There was no mistaking it, yeah, she was more than okay, don't stop. The tip of his tongue followed the curve of her breast. Her fingers wound around his hair while she held his head pressed against her chest. Bristles from his tight beard drove her to insanity.

He stopped kissing her. She felt his breath. Tugging on the back of her head, DJ released the clip holding her hair and caressed long strands through his fingers. The moonlight glistened on their faces. She wanted his lips to touch hers so badly it hurt. Nothing felt like this with the other men she'd been with.

It didn't matter if this was the romantic magic of the city's lights or the sexual magic between the two of them. Whatever it was, she took a deep breath and succumbed to the moments of carnal pleasure.

DJ slid the zipper slowly down the back of Kristina's dress. She tingled with the touch of his fingers slipping her lace panties down her legs. He pulled her naked body close to him. Kristina unzipped his shorts, popped his shirt buttons open, and then she stroked his tanned, muscular chest, wet from sweat. DJ took her hand, guiding her into the steaming hot Jacuzzi.

Water jets sprayed hard against their skin. DJ's gentle touch felt natural over her body. Both of them felt as if their souls had been together forever. Their passion heated, and it was time to move the party inside. DJ wrapped Kristina in a thick white bath towel. She tossed it on the pool deck and yanked the towel off his waist.

They plunged their bodies across the double-wide white canvas lounge chair. At that moment, they were worlds away from reality. Outside under the brilliant city lights, sex was the only thing they had on their minds. They worked their way to the bedroom, stopping for a quickie over the dining room table.

Crisp Egyptian bed linens slid under Kristina's naked body while DJ slid on top. The two of them had glorified, savage, barbaric-howling, rug-burning, sex. Mutually exhausted, they finally fell asleep before one of them had a stroke. And on that fiery February night, she fell in love, or at the very least, deep infatuation.

CHAPTER FORTY

The bright desert sun poured through the floor-to-ceiling glass walls in the bedroom. Lying next to Kristina, DJ opened one eye—just barely. He reached over to pull out a small remote control from the top drawer of the nightstand, aimed, and with one push of a button, the window dispersed a grainy sand-like substance in the core of the thick glass. Poof. The window went solid, blending in with the taupe-colored paint on the walls.

"Nice job. I won't ask how you knew about the remote control in the nightstand or the window disappearing like a magic trick until I've had a least another hour of sleep." Snuggling up next to DJ, Kristina laid her head on his warm chest.

Kristina woke to the muffled tone of her cell phone ringing. Gently pulling back the covers, she crawled out of bed to find her phone, leaving DJ snoring in the fluffy down duvet cover. With too little sleep and no caffeine yet, Kristina was slow to gain her wits. It took a second, but she remembered that she'd tucked her phone in the canvas bag filled with her shoes. Digging for her phone, she noticed the name tag on the bag: "KT." It didn't say, Kristina Truly. Her face flushed with nerves, and her stomach knotted. DJ said he read her last name on her luggage when he put it in the overhead bin. He lied. "Holy shit, who did I have sex with last night? Who's asleep in my bed?" She mumbled as she grabbed the phone just in time to catch Koo Koo's call.

"KT, oh, thank God." Koo Koo sobbed into the phone.

"Kooky, what's wrong? Are you crying?" Kristina walked to the bathroom door to secure the lock. She wrapped her chilled naked body with the hotel bathrobe hanging on the back of the door.

"KT, it's terrible. My cousin called, and something's happened to George. He might be dead." Koo Koo took a deep breath, followed by a loud cry.

Kristina dropped to sit on the velvet bench at the vanity. "George Handy might be dead? What the hell are you talking about? What do you mean?" Kristina sat shivering, trying to grasp any part of this story.

"The police found his truck abandoned in the Angeles National Park late last night. This morning, hikers found a body down an embankment. The body has been there for several days. They think it's George, but they won't know for sure until they have time to examine the body. The police said it wasn't an accident. He's been murdered. And KT, if it is George's body, you may be the last person to see him alive, and that makes you a suspect."

"Murdered? Suspect! I wanted him gay—not dead." Kristina yelled in shock and more confused.

"Kristina, everything okay?" DJ knocked on the bathroom door but used a key above the doorframe to unlock it.

"Kooky, I have to call you back." Kristina hung up the phone and grabbed one of her spiked heel stilettos.

"Stop right there," Kristina demanded, drawing back her arm with the heel pointed toward DJ. "I swear to God I'll stab you if you don't tell me who you really are right now. I want the truth. None of the stockbroker bull shit. How did you know my last name? It wasn't on my bag. How did you know how I like my martinis, and how the fuck do you know this penthouse so well?" Kristina said with her stiletto in one hand and her cellphone in the other, ready to call 911 or someone. She hadn't thought that part through.

"Whoa, whoa, whoa. Slow down, Kristina, I can explain. I'm a detective for the Special Crimes Unit—a federal agent. You can call Peter. He'll tell you we're working this case together. I'm not here to hurt you. I'm here to protect you. Put the shoe down, and we'll talk," DJ said calmly, trying to hide the grin on his face when he looked at the strings of shiny rhinestones dangling from the heat Kristina was packing.

"Detective my ass. And how? Why do you know Peter? What case? Show me your badge," Kristina yelled, ready to take a swing at DJ if he made one wrong move.

"I'm naked, Kristina. I have to pee. Let me get dressed, and I will tell you everything." DJ walked past her. He lifted the toilet seat. "You're welcome to stay." DJ relieved himself.

"That's rude, DJ, or whatever your name is." Kristina cinched her robe closed and stormed out of the bathroom.

CHAPTER FORTY-ONE

"I can't wait to hear his load of crap." Kristina shimmied into her pink yoga pants. "Where's my fucking bra?" She vented loudly. A wave of hormones rushed her body when she thought about DJ ripping her clothes off during the best sex of her life. "Damn, it's outside." She stomped her way to the patio with her mind racing, mad as hell. She tossed her hands in the air, watching her black lace bra bobbing under the water of the swimming pool. "It fucking figures. Ugh." She said in a deep growl.

"Well, you won't kiss these babies again." Kristina cupped her bouncing breasts in both hands on her way back to the bedroom to finish getting dressed. Her emotions toiled between seething mad at DJ and passionately wanting to be with him. She threw on a fuchsia sports bra under a white *Namaste* T-shirt and headed to the kitchen, praying to find a kilo of caffeine.

"Where's the fucking coffee pot?" Kristina said, practically spitting fire into the intercom in the kitchen.

"There's an espresso machine in the coffee bar next to the pantry. Open the refrigerator. You'll see a can of Lavazza and Barista brand almond milk—makes a much better cappuccino than regular almond milk." DJ answered through the intercom from the shower.

"Of course, it does. I know that. I buy that brand, asshole. Oh sure, there just happens to be a can of my favorite coffee in the refrigerator. What the hell, *detective?* Maybe you're a psychic too. Buddy, you've gotten on my last nerve. And you can stop flashing your adorable dimples at me. Crap, why'd the sex have to be so good?" Kristina heard DJ laughing in the shower. "Shit." She slid the intercom switch to off with a vengeance.

DJ walked into the kitchen with wet hair and just a bath towel wrapped around his waist. His tan, tight abs made it hard not to stare and think about last night's pleasure of rubbing her hands all over his sexy body.

"Kristina, let me do that. I make a fairly good cappuccino. Sit down and try to relax. I'm going to make us a couple of omelets." DJ took over in the kitchen like everything was hunky-dory.

"No, I'm not going to relax. And no food. You need to tell me right now, what the hell you mean by protecting me. Show me your badge and ID," she demanded, wondering how he would pull that rabbit out of his hat. He didn't have any luggage with him last night when they were together. All he had on was a linen shirt and shorts. Until they got naked.

None of this made sense to Kristina. She couldn't wrap her head around any of it. She needed an explanation before her head exploded. Pacing back and forth from the kitchen to the windows in the living room, biting and picking at her cuticles, she waited for him to start explaining what the hell mess she'd gotten into now.

"We can eat while we talk." He handed her a big coffee mug filled with a cappuccino topped with semi-foamy almond milk. Like a junkie needing a fix, she planted her mouth on the mug, closing her eyes, wishing he hadn't been so damn amazing last night.

"*Damn it*. Of course, it's fantastic." She whispered, pissed off that he was so good at everything. She held the cup firm to her lips, savoring every sip.

Butter sizzled in the pan, and the smell of the omelets filled the room. But the sweet smell of bacon, which Kristina normally loved, turned her stomach with so much uncertainty around her. The thought of food made her gag. While the omelets simmered in the saucepan, he retreated to one of the bedrooms. He returned fully dressed in Levi 501 jeans and a navy-blue T-shirt with FBI printed across the chest in large, yellow letters. Smaller writing below read, Special Crimes Unit. A green army duffle bag hung over his shoulder.

Shit, how long was I in the bathroom getting ready last night? This guy's like a friggin' magician with overnight bag, dinner delivered, and my favorite coffee, Ugh. Why is it the seemingly flawless men are always the most flawed? Just once, I'd like the perfect man to actually be the fucking perfect man. She tried to stop thinking about his body thrusting over hers.

He laid the bag on the center island in the kitchen and placed items from the bag on the countertop. "Okay, here's my Orange County police badge. Here's my Fed's ID. Here's my heat, my socks, my underwear, my deodorant—"

She stopped him right there. "*Heat*. No, no, put that away. I hate guns." Staring at DJ holding his Calvin Klein tightie-whities in one hand and his Glock 22 in the other, she'd never admit it, but he looked adorable.

"Wait. On second thought, keep the gun right there. I may need to use it." She picked up his identification. He pulled the magazine out of the gun and stuck it in his back pocket.

"Detective Richard Jakes, FBI Special Agent. Looks like you really are a dick." She read his credentials in disbelief. Sitting on a barstool at the end of the island, she buried her face in her hands to cry.

"Kristina, shit, don't cry. I'm sorry. You're right. I'm a total dick. I should've told you everything last night, but there was never a good time." DJ massaged her shoulders.

"Never a good time? A great time would have been right after nice to meet you, Kristina, and just before here's my penis." She snapped at Detective Jakes while she blew her nose into a white athletic sock from his overnight bag.

"I began to tell you early on several times. We got side-tracked. Well, then the sex thing started happening … and well, you know … everything was going so well that I guess I forgot." Nerves got the best of DJ. He had fallen hard for Kristina, but he should have spoken up sooner. He combed his hands through his hair to think. Time was of the essence. They needed to move past all of this and get to business about the case.

"You forgot to tell me you were a detective, and I was under surveillance, but God forbid you should forget the Viagra and condoms?"

"Let's stay on point, Kristina. A—You aren't a suspect in the case. You are a possible target. B—By keeping you close to me, I'm keeping you safe, and C—It was all me last night, no help from pharmaceuticals. I swear."

"Your omelets are burning." She blew her nose in the sock.

He placed two beautiful china plates with perfectly made vegetable omelets, three strips of bacon, and toasted bagels dripping with real butter on the bar for the two of them. Kristina knew the perfect cure for lack of sleep and a hangover was some good home cooked greasy bacon, so she took a bite.

"Another cappuccino, Kristina?" DJ asked with all the charm of a perfect host.

"No, I need a cold Diet Coke. I'm sure you have a case stashed around here somewhere." DJ stopped eating and headed to a small refrigerated wine cooler in the cabinets under the wet bar.

"Is Diet Pepsi okay? They must have stocked the wrong sodas," he mumbled under his breath, rummaging through the array of beverages in the cooler.

"Oh, wait. Here they are way in the back." DJ popped open the can, pouring the syrupy bubbles into the glass loaded with ice.

"Now, if I only had about three Xanax, I'd be fine," Kristina said half sarcastic, half wishing she did.

The fog cleared in her head. But reality set in: *Was George Handy murdered, and why did she need protection?*

CHAPTER FORTY-TWO

"I'll start from the beginning. Well, before I get to the beginning, I want you to know, Kristina, that sex with you was my bad. But I do like you, and I had a lot of fun with you last night. That part has nothing to do with my job." DJ's phone rang in his pocket with the theme song from *Star Wars*. "Hey, what's up? Okay. Yeah, I'll call you back." DJ walked over to the television's remote control to switch on the seventy-four-inch plasma flat screen mounted on the wall.

The local Los Angeles reporter stood in front of an evergreen tree with a monument sign behind her: Angeles National Park.

"There are still no suspects in custody for the murder of an unidentified male. Police have been looking for a man named George Handy after finding his black, Chevy Silverado pickup truck illegally parked near a popular hiking trail early yesterday evening here in the Angeles National Forest. Just a few hours ago, a pair of hikers discovered a male body down this embankment behind us. The sheriff's department has not released a statement confirming if the body is that of Mr. Handy. The authorities are asking for your help. If you have seen George Handy or know anything about this brutal crime, please call the tip line for the LAPD. This is Rachel Gomez,

L.A.CAL News, keeping you informed as news breaks." A photo of George Handy remained on the screen with a tip call hotline in bold red numbers.

"What's this about, DJ? Was that phone call about George? Is he dead?" Kristina felt weak. Nausea came over her. Resting her head back on the sofa cushion, she pulled her knees to her chest. Tears erupted like a geyser. A million thoughts whirled around her head, but none made any sense.

"It feels like I've been in a coma my entire life, and I just woke up. I'm so confused. What the hell does any of this have to do with me?" She felt totally in the dark about what was going on, and now she wasn't sure she wanted to know the answers.

The last time she'd seen George, he was very much alive and showed her an extremely healthy side of himself. *Maybe he didn't dump me? Maybe he was dead or held hostage, and that's why he never called?* Kristina felt shameful for thinking such a thing, but his murder or kidnapping versus dumping her without an explanation made more sense, which brought her back to DJ's explanation before he got the phone call. *He said he liked me. He needs to finish explaining himself right after he explains why he needs to protect me.*

"Hey, it's Jakes. I saw the news report. So, what else do we have to go on?" DJ held his phone to his ear, staring down at the carpet, rocking from his heels to his toes with one hand in his front pocket. "Okay. Got it. Yeah, that might be the break we need. It sounds like he could be one of our victims or our serial killer. Yes, she's here next to me. How are you and the girls doing? Sounds good, buddy. I'll check in later." DJ disconnected the call and laid the phone on the counter.

"Kristina, the girls are safe with our team at the hotel having lunch. And FYI, there are no stockbrokers. We're all FBI dicks." DJ rubbed Kristina's shoulders and kissed her cheek. She didn't have the energy to make him stop, and she liked it.

"Don't think I'm not still pissed at you, because I am. But let's get through this story so I can figure out just how pissed I am."

"Okay, it all started a few months ago. We found our first vic in her apartment. You know her, Jaclyn Renzo. Her landlord, who lives next door, went in because he thought she might be sick. Her car was still parked in her parking spot after eleven o'clock Monday morning. She never missed work, so when she didn't answer the door, he let himself in. Coroner estimates TOD between eight o'clock Friday night and 2:00 a.m. Saturday. The vic's hands were tied with a long rope. It appears she was killed elsewhere and dumped back at her apartment. At first, we thought by the bruises on her body that maybe she was part of some sort of *Fifty Shades of Grey*, BDSM gone too far. But the killer left a message in blood on the wall. It said: *Sorry, I wasn't Mr. Right. XO, Mr. Wrong.* The only leads we had were from the Internet dating sites she frequented, and she attended several of your relationship workshops. She'd recently filed for divorce but had been separated for a couple of years." DJ stopped to check in with Kristina. "You doing okay? Do you need a break?"

She wasn't sure how to answer. At this point, like it or not, she needed to hear everything about the nightmare that she seemed to be smack in the middle of.

"Just keep going." Kristina rested her head on the back of the sofa.

DJ tried to keep the tone of his voice calm. Nothing he had to say was going to be easy for Kristina to hear. He cleaned up the kitchen and kept the conversation moving. "Our next vic was a white Caucasian male, Kurt Bender. Lived in Newport Heights. Similar build and closely resembles George Handy. Mr. Bender was found dead in the trunk of his brand-new Mercedes. He had the same long rope around his wrists, his throat cut, and the same sort of bruising. The message was on his windshield, written in red lipstick. *Sorry, I wasn't Ms. Right. XO, Ms. Wrong.*"

Kristina interrupted, "Wait. Mr. Right, XO, Mr. Wrong? That's from my workshops and my books. Do you think the killer knows me?" The color drained from her face.

"I wish we could answer that. We don't know at this point. Mr. Bender recently got divorced, and he was quite active on the dating websites. There's no evidence he had attended your relationship workshops. We're still looking to see if he'd ever had contact with Jaclyn Renzo through one of the dating apps." DJ took a seat on one of the barstools and continued, "The next vic, you also know, Sophia Clark. Her hands were tied with tight jute rope. Like the other vics, her throat severed completely—I'm so sorry, you don't need to hear the details of the crime scene. Anyway, this vic was found in a family cabin. A page from one of your books was found under her leg. Same bloody writing on the wall. But a homeless man discovered Lila Shaw. The killers took a big risk, dumping her body behind an old building. They stayed long enough to put the same writing in her blood on the wall. Once we found the male vic, we suspected there could be both a male and a female killer or bisexual, who knows. That's where you come in, Kristina."

"I didn't meet George on the Internet, and he's never attended my workshops. Why do you think he's involved with the murders?" Kristina felt like throwing up when she thought about the victims attending her workshops. She really needed that Xanax, or stronger.

"We know you didn't meet Handy online. But I hate having to be the one to tell you this, Kristina, George Handy's quite a player. He's got over ten online profiles on several different dating sites. Every time he goes out of town to work construction, he's also working the ladies. Tinder is the most used app for strangers to hook-up, especially while out of town." DJ stared down at his cellphone, which was blowing up with one text after another.

"Yeah, DJ, I know all about Tinder, but I had no idea about George. He seems like a nice guy, but I don't know him that well." Kristina downplayed her short-lived relationship with George. She didn't want him to think she hooked up with every random man she met. It had been nearly a year since she'd had sex with anyone before meeting George. But after her quick connection with DJ, she assumed that is exactly what DJ thought of her. Now she felt a lot more regret about sex with George and DJ than she could handle.

"The vic found by the hikers at Angeles Forest was shot. We don't think it's Handy. Probably a drug deal gone bad, most likely gang-related."

"George isn't dead? We need to tell Koo Koo right away."

"We still don't know how George is connected, so we can't tell the girls anything for now."

"That's not right. George is Koo Koo's cousin. She's devastated thinking he's been murdered." Kristina picked up her cell phone, ready to make the call.

"Kristina, listen to me. They found things in George's truck that make us suspect he's involved in the murders. It's going to be more devastating to hear he may have tortured and killed four people."

"George may be a womanizer, but I can't believe he's murdering women. There's got to be another explanation." A wave of fear spread through her body for the nine hundredth time, and it wasn't even noon.

The doorbell rang. She jumped off the sofa to her feet. "What the hell, DJ." Heat rushed her body.

"Relax, I asked the house physician to give you a little something for your nerves. Jakes answered the door.

"*Thank God.* Great idea an hour ago. Better late than never," Kristina curled back on the sofa, pulled her knees to her chest, wrapped her arms tight around her legs, and buried her face in her thighs. DJ poured her a glass of cold water. She opened the bottle of pills and popped one in her mouth and then another. He snatched the bottle before she took another. For safekeeping, he stuck the bottle in the front pocket of his jeans.

"Kristina, because of the things we found in Handy's truck, I have to ask you some personal questions that could be pertinent to the case."

"What do you mean things found in his truck? I was only in his truck one time. We had run into each other at our neighborhood bar, and he gave me a lift home at the end of the night."

Kristina had followed the story thus far, but now she was completely lost. *What the hell was in Handy's truck?*

CHAPTER FORTY-THREE

The smell of warm, freshly baked chocolate chip cookies caught Kristina's attention, and she joined DJ in the kitchen. He pulled the cookies from the oven and placed them on a platter for Kristina. After the second cookie, her stomach felt worse, but she ate another waiting for the Xanax to kick in.

"I know this is a lot to handle." DJ sat on the barstool next to Kristina. He swiveled her stool around to face him. "Kristina, was George into bondage, dominatrix, satanic, or stuff like that? It's okay. You can tell me. I won't judge. Did you and he ever—"

"Whoa, wait a minute. I hated *Fifty Shades of Grey.* Oh my God, that thing I did last night, I mean . . . I was teasing with my teeth. I wasn't really going to bite it. I'm going to throw up."

"No. Stop, Kristina. You were great . . . the sex, I mean . . . Wow. What I meant to say, when you were with George, did he mention any fetishes? Did he like the rough stuff with whips, riding-crops, you know, those types of toys? Did you notice bite marks, strange cuts on his body? Was there anything out of the norm that you can remember? Maybe nipple clamps, choking during orgasm? Well, you know ..."

Kristina tried to wrap her head around everything while DJ rambled on about her one-time romp in the sack with George Handy. She didn't know if Detective Jakes actually needed to know this information or if he was fulfilling some sick little fantasy he had by asking her these questions. As the anxiety medication kicked in, Kristina felt loopy. She decided to conjure up quite a story of her sexual encounter with George, DJ's competition.

"What, you didn't bother to peek in his window while you were busy keeping eyes on me? Now, let's see. Sex with George, hmm? Nothing odd that I can think of. Well, the sex was *A-mazing*. His body's far from normal. His abs. I mean, yikes, Ryan Gosling good. No nipple clamps, no whips. I didn't check under his bed, or his closets for women chained to his slave chambers. There was a little ass slapping a couple of times. You know, like this—," She stood, turned toward DJ, and gave herself a couple of swats on the ass. Still facing DJ, Kristina gestured with both hands. "But his, well, you know—huge."

"*Okay.* I get the picture. Nothing out of the ordinary." Detective Jakes said abruptly rolling his eyes.

By the tone of his voice, he didn't like hearing about Kristina with another man. So far, that was the only thing that made her day slightly bearable.

Jakes rubbed his chin, "Well, that doesn't explain the sex toys, or whatever you'd call the stuff found in his truck." The details of the case swirled around in his head.

"Okay, Sherlock, but why would he leave evidence behind?" Kristina contributed her inquisitive questioning to all the crime series she watched on television or the *True Crime* podcast she listened to. Feeling relaxed from the drugs, she decided all of this would be easier to handle if she pretended to be a detective inspector or John Watson.

"Good point, Kristina. Why? Something may have happened that they had to flee the scene in a hurry. Maybe the killer's leaving clues on purpose. We don't know much at this point. Hopefully, someone saw something at the Angeles National Park the night Handy or whoever dumped his truck and comes forward. Forensics is checking the things found in his truck now for DNA and possible prints. One thing's for sure. We have a demented psychopath, possibly two on the loose, killing for sexual pleasure."

"Sounds to me, they're killing for some sort of revenge. All the vics are upper-middle-class, not married, right?" Kristina threw in her woman's intuition and years of profiling people's behavior and collecting data for her workshops.

"I like that you're going to work on the case already. This is why we need your help. My Special Crimes team will need access to your records of anyone who has ever attended your workshops. Give us their contact information. We need you to help us profile some of our suspects. Maybe you'll see something we're missing." DJ put his belongings back into his bag. Kristina found herself somewhat disappointed when DJ didn't stick his gun in the back of his pants. That's when she realized she had to stop watching crime shows.

"You could have asked me for this stuff without keeping eyes on me," Kristina sarcastically made air quotes mocking the trade slang DJ used earlier.

"I don't understand why you have been stalking me or surveilling me or whatever you detectives do. Why did you need to know so much about me? You could have asked Peter. He knows everything about me, and why did you have to follow me to Las Vegas? Was any part of us together last night real? Do you really have a son?" Kristina paced back and forth, thinking about everything DJ and she shared the night before ... and twice early that morning. "Well, I bet the public would love to know how their tax dollars are used for sexual benefits on an official police stakeout."

"Kristina, I'm not on a stakeout. Everything's real. You, me, and last night." DJ pointed his finger at her and then himself, back and forth, trying to convince her that his intentions were sincere.

"Please, believe me. I know it's not the perfect scenario, but I never intended to have sex with you. I mean, in this scenario. Our team's been tailing you for a few months. Peter and I needed to make sure you were safe. The female victims have attended your workshops. Now a man you know, somewhat dated, is missing, and his truck is filled with whips and bondage apparel. I'm not taking any chances. Our team's not taking any chances. We tried to keep you out of this, but it's clear, you're in danger, and we need your help. Your expertise for profiling people on the Internet and your connection to Handy could lead us to the killers. Chances are if we know that, so does the killer. You're the best resource we have. Falling for you just happened. Most of the time, you're really adorable." DJ said, winking at Kristina with a smile that could melt a girl's heart.

He almost had her believing he actually felt the same for her as she did for him, until the wink. DJ's attempt to loosen her up with his charm did soften her heart for a split second. She thought about DJ singing, "When I Met You, All My Dreams Came True." In the next second, she thought about how hard she'd fallen for a guy probably just doing his job, and that's what pissed her off again.

The second dose of Xanax had Kristina feeling loaded. "Falling for me? Ha. You need me, and I don't want to end up dead. Okay, we need each other for now. From here on, we keep this totally professional between us. If we're going to work together, I'm just part of the '*team*.' And there'll be no more, oh, my '*bad*' for having sex with you. That'll '*never*' happen again." She emphasized, team, bad, and never, using air quotes again. With the combination of adrenaline and the sedative, Kristina got a boost of exaggerated confidence. She pictured herself waving a couple of six-shooters in the air like a rootin-tootin renegade all fired up, but air quotes were all she had to show DJ she meant business. Her strong independent woman, capable of caring for herself DNA, got all tangled up with the fear of being murdered by a serial killer and her mad crush on Detective Richard Jakes. The minute she got back home, she planned to deal with Peter. He should have told her what was going on. She was furious with him too.

"It's all business from here on out, detective." Storming out of the room felt appropriate at the moment. Once she slammed the door to the bedroom, she felt like eight-year-old Krissy. Last night made her feel as though she and DJ had something special. Their conversations flowed like souls that had been together for many lifetimes. *The lights over the city, their bodies together as one, dancing, DJ singing one of her favorite songs.* Kristina ran the entire night through her head and cried.

"Damn it, DJ. Why'd you have to be so fucking perfect last night?" She tried to differentiate the suspicious feelings she felt about Jakes, the detective, there with her doing his job, and the crazy insane passion she felt for DJ, the sweet single dad who seemed like the perfect guy for her.

"Kristina, did you say something?" DJ's voice came through the intercom.

"Shit. No. Stop eavesdropping. I'm not talking to you," Kristina said, switching off the damn intercom.

Chapter Forty-Four

Without one word between DJ and Kristina, they packed their bags and got ready to leave for the airport. It seemed that neither of them felt good about this personal mess they'd gotten into. DJ tried to take Kristina in his arms before leaving the penthouse suite. Every part of her body wanted his arms around her, his lips on hers, yet she pushed him away. He should have told her everything before anything happened between them. She felt used. She couldn't trust that any part of the magic she thought they had together meant a fucking thing to him. Maybe he does this with all his assignments.

Standing at the front door of the penthouse with their bags, Kristina had to ask, "One last question, Detective Jakes." DJ stopped and stared at her with a five o'clock shadow on his strong jaw.

"What, Kristina? What's the question?" His voice was a little more stern than sweet this time. Kristina guessed she'd pushed him a little too far when she shunned his efforts to take her in his arms. She thought twice about asking the question now that DJ gave her a bit of the same nasty attitude she gave him. She cleared her throat.

"Why are you so familiar with this penthouse suite? And who the hell is Kelly?" She made sure she had the snippy bitch attitude in her voice.

DJ grinned and seemed to enjoy her feisty tone. "That's fair. I'll be honest with you."

With hands on her hips, Kristina huffed, "Now? Now, you're going to be honest with me. What an honor, coming from you." Sarcasm felt good right about then.

DJ secured his gun in his shoulder holster. "*Anyway*, as I was saying." DJ dished it right back. "A couple of months ago, I ran an undercover op here at The Arises. Las Vegas police brought us in because we worked a similar case a few months earlier in Northern California. They felt Kelly and I could help. A serial killer was murdering young prostitutes, all teenage runaways. The sonofabitch tortured those poor girls before he killed them. I went deep undercover with Kelly. She's an attractive—I mean, hardworking, smart detective here in Vegas. My cover was a high roller from out of town, a nobody who recently won big on an out-of-state lottery. That way, the other well-known local high rollers wouldn't be suspicious of why they hadn't heard of me. I needed a madam, and Kelly fit the part. And well, the rest is classified."

"How convenient. I guess what happens in Vegas *stays* in Vegas. I couldn't care less about your stupid classified secrets with Kelly, the hot detective. She probably spells Kelli with an *i*." Kristina sounded like her eight-year-old Krissy again. Scared to death, and pissed at everything, especially DJ, Kristina couldn't compartmentalize any of this mess. A good man with strong potential for a healthy, loving relationship brought out her insecurities. A man like DJ, who didn't need fixing and she couldn't control, sent her spiraling into sabotage the relationship mode. Get rid of the great guy before he figures out how dysfunctional you are, then breaks your heart and leaves you. Adding a serial killer to the mess capsized Kristina's coping skills. She rushed into the elevator without him.

"I don't even know what that means, 'Kelly with an *i.*' What the fuck does that mean?" DJ shouted at the back of the closed elevator door, hitting his palm on it. He glanced down at the large bag of Kristina's shoes, her two overnight bags, and his small duffle bag. "*Fuck.*" Jakes shook his head and waited for the elevator to come back up.

~~~~

Outside the hotel, flocks of people were hustling like a colony of ants. Alone and without Detective Jakes, Kristina felt a lot less rootin-tootin, realizing anyone could be the killer. Her throat dried, and her heart raced faster. She stood next to a security officer with eyes peeled, hoping Jakes hadn't left her to fend for herself.

Quickly catching up to her, DJ firmly took Kristina by the hand and kept walking. "Not smart, Kristina, you need to stay close to me. Like it or not, it's my job to keep your ass from getting killed." Detective Jakes had run out of patience. He didn't have time for any more bullshit. He had a serial killer to take down.

"Sorry." Kristina tightened her grip around DJ's hand. They headed for the airport to meet up with the others.

~~~~

The girls were already standing next to their gate at the airport with the other FBI agents. Their eyes were swollen and red from crying and probably too much drinking.

"Kristina. I can't believe George might be—" Koo Koo threw her arms around Kristina's neck.

"I know. It's horrible." Kristina reached out to the others, motioning for a group hug.

They all boarded the plane without a peep from any of them. Detective Jakes took an aisle seat in the front of the plane. Kristina intended to walk past him, hoping to have a well-needed chat in the rear of the plane with her girlfriends. Jakes had a different plan: he placed a tactical slide of his boot into the aisle. "Ouch." Kristina's ass landed in Jakes's lap.

"I saved your seat." Jakes scooted Kristina into the seat next to him. Koo Koo took the window seat. The other two sat across the aisle a few rows back. The flight back home seemed to take a week. Thoughts of the four murdered victims made Kristina sick to her stomach. Thinking that she could be next scared the crap out of her, and the thought of working side by side with Detective Jakes—all business, no dating— made her want to scream. She dug her hand in the front pocket of DJ's jeans to get another Xanax. He squirmed. "*Careful*, that's not the bottle."

DJ's sexual overtones caused Kristina's cheeks to warm.

"Ha, you wish." She stuck the bottle in her purse. Exhausted, she leaned her head on Koo-Koo's shoulder and dreamed about the sweet stories DJ told her about him and Richie.

As the plane landed and taxied to the jetway at Orange County's John Wayne Airport, Kristina's nerves revved back up to high alert. Seated next to DJ on the plane, they were all safe. *What happens next?* She didn't have a clue how the FBI would proceed to catch a serial killer. *What if the worst is yet to come?* Cold chills breezed her body. She picked at her cuticles, waiting for her bags to circle the luggage carrousel.

~~~~

"Good, it looks like everyone has their bags." Detective Jakes gathered around the girls with his team. "Kristina, our team will make sure you and the girls get home safely. We'll have eyes"—Detective Jakes stopped himself mid-sentence—"our team will be in unmarked vehicles outside your house all night. But if you need anything ..." his demeanor had shifted. The minute his team showed up, Detective Jakes was all business.

"I'm sure I'll be fine." That was a bald-faced lie because she was fucking scared to death. That was the truth. She thought about the guy pulling out of her neighbor's driveway, wondering if he'd also followed her out of the parking lot of the hospital.

"Wait, Detective Jakes, a question. Was it one of your guys that pulled out of my neighbor's driveway in a silver Lexus?"

"No, we were in the FedEx truck. We lost him. Don't worry, Kristina, we aren't going to let anything happen to you. We've—"

Kristina rolled her eyes and interrupted him, "Yeah, yeah, I get it. The FBI knows how to take care of business. I feel much better knowing you'll do whatever it takes to keep me safe." Dishing out more sarcasm made her feel like she had some control. "But having fantastic sex with me, really Detective? What a sacrifice. You really took one for the team," she mumbled under her breath as she climbed in the back seat of the town car with the girls and headed home.

CHAPTER FORTY-FIVE

"We checked upstairs, and in your backyard, everything looks secure. We'll be right outside, Ms. Truly. Don't hesitate to let us know if you'd feel safer with one of us inside with you tonight." Two uniformed police officers secured Kristina's house for the night.

"Thanks a lot. I appreciate it. I'll be fine. Good night." Kristina locked the deadbolt and pulled down the window shades in the living room and kitchen. It felt nice to be home. The chirping crickets of Peter's ring tone sounded on her phone. Kristina ignored his call, kicked off her tennis shoes, and headed for the shower. She didn't have the energy or the patience to hear Peter's censored FBI bullshit about his involvement with Detective Jakes and the case. It was too late to phone Angel, and they'd need to keep Deedee Marie in the dark about all of this. How would I even start the conversation? *Hey mom, don't worry, but there's a serial killer after me. Oh, hell no. I'll never put Deedee through that.*

Thoughts of finding another dead body soon, possibly hers, tightened her chest. She cranked the shower knob to steaming hot. The warm spray calmed the shaking inside her. Before crawling into bed, she debated taking another Xanax. A Snickers bar sounded good too, but the sharp pains in her stomach were a good sign it wouldn't stay down. Not even a bottle of wine or a magic wand would help her tonight. Ms. Prissy curled herself under the down comforter beside Kristina's legs. Snuggled in her safe cocoon, Kristina played meditation music on her iPad, and before a single tear rolled down her cheeks, the fog in her head turned to deep sleep.

~~~~

Ding-dong, Dingggg-dong, ding-dong, ding-dong. The numbers 4:13 a.m. shone in bold blue numbers on her digital alarm clock. Fumbling, she turned on the lamp next to her bed. Her tired eyes cowered to the bright light.

Ding-dong, knock, knock. "EEEEEOW." Ms. Prissy hissed. "Aw, sorry, baby. My foot got your tail, poor baby." She hurried to see who the hell was ringing the bell at such an ungodly hour. Nervous, but mostly pissed off, she looked through the peephole. "What do you want, Detective?" Kristina rolled her eyes, waiting for a response.

"Kristina, open the door, let me in. I need to talk with you about the case."

"Uhh, I'm in no mood for you or your bullshit. I'm sleeping," Her tone of voice was curt. Before she could open the door, she needed to wipe the schoolgirl crush grin off her face. She couldn't let Detective Jakes know that despite her best efforts to dislike him, there was something she liked—a lot.

"Come in. What's going on? Why are you here at four in the friggin' morning?" She closed the door and locked the deadbolt.

"Ouch. What the hell?" DJ felt Ms. Prissy using his pant leg for a scratching post.

"Detective Jakes, meet Ms. Prissy. Prissy, meet Detective Jakes," Kristina made her introductions between yawns.

Waiting for DJ to answer her questions, she headed for the sofa to cuddle up with a soft chenille throw.

"Kristina, where are the lights? I can't see. Aw, shit. What the—"

In the dark, DJ couldn't see the smile on Kristina's face. "Careful, don't trip over the ottoman."

DJ stumbled his way to join her on the sofa. "Jesus, why is it so cold in this house?" DJ draped part of the throw over his legs.

"I'm over forty. I like it cold. Why are you here?" Kristina couldn't stop yawning. She needed a lot more sleep.

"The team outside your house was called to work another case. I volunteered to keep eyes on you." DJ teased with a nudge of his elbow.

"Ha-ha, Detective. You're pretty cocky for a guy who's going to be sitting in his car outside of my house alone for the next few hours." She pulled the blanket back over to her side. "What's the information you have about the case?" A long yawn rolled out. She closed her heavy eyelids.

"Kristina, go back to bed. You're exhausted. We can talk in a few hours. I'll sack out here on the sofa. Go to bed." DJ pulled Kristina to her feet and led her by the hand upstairs to her bedroom.

Already half asleep, she crawled back into her warm bed, "Shouldn't you be home with your son?"

"I have a hall pass, remember. We left Las Vegas a day early. My pass is still good."

Safe with DJ next to her, without another word, she fell back to sleep.

~~~~

Kristina opened one eye, "You awake?" She tapped DJ's arm. He pulled his phone out of his pocket to check the time.

"Yep, I'm awake. Wide awake." He rolled over and buried his head under a pillow.

"What happened to you sleeping on the living room sofa?" Kristina yelled through the bathroom door.

Detective Jakes lay fully clothed on top of Kristina's comforter. Ms. Prissy took to kneading his arm with her claws. "Ouch, ouch. Shit, Ms. Prissy, you should work for the mob." Prissy jumped on DJ's stomach before hitting the floor on her way to the kitchen.

"Well?" Kristina tossed DJ a new toothbrush. "The toothpaste is on the sink."

DJ headed into the bathroom. "I knew I'd never survive downstairs in Siberia. Freezing to death on your sofa isn't how I want to go. Sleeping next to you, I had a fifty-fifty chance of survival. I'll take my coffee black unless you've got real half and half, no almond milk, please."

DJ joined Kristina in the kitchen with his shoulder holster on, gun fully loaded. He sat at the dining room table. Kristina poured their coffee. Ms. Prissy walked across the table, looked at DJ, took a swipe toward him with her paw, then stuck her back leg in the air, and licked herself.

"Prissy, girl." Kristina scooped the ball of fluff in her arms, kissing her face. "Don't worry. He's not staying long."

DJ responded to a text he'd received. By the look on his face, Kristina knew this morning had just taken a bad turn.

"Kristina, come sit down. We need to talk about the case."

"What's wrong, you're scaring me. Did they find another body?" She paced the kitchen. *Breathe in through my nose, out through my mouth.*

"There's a woman reported missing. She's an attractive blonde, filed for divorce five months ago. She's posted stuff about attending your workshops on her Facebook." Detective Jakes stared at the screen of his smartphone, enlarged the photo, and looked closer.

"Kristina, the team sent me her picture." DJ looked at his phone again and then at Kristina, then back at the picture. "This is weird. The resemblance is uncanny—she looks like you." DJ turned the photo of the missing woman toward Kristina.

She collapsed into the seat of a chair next to DJ at the table.

"Are you okay?" DJ tucked a strand of Kristina's hair behind her ear out of the way of her eyes.

Kristina stared at the picture, her hand over her mouth.

"You're scaring me, Kristina. Do you know her?"

"Please, DJ, don't let them kill her. She's my sister."

CHAPTER FORTY-SIX

"Kristina, what do you mean? Who's your sister?" DJ looked again at the picture on his phone, then at Kristina.

"The woman in the picture. We have the same father. Her name is Taryn Kennedy, but that's her married name." Still looking at Kristina and then the picture, DJ finally set the phone down.

"Shit. It's worse than I thought. I'm sorry, Kristina. I didn't realize you had a sister. Your brother and mother are in your background info but no sister—what the hell? Does Peter know you have a sister?" Running his hands through his hair, DJ paced the kitchen.

"She's the same age as Timmy, my brother. When I was eight, my father walked out on us to live with his other family. I never saw my dad again. Well, I went to see him at the hospital the day he died a couple months ago. When I saw Taryn at my workshops, we looked so much alike. I knew she had to be my sister. The first time she came to a workshop, Angel nearly passed out when she saw her at registration. Even our mannerisms are similar. You'd think we grew up together. Our voices sound identical. I saw her in the hospital with my father the day he died. I guess I should have told

Peter, but he's been so busy planning his engagement with Beth." It wasn't the time for pettiness, but Kristina scrunched her face with the mention of Peter's fiancée.

"Well, mostly Peter's been working his ass off to find a serial killer and keep your butt safe but go ahead with your story." Detective Jakes poured another cup of coffee.

"Okay, noted, Detective. Anyway, at first, I wanted to confront Taryn, but I wasn't sure if she knew anything about Timmy and me. Growing up, we never really spoke about my father or his other family. My mother never fully got over his betrayal. She was shocked to find out he'd been having an affair and even more shocked when she realized he had no intention of helping her financially with Timmy and me. A few days after my father left us, I overheard Aunt Mimi telling my mom about my father's mistress being pregnant with a baby girl. It caused a lot of emotional issues for me to think my dad loved his new daughter and not me."

DJ felt Kristina's pain as he listened about her childhood. Now he understood where Kristina's insecurities were coming from. After his wife Anne died, he worried about Richie growing up without a mother. *What fucking parent intentionally leaves their kids?* DJ knew they needed more time together, but eventually, he'd help Kristina with her trust issues. She deserved a good man, and he hoped they'd figure out their messy relationship together.

"At my workshops, we have the attendees break into teams. I go around the room and observe each person's interaction with their teammates. After the first couple of workshops, I realized there wasn't a mean bone in Taryn's body. She lacked confidence. She seemed timid, sort of nervous like she'd been beaten down by someone. I felt sorry for her, so whenever I could, I gave her a little extra attention. Even though it was against everything I felt about her when I was growing up, she's hard not to like. She's a sweet person. Whenever I got the chance, I'd make sure to tell her that she was a strong, intelligent woman with a lot to offer. Angel gave her extra praise and encouragement as well.

At the last workshop she attended, she asked if we could walk out to the parking lot together. It made me nervous. I'd hated her for so many years, and I felt ashamed of blaming her for my fucked-up childhood. I wasn't sure I was ready to talk about it with her. Luckily, she never brought it up. I guess she wasn't ready either. She told me that I'd helped her a lot and hugged me, and we said goodnight. After that, I had a change of heart. I wanted us to get to know each other. I hoped she might open up if she were being abused, and maybe I could help her. I decided to ask if we could meet for dinner the next time I saw her, but she hasn't attended the past couple of workshops. The hospital was the first time I'd seen her in months. She didn't see me at the hospital, and besides, that wasn't the time to talk about things."

Detective Jakes listened as he made them each a bowl of hot oatmeal and tidied up the kitchen.

"Kristina, we don't have a lot of time. If we're going to find your sister alive, we need to work fast. Call Angel and have her meet us at your office. We need to start putting the pieces together quickly." DJ threw the kitchen sponge in the sink. "There's one more thing, Kristina. We've hired the Jewish Mother Mafia to help with the case. Go jump in the shower. I'll meet you downstairs in thirty minutes." He headed toward the downstairs bathroom.

Wait, what did he say? Kristina spun around on the balls of her slippers like she was wearing ballet shoes. *They hired the JMM? What the . . .?*

Kristina sat on the lid of the toilet seat. Through the slightly fogged glass, she watched DJ lather his well-defined abdomen with the bar of soap. For a second, she forgot what she'd barged in to say. "Oh, yeah. DJ, what the hell does the Jewish Mother Mafia have to do with anything? What possible good can a bunch of nosy Jewish women do to help find serial killers?" She tilted her head to get a better view of DJ's naked body while his biceps bulged shampooing his hair.

"If you're not here to join me in the shower, Kristina, then go upstairs and get ready. We'll talk about it on the way to the office."

CHAPTER FORTY-SEVEN

Arriving at the office early on Sunday morning, Angel forwent her designated tenant parking space at the business park where they rented their office unit. On weekends, parking spaces were abundant, so Angel whirled her car into the nearest space reserved for property management. She arrived at the office ahead of Kristina and Detective Jakes. Angel slipped her key in the office door. There wasn't time to flip on the lights. Her purse made a loud thud when it hit the floor as she tossed it toward her desk and headed straight for the restroom.

~~~~

Detective Jakes motioned Kristina to stay back with a strong arm across her stomach. He put his finger over his lips, signaling Kristina to be quiet. The door appeared unlatched and the office dark. He pushed the door open slowly and pulled his gun. He heard the toilet flush. He flipped the light switch.

"*Fuck.*" Angel's jaw dropped. Her yoga pants were down around her knees. "Who the hell are you?" she shrieked, looking down the barrel of Detective Jakes's pistol with Kristina clinging to the back of his shirt, peeking out from behind. Angel tugged her skintight spandex pants up over her curves.

DJ tucked his gun in his shoulder holster, then offered his hand for Angel to shake. "You must be Angel. Pleased to meet you. I've heard a lot about you. FBI's Special Crime Unit, Detective Jakes. Thanks for meeting us. Sorry to startle you like this, I promise I didn't see a thing. We'll try to explain, but people's lives are at stake. There's not a lot of time, and we need your help. Kristina can take it from here. I'll be in my car downstairs. I need to get some files and make some calls. When I get back, we'll need to discuss the plan." Detective Jakes flashed Kristina a *good luck* grin with a raise of one eyebrow on his way out the door.

"Good grief, Kristina Melanie. What in the *hell* have you gotten into?" Angel shook her head, pissed, thinking about Jakes seeing her with her pants down. "For godsakes, what happened in Las Vegas?" She picked her purse up off the floor and dropped it on her desk.

Kristina pulled two cans of Diet Coke out of their small compact refrigerator, cracked both open, placing one in the middle of Angel's desk.

"Girlfriend, you're going to need to sit down. I have a lot to tell you, and none of it's good."

For the next twenty minutes, Kristina only stopped talking long enough to take a breath between gulps of Diet Coke. While she explained the seriousness of the situation, Angel didn't utter a word. Listening to Kristina's explanation about the victims and the gruesome murders, the expression on Angel's face matched how Kristina's stomach felt.

"And . . ." Kristina could not bring herself to tell Angel Taryn was missing.

"What, Kristina? Spit it out, what?"

"FBI thinks there's a chance two killers are working together, and we think they have Taryn." Kristina had a hard time getting her breath, thinking about her sister possibly found murdered.

"No. Oh, my God. No, no, no, KT. I can't wrap my head around any of this. Are you in danger?" Angel's hands trembled as she wiped the tears from her cheeks.

"Yes, Angel, I'll be honest. The Feds believe I'm in danger. But they're keeping a team outside my house and on my ass twenty-four-seven. They won't let anything happen to me. I promise."

"KT, do you think George is somehow involved?" Angel wiped her nose with a tissue and tossed the box to Kristina.

"Honestly, I just can't bring myself to believe George is a killer. But it doesn't look good that he's missing, and they found bloody ropes and whips in his truck. We have to help the FBI stop whoever's doing this. I pray we aren't too late to save Taryn." *Breathe in through my nose, out through my mouth.* Kristina fanned her face with both hands to keep from hyperventilating as a flash of fear overwhelmed her.

"KT, what about her husband? I think she said his name's Tom. Yeah, that's it, Tom Kennedy. Remember we thought he might be abusing her? We could see through her makeup that she had a nasty bruise on her face at the last workshop." Angel touched her cheek at the thought of Taryn's beautiful face battered and now possibly even worse.

"Tom Kennedy's got a strong solid alibi. There's documented proof he wasn't in town at the times of the murders. He works out of state a lot, selling high tech security systems to large corporations. The company's president provided records of everything the Feds asked for, his travel schedule, and all that sort of stuff. The other victims' spouses have been checked out and have rock hard alibies. At this point, Angel, it could be a killer, two killers, or someone bisexual. Truthfully, it could be anyone. FBI's looking into a possible person off the Internet, someone from our workshops. There are no solid suspects."

"KT, what about the JMM? How do they fit into all of this?" Angel followed the details of the case intensely.

"Right, the JMM. It turns out that they are not a bunch of overbearing Jewish mothers. They're a group of shrewd businesswomen, from Harvard, MIT, Princeton. All are highly educated, and they are extremely tech-savvy. They started off watchdogging the internet for predators on the GoodJewishdating.com site. They found out there were criminals in prison with internet access. Sex offenders were targeting children, and just a lot of bad people getting away with doing horrible stuff on the internet. They had the skills and decided to start a business. Now they're highly paid cyberspace security consultants for the FBI and other large corporations. Basically, they're a group of brilliant women who hack into bad people's personal lives to help get justice. They do things that the FBI can't be caught doing. The Feds put them on this case a month ago. Their job is to look for similarities between the victims. See if any of the victims have dated the same people, maybe have the same divorce lawyer or anything the victims may all have in common. So far, what the women have in common is they've attended our relationship workshops."

Kristina took a deep breath, "The JMM has already helped solve a few very high-profile cases. In fact, I'm flattered that they wasted their time contacting me over a little thing like wine with Erwin, the podiatrist."

"KT, my head's spinning. But I need to ask a personal question. And please know I mean no disrespect to bring this up, considering the horror that's happened. But KT, girlfriend, you need to get over being pissed off at Detective Jakes. So what if he didn't tell you what was going down? Yes, I agree he should've told you sooner than later, especially before having sex with you. However, if he'd told you what was going on, you'd never have gotten to know DJ, the gorgeous single dad, who works for the FBI. He's as close to perfect as God could manage in a male. After you heard about the murders, do you really think you'd been up for having a good time? Never, it would have ruined the amazing night that you and DJ shared. Listen, KT, he's been watching you for over a month. He's seen the raw, uncensored Kristina Truly and obviously likes what he sees. I'm telling you, girlfriend, give Detective Jakes a chance. Don't be pulling your typical, 'I can't trust men' bullshit. You buried your dad, now quit blaming all men for your daddy abandonment issues. Detective Jakes is a great man. If you don't snag him soon, there'll be some other chick all up in that sexy detective's business faster than you can say, *'Oh, shit, I fucked up. You were right, Angel.'* I'm just saying, KT."

"Well, I can't trust him. He wasn't honest with me. Yes, he's adorable, but that doesn't mean I'm going to date a guy I can't trust. I mean, after all—" Angel pursed her lips and quickly gave Kristina a wide-eyed stare, indicating, button it, stop talking. "Is he right behind me?" Kristina mouthed silently. Angel nodded yes.

Detective Jakes stood in the doorway behind Kristina with his arms full of folders stamped Classified. "Are you still beating the same dead horse, Kristina?" DJ shook his head as he set the files on her desk. "It wasn't my smartest move, but I'm not going to keep apologizing. I told you everything when it was appropriate. You need to get over it. I've got killers to catch. Seriously, this sort of shit is why I stay single." Detective Jakes kept mumbling while he made himself at home seated behind Kristina's desk. Angel gave Kristina one of her looks like *KT, don't do it*, but of course, she did it.

"Get over it? Well, I'll tell you when I'm over it, and I'm *not* over it. And this sort of shit is exactly what women have to put up with from men and why *I'm* single." Kristina stormed out to the deck through the double glass doors to calm down and call Poodles.

"Angel, I'm sorry about that. I should've ignored her comment. She's right. I should've told her what was going on the minute we went back to the penthouse. But what's done is done. I'm crazy about her. Help me out, Angel. I'm a nice guy. Put in a good word for me—please." DJ flashed Angel his friggin' dimples. They sucked her in too. She also loved how Detective Jakes handled Kristina. He seemed like just the guy to give Kristina back the same headstrong attitude and show her what it feels like to date a good strong man for a change.

"Detective, you focus on keeping our girl safe and catch the sonofabitch that has Taryn. I'll work on KT. You know she's a handful—right? But her tough girl is all a façade. She's been hurt a lot in her life by people she loves, but she's working on herself, and there's no one with a bigger, loving heart than KT. She really cares about helping people find happiness. The people who attend our workshops mean everything to her. But she can be crazy as bat-shit at times." Angel patted DJ's back on her way to the file cabinet.

"Don't worry, Angel, I'm never going to let anything happen to her. I can handle that feisty, sweet badass. The first time I laid eyes on her, I saw through her 'I don't need your help bullshit.' I saw right away that she's smart, she's kind, she's beautiful inside and out. That's what I love about her. But we've got a terrifying job ahead of us to catch some sick bastard, and right now, she's causing me nothing but trouble."

CHAPTER FORTY-EIGHT

On the phone, Peter reminded Kristina about the night she went out with Drake Toucuti, who turned out to be a psycho psychotherapist. She hurried back inside the office.

"Angel, do you remember Drake, the therapist that went psycho on our date? Kristina made sure not to make eye contact with DJ. She didn't want him to think she was over anything just because he said to get over it.

"Crap, KT. That's right. He was into kinky bondage weird stuff. If you ask me, he's nuts enough to kill people."

"Oh, for sure. He's nuts. But he also mentioned that some of his patients blamed me for their divorce. He said he considered some of them deranged. Remember, right before I dropped the hot coals on his crotch, he told me I should watch my back."

DJ popped his head up from the stack of files he was going through. "Kristina, I remember that guy at the restaurant on the ocean." DJ had his detective hat on, and he meant business.

"Oh, my God, I did see you that night. On the plane, you pretended that wasn't you. I knew it. But whatever. His name's Drake Toucuti. He's a psychotherapist, literally and figuratively speaking. I guess you know we met for dinner one night. But what you may not know, unless you had a microphone hidden somewhere, he told me a couple of his patients blamed me for their spouses leaving them. I didn't take him seriously at the time."

"Shit, we need access to this guy's patient files. This could be the break we need in the case." DJ got on the horn with FBI headquarters.

At their small conference table, Kristina sat with her laptop, perusing thousands of old emails from every man she'd ever been in contact with online, or through a friend, a book signing, or ever talked to period.

No one felt much like eating, but Angel had a pizza delivered. She insisted they all take a minute to try to eat something.

DJ corresponded throughout the day with his team. Kristina heard him on the phone with the JMM. It sounded by his conversation that they had some intel they were running. So far, all the leads were a shot in the dark, nothing substantial. More pressure set in. Every minute that passed gave Kristina less hope of finding Taryn alive.

~~~~

Joan at the FBI called DJ to let him know they'd found information about Drake Toucuti. DJ finished his conversation, and he didn't seem happy with the latest news.

"Goddamn it, Toucuti's been missing for the past three days. Another therapist in the office reported he came into work and noticed the door to Drake's private office had been pried open with a crowbar. The place had been tossed. Every fucking patient's file gone. No prints, nothing. The place was wiped clean. Security footage blank." DJ slammed his hand on the desk. Combing his fingers through his hair, he walked out to the deck, closing the glass doors behind him.

The news about Drake felt like someone had just thrown kerosene on a fire already burning out of control.

Angel and Kristina had scoured their files, database, social media, and they ran scenarios about past workshops, trying to remember anything out of the ordinary but found nothing that made much of an impact on the case.

They had more suspects than time. As the hours ticked away, they all knew it wasn't going to get any easier.

DJ stuck his phone in his back pocket, adjusting his gun in his shoulder harness as he walked back into the office. "Ladies, it's time to call it a day. You both need to go home and get some rest. Kristina, a team will drive you home and stay with you tonight. Angel, another team will follow you home just to be on the safe side, and they'll be there all night."

"What about you? Are you leaving? I'll give you a key to the office." Angel handed Detective Jakes a spare key, turned off her computer, and headed for the door. She hurried, thinking DJ and Kristina needed to be alone for a minute.

The first musical note to the Star Wars theme played, and Detective Jakes answered his phone immediately when he saw the caller's ID.

"Stay focused. Hold tight—SWAT's en route. I'll be there in twenty. Kelly, you need to stay focused. Don't let that mother fucker fool you. He won't hesitate to kill you or hostages."

Without a word, Detective Jakes ran out of the office like a
bat out of hell.

CHAPTER FORTY-NINE

Lying in bed, Kristina stared out her window at the beautiful morning scarlet sky. She heard her Grandmother's voice echoed in her thoughts, *Remember Krissy: red in the morning, Shepard's warning, red at night, sailor's delight.* She savored the peacefulness but knew the reality that haunted her based on predictions of strong winds and heavy rains by early evening and an El Niño storm to hit California hard late in the season.

Dread of the unknown regarding the case snatched her few moments of serenity. Thoughts of Taryn tore at her heart, and she prayed the universe would keep Taryn safe and help them find her unharmed soon. Kristina forced herself out from under her warm, safe covers.

As she stepped into her large whirlpool bathtub filled with the perfect warm temperature and eucalyptus bath salts, her cell phone rang. The "When I Met You" ringtone Kristina programmed for DJ's caller ID continued as she dried her wet hands before she answered the call.

"Hey, what's up?" Kristina said, relieved to hear Detective Jakes's voice. After the phone call overheard at the office, she'd spent the night unable to sleep, worrying that something horrible might've happened to him.

"Good morning, it's Detective Jakes." Assuming by the

way he greeted her, there had to be someone with him. Clearly, he wanted that person to know he and Kristina were all business. "I'll meet you and Angel at your office later today. I'm finishing up paperwork on a case we closed last night. A police officer will be by this morning to drop off a stack of books with criminal photos. Go over each photo with a fine-tooth comb. See if you or Angel recognize anyone. Take a picture with your phone of anyone who looks even vaguely familiar, perhaps from a workshop or staff at the hotel or even the grocery store, and send it to me right away. Look for the slightest familiarities in their eyes in case they have changed hair color or style. I'll be tied up for several hours. Text if you need me. Hopefully, you'll recognize someone from the photos, and I'll put the JMM on them."

Kristina could hear a woman's voice in the background. "Is that Kelly? Kelly from Las Vegas?" Kristina wanted to know, but yet she didn't want to know.

"Kelly, give me five minutes. Order me two eggs scrambled, bacon well done, two pancakes, and a pot of coffee. I'll be right in," DJ said just before answering Kristina's question that she wished she could retract.

"Yes, it's Detective Kelly from Las Vegas. The case she's been working crossed over state lines. Last night she took down a fucking Honduran Kingpin selling teenage girls for sex slaves. It ended in a deadly hostage situation in Santa Ana. The sonofabitch shot two girls before a sniper took him out. Kelly ran negotiations, and she did a hell of a job," DJ said with all the passion of a truly dedicated FBI agent. It was clear from his exasperated tone that he was pretty fed-up with her. Kristina just listened but felt horrible about pushing DJ to such frustration by stepping over the line concerning his job. "I'm an FBI agent," he continued. "In my job, I see the fucking worst of people. I don't need that in my personal life too, Kristina. I haven't seen my son in four days. I haven't slept in thirty-six hours. I don't need more shit right now. I need support from the people I care about. I won't be in a relationship with someone who doesn't trust me, Kristina. You know, you were right. Let's just keep this strictly business between us. Fine with me." DJ hung up before Kristina could say a word.

Another wave of nausea knotted in Kristina's stomach. Tears rolled down her face until the bathwater was cold. More loneliness and regret set in, but nothing compared to the fear Kristina felt when she thought about losing DJ, or Taryn, or both. Ms. Prissy was having a hissing-fit about something as Kristina walked in the kitchen to make coffee.

"Ms. Prissy, what's going on this morning? Whatcha so upset about, pretty girl?" Ms. Prissy hissed viciously, scratching and batting her paws at the sliding glass door that led to the backyard. "Prissy, what's out there? You see a bird you want to go after?" The winds were already starting to pick up even though the weather report said it wouldn't start raining until later in the evening. Cuddling Ms. Prissy in her arms, they both looked out the sliding glass doors at the leaves falling from the swaying tree branches.

"Oh, no. Prissy girl, is that what you were trying to show me?" One of Kristina's security cameras had fallen, possibly from the wind or poor installation. Either way, it needed to be repaired pretty damn fast.

~~~~

"Hello, this is Ms. Truly. One of my security cameras fell off the wall in my backyard. Your installer was in a rush the day he was here. I don't think he installed it properly." Kristina flipped on the television to hear the news while she spoke with her security company.

"I'm so sorry, Ms. Truly. I apologize for the poor installation. We are happy to replace the camera and install it properly so that it won't fall again."

"Thank you, and I'd also like to follow up on the status of my new security system. I received a voicemail the other day, letting me know my cameras were on backorder, but I haven't received a call or email with an update. Why is it taking so long to get new cameras installed? It's imperative for me to watch my house on my phone." Even with the FBI watching her every move, she wanted her new cameras and security upgrade installed as soon as possible. It couldn't hurt.

"Ms. Truly, I'm looking at your account, and your new system was canceled. Our notes say Mr. Truly called and canceled the new equipment."

"There must be a mistake. I'm not married, and there's certainly no Mr. Truly," Kristina snapped.

"No problem, we have everything in stock at one of our warehouses, and I apologize for this confusion. I promise I'll look into this. I understand the urgency. However, I can't promise an installer can come today, perhaps tomorrow. Due to the heavy winds, we have more than usual service calls today. Our installers are already out on calls, but I'll see what I can do."

"I never canceled my order, and as I said, there's no Mr. Truly. There's been a mistake. Please, see what you can do. Have the tech call me at least thirty minutes before they arrive. I'll be at my office. I can be home in fifteen minutes. They didn't call the last time I had them out for a repair. They left a note on my door, and it took me a week to get a tech back out," Kristina said sharply, hoping he would make sure to do as she asked this time.

"I completely understand. We are a national company with several thousand customers, so things like this happen from time to time, and perhaps we have another customer with the same last name. I'm not sure what happened, but I assure you I'll look into it. I will be sure to notify the installer of your request for a call before arriving. Typically, we give you a window of time, either morning or afternoon, but I've put a note in the computer to call thirty minutes before showing up. Again, I can't promise we can be there today, but we'll definitely try. Thank you, Ms. Truly."

~~~~

Ready to start her day with Angel looking at photos of people with a criminal record, Kristina started to turn off the television before setting the security alarm.

"Breaking news." Kristina stopped. "The body found in the Angeles National Forest last week has been identified as

Juan Vasquez. Police suspect the murder is gang related. Police are still on the lookout for George Handy, whose truck was abandoned here in the park." Kristina snapped off the TV. She couldn't stand to hear anymore. She phoned Koo Koo to make sure she was okay hearing the news George was missing but presumably still alive.

"Koo Koo, it's KT. Just checking on you. I'm sure you've heard the body wasn't George. Call me when you get this message. Love you."

The drive into the office took a little longer than normal because of the weather. The rain started early, which slows down traffic in California. It gave the Feds in the unmarked car tailing behind her an opportunity to relax. No one on the road was driving fast enough to cause them to lose sight of her car.

When she arrived at the office, Angel had already started the coffee. She looked worn-out. Every minute that passed, they feared receiving bad news about Taryn.

"Angel, did you get any sleep last night? Promise me, girlfriend, you will speak up if this is too much. You don't have to be here. It's a lot, and you have a family to take care of. Please go back home and sleep for a couple of hours. I'll be fine." Kristina wrapped her arm around Angel's tense shoulders.

"I'm okay, KT. I've prayed all night that we get a break in the case, and this will all be over soon. What about you? You look cute this morning. I haven't seen you wearing those boots in a while. I thought they were a little too big. The skirt's cute too."

"Thanks, the boots are a bit big, but they're great in the rain. I'm wearing extra thick socks. I'd forgotten how cute they are. They have this cool little pocket inside each boot just big enough to stash money, credit cards, even a lipstick, so you don't need a purse when you do the Boot Scootin' Boogie." Kristina showed Angel a few of her smooth moves, country style. It felt good to hear Angel laugh.

"Hey, KT, see if this will fit in the pocket." Angel handed Kristina the high-tech stun gun that Peter sent over. "It's all charged up."

"That's crazy, Angel. I can't walk around with my Taser in my boot. What if I stun myself?" Curious, Kristina slipped the Taser gun in the hidden pocket in her left boot. "Wow, look at that. It fits inside the pocket perfectly. There's still plenty of room. I feel like a Bond Girl. Cowgirl by day, Bond Girl by night." Kristina gave her leg a couple of quick kicks in the air to make sure the stun gun stayed tight in the pocket.

"Be careful, Kung Fu Kitty. We don't want you to burn your leg in half if that thing goes off. Not to change the topic, but have you heard from Detective Jakes? I thought about him running out of here last night. Something must have been going down." Angel poured each of them a cup of coffee with a heaping splash of almond milk.

Kristina grabbed a tissue to wipe her eyes. By this time, the fight with DJ felt worse than ever. Her stomach turned, and her heart broke.

"I spoke with him. He helped stop a sex trafficking case with Las Vegas Kelly. Our conversation didn't go well. He overreacted when I asked about Kelly. I mean, Detective Kelly. He's got a lot on his plate, and I'm adding to his stress. I feel really bad about it and so stupid. I'm just hoping when this nightmare is over, he and I can be friends. But I'm pretty sure by our phone call, that's not going to happen."

Looking at Angel would have made Kristina start crying again, so she flipped open a police photo book, hoping she'd recognize someone that could be killing innocent people.

"KT, we're all running on too much adrenaline. I'm sure everything will be fine with Detective Jakes once they have the monster in custody. Girlfriend, we all just need to take a deep breath. He'll be fine."

For the next three hours, Angel and Kristina looked through photos. A few people looked familiar, but they ended up being from an episode of *48 Hours*. The JMM emailed Kristina with photos of men and women on the Internet that had connections with one of the victims. Everything led to a dead end. DJ hadn't called all day, and it was getting late. Angel and Kristina were hungry and felt they were wasting precious time. They knew the FBI had their own agenda, and they weren't briefed on every detail of the case, but they were losing hope fast.

"KT, I'm so worried. Do you think the FBI is doing everything they can to find whoever's responsible? We haven't heard from anyone today other than the JMM." Angel laid her head on her desk.

It was late in the day, and the sun would be setting soon. Dark clouds rolled in, and temperatures dropped. Kristina's phone rang. She'd misplaced her Bluetooth earpiece again, so the actual phone rang loudly, startling her and Angel. She'd hoped it was DJ, but the ring tone indicated Lois and Jim's cell.

"Hi Lois, how are you? What's up? Everything okay?" Kristina asked.

"Hi, KT. Sorry to bother you while you're working, but there's a man in a uniform outside your house looking at your security cameras. Do you want us to go over and talk with him?"

"Ugh. I told them to call me before they came. If you can, please tell him I'll be there in fifteen-twenty minutes. Let him know to start in the backyard. Until I get there, he can start replacing the camera that fell down."

Kristina heard Jim yell in the background, "Hey buddy, Kristina will be home in twenty minutes. Go through the gate, start working on the camera that fell in the backyard. She'll be right home."

"Okay, KT. He's going around back. Jim and I are heading out for an early dinner and grocery shopping. We don't want to get caught in the eye of the storm. See you later, dear."

"Thanks, Lois. I appreciate it," Kristina said.

"Angel, one of the security cameras fell off the wall in the back of my house this morning. They have my new equipment to install, so I need to run home and show them where I'd like my new replacement security cameras and a few additional cameras. I want to make sure they install them right this time. It shouldn't take long, but there's no need to come back to the office. DJ said he'd come by later today, but it's late, and I guess he's not going to show. But you know, Angel, I do trust him. I really do for some reason. My gut feeling is he cares about this case, and he's doing everything he can to find Taryn. I'm sure he's working on important stuff. We have to trust him and keep our hopes up. Why don't you leave too, Angel, you have to be starving. We haven't eaten all day." Kristina gathered her things.

"I'll pack it up soon. The JMM just sent over a couple of emails. I'll see what they want, and then I'll head home. Drive safely, KT. It's wet out there and looks like it's ready to downpour any minute." Angel went back to working on the computer. Kristina blew her a kiss on her way out the door.

~~~~

Detective Jakes walked in with Chinese food for the three of them. "Hey, Angel. Where's Kristina? I've called her three times and sent her two texts. I assume she's pissed about what I said on the phone this morning, but she has to take my calls. This is bullshit. I've felt bad all day because I didn't mean any of it. I needed to blow off steam, but she can't just be pissed and not take my calls. Where is she?" DJ took the food out of the plastic bags.

"Wait. KT's not mad at you. She felt really bad about pushing you to that point. She said she hoped you two could start over as friends. She even said she trusted you. She left about forty-five or fifty minutes ago to meet the security guy at her house. One of her cameras fell on the patio this morning." DJ cut Angel off mid-sentence.

"What do you mean, she left? There's no way a security installer can work in this weather, and it's too late in the day to start installing cameras. Angel, call her phone to see if she answers." Detective Jakes handed Angel her phone from the corner of her desk.

"DJ, you're scaring me. Your team's with her. Why are you so upset?" Angel said, concerned with the look on DJ's face.

"That's why I called her. The team got called to take care of another case. I told them to take off. I told Kristina on her voicemail and text, don't leave the office. The team's gone, and I'm on my way. Fuck." DJ ran his hands through his hair.

DJ and Angel's anxiety raised an octave when Angel's phone rang. Angel looked at the caller ID. She didn't recognize the number.

"Hello, this is Angel."

"Hi, I'm looking for Ms. Truly. We've called her several times, but she's not answering, and she gave this number as an alternative contact number. This is her security company. She wanted us to call her if we could make it out today, but I wanted to let her know we won't be there today. Besides the bad weather, we have to have a tech pick up her new equipment across town, and he can't pick them up until morning. Weather permitting, we can be there tomorrow afternoon." The coloring ran out of Angel's face as she listened to the man on the phone.

"DJ, something's wrong. That was KT's security company. They aren't installing her cameras until tomorrow. KT's in trouble."

CHAPTER FIFTY

The dreary weather caused a slowdown in traffic on Kristina's drive, which gave her and Koo Koo a few minutes to get caught up on the phone before she arrived home to meet the security installer.

"Kooky, meet me at my house later tonight. Let's have a sleepover. I could use some girl time and a bottle or two of merlot." Kristina chatted on the phone while navigating her SUV through the flooded streets from the heavy rain earlier.

"KT, it will do us both good to drink lots of wine, have a good cry, and a few laughs. We need to get our minds off things even if it's just for a few hours. See you between five and six. I'll bring a tub of caramel fudge delight ice cream. You have the wine ready."

There were no signs of the installer when Kristina pulled next to the large utility van backed into her driveway. She grabbed her purse and hurried to the front door to meet the installer in the backyard. She slipped her key in the slot on her door handle, then the deadbolt. The deadbolt wasn't locked. She hesitated. When she left the house that morning, she had so much on her mind and couldn't remember if she'd locked it. Her stomach knotted. The unmarked car with her police team wasn't parked across the street. Panicked, her heart raced. *Something's wrong. They should be there.* She slid the key out of the lock as she turned to run toward her car. Kristina's back slammed against a large man's chest. His hand gripped around her throat as he pulled her from behind through the front door.

"Listen to me, or your furry little friend dies, and so do you." Like a noose, his fingers tightened around her neck. Kristina tugged the man's hands to pry his fingers from choking her. She couldn't breathe. He slammed her head against the back of the front door as he closed it, latching the deadbolt. Her body fell limp. Zip ties bound both wrists tight, painfully tight. Stumbling to keep her balance, she gave a swift kick toward her attacker. She kicked again but missed, and his hands pinched into her shoulders. She couldn't see his face.

"Help me. Help, someone help." Kristina screamed, but they both knew no one could hear her. A stinging slap hit her face full force, then another backhand, spinning her into the corner of the wall. Another blow of his fist buckled her knees. Her head slammed into the ceramic tile floor, face first. Her phone vibrated in her back pocket, and she could hear DJ's ring tone through the earpiece under the ottoman.

"Answer, answer . . . DJ. Help." Kristina screamed, praying it automatically answered the call.

"Kristina, hello? Bad connection, I'll call you back." Detective Jakes's voice faded.

The attacker secured thick silver duct tape over her mouth. Please, DJ, help me. Her mind raced, but she had little hope that things would end well.

Her earpiece announced again, "DJ calling. Answer or ignore?" She could only manage a low muffled scream. The attacker took the phone from Kristina's pocket and silenced DJ's call into voicemail.

"EEEow. Hiss." Ms. Prissy lit into his pant legs with her fierce little claws. She pounced again, and her claws caught his jaw, drawing blood.

"Fucking cat. *Bitch.*" The stranger grabbed the back of Ms. Prissy's neck and threw her into the bathroom and slammed the door. A sickening feeling lurched upwards in Kristina's stomach. With the tape over her mouth, she would choke to death if she threw up. Taking several deep breaths through her nose, she continued to swallow to maintain control.

"Stupid fucking cat," The attacker pressed his knee into the small of her back. Kicking for her life, Kristina gave it all she had. A few swift backward kicks with her boots caught his chest as he leaned over her, but his six-foot-five massive build left Kristina like a little ragdoll in his grip. Despite Kristina's efforts, he managed to duct tape her boots together at the ankles and then jerk her up from the floor to her feet. Blood splattered the wall from the gash above her eye. Dazed, Kristina struggled to stand up. The blood dripped down her forehead, seeping into her eye and down her face.

Kristina hopped toward the kitchen, praying he'd left the sliding door open. He pinned her face down over the dining room table, laughing as he squeezed his grip around the back of her neck. She recognized his face. It was the man in the Lexus. *Who the hell are you? What did I ever do to you?* She tried desperately to put pieces together.

DJ called again. The ringing distracted the attacker enough that Kristina managed to get loose from his hold. She jump-kicked with both feet, attacking his shin as she fell to the kitchen floor, knocking the wind out of her.

"You want to die right now, bitch?" He picked her up off the floor by her hair. She could hardly breathe. A text sounded on her phone, and he read it. "Aw, poor Kristina. You've got no one outside watching you. Your boyfriend's on his way to your office, and his team's on another case. Oh yeah, he says, don't leave the office. He's picking up Kung Pao chicken. Now, let's go, you cunt."

His fingers dug into Kristina's arm like a vice grip as he forced her toward the laundry room that led to the garage. She felt the duct tape give way around her bulky cowboy boots with every shuffle she took. Pretending her feet were still tightly taped, she took tiny steps. He opened the laundry room door into the garage. The van's rear door butted up to the garage. As the garage door slid up, Kristina gave one swift kick, digging the heel of her boot in the same shin she kicked before. Knowing damn well, if he got her inside the van she'd be dead, she fought like a wild banshee.

"Ow. You ... fuckin ..." He lost his grip. Kristina managed to free one boot from the duct tape and ran toward the street. Her neighbor across the street backed his car out of the drive but headed in the opposite direction. The attacker's hand grabbed her collar from behind, securing both of his arms tightly around her waist. Her ribs felt like they were going to crack. Another car sped by without noticing Kristina's silent plea for help. Kicking like hell, she got some good licks in, but she was putty compared to the attacker as he dragged her back to the van. Her head hit the side of the van as he threw her in the back and locked the door.

~~~~

A pool of blood saturated a wad of Kristina's hair draped over her face as she woke up. Her hands were bound behind her. A plastic zip tie cut into her legs, tightly wrapped below the crease of her knees. The duct tape was wet against her mouth. Kristina shivered. The cold metal underneath her numbed her back through her thin blouse. She realized she was lying on the floor of a van. Listening carefully, she could hear the rush and scraping of pavement under the tires, but she had no idea where she was going or why her head felt like it was split open. Her memory was foggy. Lying on her stomach, she vaguely remembered being at her office with Angel, but she wasn't sure if that was today, or how much time had elapsed. Severe pain throbbed in her head. The van swerved, knocking her shoulders into the tire hump. She kicked her boots hard against the metal floor bed, making a few loud thuds. The van kept moving, tossing her around at every twist and turn. The vehicle came to a stop. Kristina's heart pounded harder and faster. Moments later, they started moving again, slower, turning right, then the driver used the turn-signals before making a left. Slowly, she began to remember everything. *Fuck. I've been kidnapped by a serial killer.*

CHAPTER FIFTY-ONE

"Angel, call Peter. Tell him to suit up, pack full heat, and meet me at Kristina's. And Angel, get your ass home. Lock your doors and stay there." Detective Jakes ran out the door, jumped in his car, and sped toward Kristina's house.

"This is Detective Jakes, FBI. I need all units in the area of 1440 East Noble Drive, Newport Beach. Code 2. No lights, no sirens. Possible serial killer with the intent to harm the owner of the house, Kristina Truly. I'm there in fifteen."

"10-4 copy that. I'm turning the corner now," one police unit responded.

"Copy 10-98. We're right behind you," another unit responded.

~~~~

Angel's hand shook, holding the phone. She put the call on speaker, "Peter, Kristina's in trouble."

"I know. I got the call from SWAT. I'm en route. Angel, go straight home, get Jermaine and the kids. Go to your mom's. I sent a black and white, so you'll be safe. Don't leave your mom's. Go now." Peter gave Angel strict instructions.

"Jermaine, listen to me. Take the kids and go to my mom's. Don't ask questions. I need you to leave now. *Right* now. I'll meet you there when I can. I'll call you later and explain, but right now, a black and white is outside waiting for you. I love you. Go right now." Angel grabbed her purse, locked the door behind her, and headed for Kristina's house.

~~~~

"SWAT's got boots on the ground in five." The voice came over Jakes's radio.

"Roger that," Detective Jakes responded, clipping the radio receiver to a hook next to his steering wheel. He accelerated, plowing through a red light, missing a car turning left by a quarter inch. He shoved his car into park, snapped the magazine in his Glock, and headed toward the front of Kristina's house. Patrol officers had the house surrounded.

Peter jumped out of his car. He wore a bulletproof vest, his sniper rifle pointed.

"No. Angel, get back in your car—*Now*," Peter whispered as he pushed her back in her seat. "Angel, if you want to help Kristina, go to your mom's. I'll call you when I can. Please, Angel, go." Peter held his gun aimed at the house. His body blocked Angel from getting out of her car.

"I'm not leaving, Peter." Angel didn't back down.

"What the hell's going on?" Koo Koo walked up to Angel's car parked in front of the house.

"Damn it, Koo Koo, what are you doing here? Angel, take her for a glass of wine and get out of here." Peter raised his voice, trying his best to keep the girls out of harm's way.

"KT asked me to spend the night." Koo Koo looked around at all the activity, totally confused.

"Shhh." Angel put her finger over her lips and opened her passenger door, motioning Koo Koo to get in.

"What the hell's going on?" Koo Koo lowered her voice. She sat in Angel's car, looking around at the mess she'd walked into.

"Angel, where's Kristina?" Koo Koo gripped her purse and carton of ice cream tight to her churning knotted stomach.

"Officer, get these two out of here now." Peter turned the safety babysitting over to one of the uniformed cops and approached the front of the house where Detective Jakes stood talking with SWAT's deputy chief.

"The house is clear. Sorry, Jakes. Looks like they have her," the chief explained. Five SWAT officers walked out of the front door. The exterior lights came on, revealing that all security cameras were disconnected.

"*Goddamn it.*" Detective Jakes combed his hands through his hair while he contemplated their next move.

"Jakes, we're going to find her. KT's tough as nails when she needs to be. She'll be okay. She has to be okay." Peter stopped himself from thoughts of the worst. His special ops training kicked in, hard, and he knew not to allow personal feelings to drive this operation. It was time to find the sonofabitch responsible for this nightmare—time was wasting.

Peter placed his hand on Jakes's shoulder. "We'll set up a station here to save time. Let's look inside and see if they left us any clues." They walked into the house. Angel and Koo Koo followed right on their heels.

Without saying it, everyone knew by the looks of the living room there had been a serious struggle. Frustration and fear continued to boil Detective Jakes's blood. Just before putting his fist through the wall, he stopped when he saw blood on the tile floor.

"Get a sample of the blood to the lab. Tell them I need it back A-SAP." Detective Jakes barked orders. "Where's Ms. Prissy. Anyone see the cat?" Jakes sounded panicked.

One of the police officers put his ear to the bathroom door. "Sounds like it's in here, Detective." He went to open the door.

"No, don't. I'll get her." Jakes opened the door, praying to see Ms. Prissy unharmed. She had clawed at the door until her paws were red and swollen. Jakes scooped her up in his arms. "You're a furry little fighter, aren't you, Prissy girl? I promise Kristina will be home soon." He kissed Prissy's head and secured her in Kristina's bedroom. He took the stairs down two at a time.

"Okay, let's get started." Jakes looked around the house. Peter had already set up in the living room with a portable FBI camp complete with high-tech devices right out of a James Bond spy movie.

"What's going on? Who are you people? Peter, Angel, where's Kristina? What's happened to Kristina?" Lois and Jim stood at the open doorway with concern in their eyes.

"Lois, Jim, did you see the man's face that was here dressed like a security installer?" Angel jumped off the sofa and stood in front of Jim. "It's really important. Did you get a good look at the man's face?" Angel's voice was sharp and to the point. Her nerves were getting the best of her, and things were just heating up.

"Not really. He was tall, over six feet-four, six-five maybe. Dark wavy hair, looked like he could be Italian, maybe Middle Eastern? I don't know. I'm sorry. I can't see that well, and I didn't have my glasses on." Jim's hands shook the more he tried to explain.

"It's okay, sir, anything you can remember will help us. Take your time." An officer taking notes chimed in.

"Okay. He had a heavy build, not obese but a big man. Oh, he had a thick beard covering his face. He wore a red baseball cap, Anaheim A's, pulled down near his eyes. I remember that because I'm a Dodgers fan. A shiny van was backed in the driveway. Dark blue or black. I couldn't tell which. That's it. Lois and I left for dinner. What does this have to do with Kristina?" Jim didn't look good. He coughed with a rattle in his lungs. Lois fumbled in her pocket to pull out an asthma inhaler, handing it to Jim. After a puff, he could breathe easier.

"We'll take Ms. Prissy to our house and take care of her until Kristina gets home." Lois wiped tears from her eyes. It was obvious things didn't look good. Lois worried about Jim's weak heart. She needed to get Jim home.

"Angel, walk Lois and Jim home. Take Prissy too." Peter pulled Angel aside. "Keep the details brief. I'm afraid it's too much stress for Jim's health."

By the time Angel got back from next door, the lab results were back.

"Detective Jakes, the blood found on the tile is O negative, same as Ms. Truly. That's all we have for now." An officer handed Detective Jakes a printed copy of the results.

Jakes tossed the paper to the ground and combed his fingers through his hair, pacing the living room.

"Detective, we traced her cell phone signal and found it in a dryer in the laundry room. We dusted for prints. It's been wiped." An FBI agent handed Jakes the phone. The perp had read Jakes's text and knew there was no security backup outside the house. Jakes's emotions were at their peak. Peter stayed focused on the computer and other devices.

"Wait, I just remembered. Kristina has her Taser gun with her. Peter, the new one you gave her from the FBI. I completely forgot about it. I turned it on. She should have a GPS signal. Track it, Peter." Angel hurried over to Peter's side.

"If they tossed her phone, I'm sure they tossed her Taser. They threw everything in her purse on the floor," Jakes snapped dismissively.

"No, she had on her cowboy boots. There's a pocket inside the leg of the boots. We stuck the gun in the pocket to see if it fit. We got sidetracked, and she never took it out. Track it, Peter, hurry," Angel demanded.

Koo Koo sat on the ottoman with both fingers crossed as Peter pulled up a software program to find the signal from the X56 Taser gun's GPS.

"I got it. She's moving East on the 91 Freeway." Peter picked up a handheld walkie-talkie. "All units be on the lookout for a black or dark blue van headed East on the 91 Freeway.

Highly dangerous situation, possible serial killer has a female hostage. Repeat all units, East on the 91." Peter continued tracking Kristina's signal.

loud clap of thunder exploded, followed by streaks of silver across the sky. The living room lights dimmed, then went out completely.

Peter picked up another transmitting device. "We need a backup generator—now."

Seconds later, the lights came back on without the help of the generator. Peter kept his eyes on his computer screen. "Damn it. We lost the signal. We lost her."

CHAPTER FIFTY-TWO

The van stopped moving. Kristina's heart filled with dread. A garage door opened, and the van rolled about ten feet before coming to a final stop. Boots tapped on the concrete garage floor, moving toward the back of the van. Even if Lois and Jim described the van to the FBI, they'd never find it hidden in a garage. Kristina had to trust that Detective Jakes and Peter had a few tricks up their sleeves and would track her down. Hopefully, sooner than too late.

She fought like the devil as the attacker dragged her from the van. Her legs and arms were bound and her mouth covered with tape. He penned her face to the rear door of the muddy van. He held a firm grip on the back of her neck. "Look stupid, do you wanna die right here? Don't you want to take your last breath lying beside your baby sister? She fucking looked up to you her entire life, and you didn't even know the bitch existed. But for some reason, she idolized you. You and all your perfect relationship bullshit. Well, guess what, now you two can burn in hell together." Parts of this nightmare were starting to make sense. Clearly, Taryn's husband, Tom Kennedy, wanted serious revenge. Fear that he had already killed Taryn yanked tight the large knot in Kristina's intestines. And she had no doubt she was next.

Taryn's ex-husband's rock-solid alibi took him off the FBI's radar, making the hope of them finding Kristina seem like a bad bet, so she needed to figure out what the hell to do next. At this point, staying alive seemed like a longshot too. But for now, she was still breathing, and she would take one moment at a time.

"Dipshit, did everything go as planned, or did you fuck something else up?" A beautiful, well-dressed brunette woman met them at the door leading to the house from the garage. When Tom carried her into the house, Kristina thought she vaguely recognized the woman. *Who is she?* Kristina made mental notes in case of an escape. She wanted to make sure that bitch went to prison.

"Smooth as glass, babe. We might need to sedate her until I get rid of her. She's a fighter." Tom carried Kristina through an enormous foyer lined with expensive marble and ornate antiques. A strong scent of cinnamon filled the room from a candle with three wicks burning next to a cut crystal vase of fresh-cut white roses on a white marble table. Nothing Kristina could see gave her any clues as to where she was, but by the size of the house and elegant furnishings, they weren't in the barrio.

"No need to sedate her. She'll calm down. If she doesn't, her sister will pay the price. We'll see how much sisterly love those two can handle. It's such a pleasure to finally meet the beautiful Kristina Truly. I bet you don't remember meeting me, Virginia Van Heed? I introduced myself at the luncheon, *Women at the Top.* You left early. Did you think you were too good to watch me receive my cheap-ass plaque? I donated a hundred grand to an entire school district of fucking shithead children, and all they could do to show appreciation is a nasty ass plaque. Well, Kristina, you can call me Ginny." Virginia Van Heed, a prominent figure in the area, stood holding a riding crop, tapping the tip in the palm of her hand. Then she took a gentle swipe along Kristina's face before she tapped Tom's crouch as she let out an obnoxious flirtatious giggle.

Tom dropped Kristina like a sack of rocks in a high back soft leather chair.

"I'm going to cut the zip ties from around your legs so you can walk. If you don't behave like a good little girl, your baby sister is going to pay for it. I'll beat the shit out of her every time you misbehave. Got it?"

It sounded like Taryn was still alive. Kristina nodded her head in agreement. Her Taser gun cut into the side of her calf while her legs were bound tight. She knew if she could keep her boots on, somehow she'd figure out a way to get Taryn and herself out of there alive. The Taser's GPS was on, but with all the security equipment Kristina saw lining the walls of the garage, she had little hope. The sophisticated security equipment could easily block signals in and out.

Tom had his vice grip on the same arm already bruised from earlier at her house, making the pain intense, nearly unbearable. Not to mention the welt across her cheek from Tom's fist and the gash in her head from hitting the tiles back at her house. But she had to shake off the throbbing pain, stay focused, fight and flight, her adrenaline pumped at full throttle.

"Let's get her downstairs." Ginny led the way. Tom dug his fingers into Kristina's arm when she pulled away from his side. Ginny didn't look a day over thirty-five with her face pulled tighter than a pair of Spanx. Ginny's caricature appearance, with her tiny waist and disproportionate silicone breasts, made Kristina think of Jessica Rabbit. You could use her lips for lifeboats with all the Juvederm injections. Kristina imagined Ginny's breasts bursting as her body deflated, shooting like balloons around the room.

They took Kristina down two flights of stairs to a basement. Not your average dingy dungeon type basement, this looked like something on an episode of *The Lifestyles of The Rich and Famous*. Kristina realized that's exactly where she'd seen this house—on television. Kristina pieced some of the puzzle together. She remembered seeing Ginny on the news, not at the luncheon. Kristina remembered the media made a big deal about Ginny's donation of the new security systems to the city of Anaheim Unified School District and police stations. Virginia Van Heed built a small family security company her father started into a multimillion-dollar corporation, but there had also been rumors the donations had plenty of strings attached.

Some of the pieces were coming together. It didn't answer all of Kristina's questions, but at least she knew how Tom got in her house without setting off her security alarm and who canceled her new security system. Also, she knew why Ginny, the president of the security company that Tom worked for, eagerly turned over documentation to the FBI securing her lover's alibi. She'd gone to great lengths to keep the local police and the FBI off their trail.

Tom followed behind Ginny with his chest puffed up like a tough guy, maltreating a defenseless woman with her mouth taped shut and her hands strapped behind her back. Kristina watched with intense focus. Tom seemed like a child begging for approval, which gave Kristina hope that her psychological insight would eventually give her the advantage to come up with a plan to get Taryn and her the hell out of there alive.

They continued down a long hallway past several closed doors. Behind one door, Kristina heard someone moaning in pain. It sounded like a man's voice.

Ginny slapped the door with her whip. "Drake, stop whining. I've had enough of your whining," Ginny said, looking back at Tom and Kristina. "He's your problem. You need to get rid of him soon." Ginny shook her head. "You sliced a couple of women's throats then brag to your therapist about it? Jesus Christ, Tom, you are dumb as shit sometimes."

"Stop dwelling on it. I've got it handled. Just a few more details to take care of, and we'll have planted all the evidence we need to frame your ex for the murders. Poor bastard won't know what hit him when he falls over the cliff. We've already gotten rid of four bodies, and we've got four more, no big deal, just stick to the plan." Tom pushed Kristina to the side as he and Ginny groped each other like something out of a bizarre sex film.

"Oh, and Kristina, you shouldn't put your vagina where it doesn't belong. George Handy's one of my boy toys, and I'm not good at sharing. But I'm pretty sure he's learned his lesson. Right, George?" Ginny tapped her knuckles on another closed bedroom door. Again, there was a disturbing sound—a male voice moaning—coming from the other side of the door. Kristina made a mental note in case she could somehow sneak into the room to help George escape with Taryn and her. Drake Toucuti, she'd leave behind. But by the sound of George Handy's moaning, he did not seem like he'd be in any shape to make a run for it.

Ginny took out a key she had tucked in her bra between her cleavage to open the doors across the hall. "Once you're done with her, let's get started tying up loose ends." Ginny kissed Tom's cheek, and then out of nowhere, she bitch-slapped the palm of her hand across his face, laughing as she walked away.

"Thanks, baby. Felt great," Tom said, practically jerking himself off with a perverted sick grin and his ego beaming as Ginny walked away. He gave Kristina a nasty look as he shoved her through the bedroom door that Ginny unlocked. Lying in the middle of a large king-size bed, Taryn woke up, startled. She wore a black leather corseted bustier with a pair of lacy G-string panties, and her petite legs were adorned with black sheer top-laced thigh high stockings. Taryn hurried to her feet, fully cognizant of the rules: no eye contact with Tom, her Master. Fear weathered her sweet face.

Tom secured the door as he let go of Kristina's arm. "Taryn, where the hell are your shoes? You know better than to let me see you without your fucking heels on." Tom took a powerful swing with the back of his hand to Taryn's face. Kristina tried to come to her defense, but he shoved Kristina to the floor.

Tom took a switchblade knife out of his pocket to cut the zip-ties around Kristina's wrists. She held her breath, hoping that was all he was going to cut as she sat motionless on the floor. With one pull, he ripped the duct tape off her mouth. "Aw, sweetheart, that's going to leave a welt, but it won't matter because the maggots will have eaten most of your pretty face before your FBI boyfriend finds your mutilated body. Now, be a good little girl and do as Daddy says, slip on one of the leather outfits hanging in the closet. I'll be back, and Taryn, sweetie, you'll have your heels on, right?" Taryn shook her head yes, still looking down.

"On second thought, bitch, I'll tell you what I want you to wear. Take off your clothes. You won't need them anymore. They'll make a colorful display in the fireplace," Tom said to Kristina.

Kristina trembled, slipping her jeans skirt off over her boots. "The boots, stupid. Take your boots off." Tom watched, twirling the switchblade in his hand like it was a baton. Kristina removed her cowboy boots carefully. More panic set in. She tucked the boots tightly by her side as she took off her blouse.

"Here, put your fat ass into this lacy G-string and bad boy leather corset. Now, you two sisters are dressed like twins." This wasn't the time to provoke him, so Kristina did exactly what she was told to do. Tom picked up her pile of clothes and her boots. Kristina's heart raced, and she felt lightheaded with fear. She held her breath.

"You know, I love a whore in cowboy boots. Here, put em on with your leather." Tom started to toss the boots to Kristina.

"Wait, I'll take them. I mean ... thank you. I'd love to wear my boots for you." Kristina took them out of Tom's hand.

"Thank you, Daddy. Say it, bitch ... let me hear you thank your daddy," Tom said in the same way you'd talk to a two-year-old.

"Thank you, Daddy, thank you, thank you so much." She nearly threw up, but she needed to keep her boots. They were the only hope they had left.

CHAPTER FIFTY-THREE

"Kelly, what are you doing here?" Detective Jakes looked surprised to see Detective Kelly standing in the living room.

"I'm here to help. Stopped by the station on my way back to Vegas to say goodbye. Joan said you were here with Peter and the team. She told me the case you're working took another bad turn. Figured you might need my help. Hey, Peter, haven't seen you in a long time. Congrats on the engagement. What can I do?" Detective Kelly joined Peter to get up to speed on the case.

"Oh, boy. That's Detective Kelly?" Angel whispered to Koo Koo. "Whoa. She missed her calling as a Victoria Secret model, and she's British. She's friggin' hot." Koo Koo gave Detective Kelly a complete once over with bugged-out eyes.

Detective Jakes knew he couldn't worry about feelings getting hurt. He had to find Kristina, and the more time they wasted, the less likely they would find her alive. The fling between him and Detective Kelly happened over six months before. There had been nothing between them since. Jakes and Detective Kelly had a mutual friendship with occasional benefits, nothing more. Jakes felt guilty, not about his friendship with Detective Kelly, but he never thought he'd have feelings for another woman like he had for his wife and falling for Kristina really did a number on him.

Detective Jakes needed a minute to clear his head. Sitting alone at the dining room table, he pictured Kristina and him sitting together the day before, drinking coffee, eating oatmeal. Too bad she didn't join him in the shower. He couldn't think about anything but the crazy chemistry he felt the second he laid eyes on her. His hormones skyrocketed when he saw her boarding the flight to Las Vegas. It felt like some sort of universal intervention. He'd never felt like this before, other than for his dead wife, Anne, who had teased Jakes through the years saying if she went first, she'd bring him someone very special.

"So, what do we have, Jakes? Where you at with the case?" Kelly joined him in the kitchen while the team carried on in the other room. She rubbed Jakes's neck and shoulders. With his elbows on the table, he buried his face in both hands. Kelly's plump full lips softly grazed his face as she kissed his cheek.

"No, please. Not now, please. I mean, thanks for your help with the case but—" Detective Jakes lowered his voice so the others couldn't hear. He got to his feet. Kelly hadn't seen this side of him before now.

"This isn't just another case to you. This is personal, isn't it? You care about this woman." Kelly smiled, slapping Jakes's tight buns with her hand. "Good for you. You deserve it. Come on, baby, let's catch this sonofabitch and find the woman who's making you crazy in love with her." Kelly and Jakes joined the others.

~~~~

"Hey, everyone, listen up. The JMM's on the phone. They've got something," Peter shouted. You could hear a pin drop. "Go ahead. I've got you on speaker." Peter turned up the volume on the phone. Jakes got closer.

"Detective Jakes, your hunch paid off. There's a connection. We dug deeper into the connection with Tom Kennedy and the president of the security company he works for. Come to find out Tom got the job because Taryn went to elementary school with Virginia Van Heed. She goes by Ginny, the president and CEO of the security company. We thought it odd Ms. Van Heed didn't mention anything about her friendship with Tom's wife when she came in for questioning. Made us question Tom's alibi. Jakes, just like you thought, his alibi was a little too perfect. So, we kept digging. We hacked. Excuse me, scratch that, we found surveillance tapes from everywhere Tom allegedly stayed when he was out of state working. Ginny supplied us with documentation to prove Tom wasn't in town the weeks of each of the murders. We tracked every convenience store, every ATM. If he had a receipt, we found the video camera tapes to see if he was really there."

The phone line crackled. The connection skipped in and out. Claps of thunder shook the house. The house went dark again. The technicians powered the generator, and they were back in action. Almost ….

"JMM got disconnected. There's a full power outage in upstate New York. They must've lost their phone connections. Shit, the JMM all work out of their homes in the Adirondacks, and their cell tower isn't working." Peter had a panicked look on his face.

"Do something. Someone's got to do something." Angel felt like she could have an anxiety attack at any moment.

"Wait, I've got KT's GPS signal again. She's somewhere in Anaheim Hills. No, no—fuck. We lost the signal." Peter stayed focused on his electronics.

"Listen, that's a good sign. If her GPS is still active, there's a chance she's still alive." Detective Jakes felt hopeful for the first time in several hours.

"But what if they tossed it somewhere to lead us on a wild goose chase? Koo Koo gasped for air to keep from going hysterical. Angel held Koo Koo's hand to settle her down.

"Koo Koo, listen to me. If Detective Jakes says it's a good sign KT's alive, we have to trust his instincts. KT told me today she trusted him, and you know she doesn't trust anyone."

"Okay, you're right. She doesn't trust anyone." Angel and Koo Koo shared a slight smile thinking about KT's trust issues with men.

"Goddamn it, Peter. Get the JMM back on the line. I know you've got access to the NSA's cell towers. I don't give a shit if it's legal, get the fucking JMM on the line." Detective Jakes's anxiety escalated with every second wasted.

"I'm already on it, Jakes. And don't ever question what I'd do to save Kristina and put this sonofabitch away. You understand? Okay, I've got them back."

"Go ahead, JMM, we can hear you," Peter said. His eyes never left his computer screen as he continued working with his technical equipment.

"Okay, where'd we leave off? So, we digitally formulated a replica of Tom's body frame. We dubbed it into the security tapes of the hotels he stayed in. We can clearly see a man checking in on the day of one of the murders. He fits Tom's description to a T, but what gave us reason to question it was the man checking into the hotel made sure to be seen on nearly all the hotel security cameras. Someone who works in the high-tech world of security would know how to position themselves well enough to be seen but not a complete view of their face. He made sure to be on camera every chance he got. So, we compared the digitally accurate Tom that we created with the exact measurements of the man caught on camera in the videos, and they don't match. The man on the hotel tapes giving Tom his airtight alibi, isn't Tom. Looks like they could be twins at a glance, but the man on the videotapes is a half-inch shorter than Tom, his waist is an inch smaller, his left ear's an eighth of an inch bigger, his nose a sixteenth—well trust us, it's not Tom."

Detective Jakes secured the straps on his bulletproof vest. "They've got Kristina at Virginia Van Heed's mansion in Anaheim Hills. Let's go."

CHAPTER FIFTY-FOUR

"Taryn, thank God. You're alive. I've been so scared you'd been . . ." Kristina threw her arms around her sister. They held each other, shaking, and scared to death.

"Kristina, I'm sorry I've caused you so much trouble. Tom's going to kill us." Taryn sat on the side of the bed with her face in her hands, sobbing.

Kneeling in front of Taryn, Kristina placed her hands on Taryn's knees and whispered, "Taryn, look at me." Taryn slowly made eye contact. "We're together, okay? We're stronger together, and we are going to get out of here." Taryn nodded in agreement with a tearful sniff of her nose.

"Honey, listen to me. Do you know they have two men locked up in the rooms down the hall?" Kristina asked.

Taryn shook her head no and held up three fingers. "They have Randy, Ginny's husband, also unless they already killed him. She struggled to catch her breath.

"Shit," Kristina blurted out. Taryn placed one finger over her pursed lips, reminding Kristina to keep her voice down. Kristina mouthed in a whisper, "Do you know they've already brutally murdered four others?" Taryn nodded her head yes.

"I'm sure they have cameras in this room and listening devices. The house is full of high-tech security. So, we have to keep our faces down away from the cameras as much as possible. We can't let them see us talking secretly too long. We'll make sure they only hear what we want them to hear. Otherwise, we keep our heads down. Taryn, I have a Taser gun in my boot. It's a longshot, but somehow we have to take Tom down long enough to make a run for it. Okay?" Kristina tucked Taryn's hair behind her ear to see her face. Taryn nodded in agreement. In case they were being watched, Kristina didn't want to stay knelt down too long. Pacing the room served a dual purpose: it helped her think and looked good for the cameras.

Taryn approached Kristina with another embrace. This time she spoke softly in Kristina's ear, "I overheard them talking earlier. Ginny has a social event to attend later tonight with the mayor of Anaheim. The minute she leaves, Tom will come in here. Every time she leaves, he comes here to have sex. He'll want sex with both of us. That'll be our chance."

They sat on the floor close to one another, leaning their backs against the wall. The large four-poster wooden bed partially blocked the two of them from a clear camera shot. Huddled together wearing their ridiculous black shiny patent leather and lace get-up, they had nothing to do but wait, praying Ginny would leave as she mentioned earlier.

"I wish it had been different for both of us growing up. I just want you to know I don't blame you for my father, I mean our father, walking out on my brother and me." Kristina's voice cracked, watching terror in her sister's face.

"May I ask how did you get involved with Tom and

Ginny? You're so sweet." Kristina gripped Taryn's hands tighter.

"Ginny and I met in first grade and grew up together. I met Tom online on Tinder. I'd just gotten out of an abusive relationship, and then I met Tom. My self-esteem has never been good. My dad . . . our dad, he hated me. I was the reason he left you and Timmy. Mother and Dad were having an affair, and Mom got pregnant with me. So, they got married." She took a deep breath. Her painful past lined her face. "I could never live up to you, Kristina. Nothing I did was good enough for Dad." Taryn swallowed the knot in her throat. "As long as I can remember, he's been a miserable drunk. After a couple of beers, he'd call me Krissy. He'd beat me with his belt when I stood up to him. I didn't care. With every whack, I screamed louder, 'I'm not Krissy!' Once, he nearly killed me, so I learned to shut up. My mom never stopped him, and my brothers are just like Dad." Tears glistened in Taryn's eyes. Kristina wiped Taryn's cheeks with her fingertips. Taryn pulled herself together.

"I married Tom after dating only three months. I didn't find out until after we were married, he lost his job because he took a swing at a co-worker. His temper and our deep financial debt are what started me reading your books. Tom needs prescribed antipsychotic meds. He's mentally ill but often refuses to take his meds. Dr. Toucuti, his psychiatrist, says he should be institutionalized. Tom tried to suffocate me more than once in my sleep." She stopped abruptly, pointing her finger toward the door. The two jumped to their feet when they heard someone in the hallway, turning the doorknob.

"Dumbass, get downstairs. I have shit for you to take care of before I leave. If this fucking rain ever lets up."

The two took a breath. They heard a key turn in the lock, and Tom's large feet retreat down the hallway.

"Whew." Kristina closed her eyes, crossing her hands over her chest. The two sat back in their hiding spot from the view of the camera.

Nerves caused Kristina to shiver. "Taryn, was Tom always abusive?" She gave her forearms a brisk rubbing to warm up.

"Six months after we married, Tom wanted me to be his submissive. At first, it was just harmless, playful sex. It got more controlling and violent within a few months. I didn't find out until later that shortly after Tom and I married, he and Ginny formed a tight Mistress/Slave relationship. That's why she hired Tom. Mentally, I couldn't leave him until I read your books and attended your workshops. Ginny's a sadist who dominates and abuses men. I became very close with her husband, Randy. He attended your workshops too. Ginny has to pay Randy fifteen thousand a month in their divorce agreement. I guess the lack of control over Randy is what triggered her plan to kill him. The three women they killed were just sweet girls Randy and I met through the workshops. We all went to dinner a few times, and now they're dead." Taryn wiped her eyes. "I overheard them talking. They're planning to pin the murders on Randy. They'll make it look like he killed himself, leaving a confession note admitting to killing the three women and one of Ginny's ex-lovers." Taryn and Kristina each used a corner of the bedsheet to wipe their noses.

"Sounds like they're also planning to blame Randy for the murders of Drake Toucuti and George. They're both locked in rooms across the hall. I'm sorry, Taryn. I dreamed about how much I wanted Dad to love me, but I never wanted it to be at your expense. We both deserved better. We both get out of here alive, or we both die fighting. These two psychopaths will pay for what they've done. I promise you that. My friends will make sure of it." Kristina felt weak and unsure how much more she could take. *Breathe in through my nose, out through my mouth.* Trying to stay focused and hopeful, she thought about the people she loved so much.

The torrential downpour threw the rain sideways against the small basement windows six feet above their heads. Those windows allowed a sliver of light, and they'd be able to see headlights if Ginny left for the evening.

Thunder clapped loudly. Silver streaks of lightning flashed. The ceiling's recessed lighting dimmed, going off for a second then back on.

"Randy and I were blind-sighted one weekend. Ginny and Tom said the four of us were going to Palm Springs for the weekend to relax. We panicked when we walked into a private resort filled with slaves and masters into BDSD and having orgies. It was *Fifty Shades of Grey* on steroids with Ginny and Tom jumping right in. Randy and I got the hell out of there. We drove straight back to Orange County and met with our attorneys that afternoon. I helped him grab a few things from this house. That's when Randy told me that Ginny didn't just have a sexual fetish for hurting men, but she was clinically psychotic, and we could be in serious danger. He said Ginny had always hated me. All those years she pretended to care about me, she actually despised me. Jealous over the attention her father gave me. Her dad knew I couldn't afford to go to summer camp, so he always made sure my fees were covered. He took me on all their family vacations. I felt like I was part of their family. He was a good man and loved Ginny beyond belief, but for her, it wasn't enough. I always felt her mother's death wasn't an accident. Ginny's a very sick woman."

Kristina's heart pounded harder. "How did Tom kidnap you?" It pained her to hear the heartbreaking truth about Taryn's life. It was far from the fairytale Kristina dreamt about growing up. *Taryn, the lucky little girl. She's got a daddy, and I don't.*

"The morning Dad passed away, Tom was in the parking garage standing next to my car after I left the hospital. He said he was there to visit Dad. Of course, the two assholes got along well together. I'm still not sure how he knew Dad was sick unless one of my brothers let him know. I told him Dad was gone. He wiped his eyes like he was upset. I saw through his act, and I got a bad feeling something was up. I went to open my car door, and that's when he forced his hand around my mouth. The last thing I remember is hearing Ginny's voice from behind me. I heard her say, 'Get her in the car.' One of them must have given me a sedative. I really don't know what happened. I woke up locked in this room." Taryn's eyes grew dark. Remorse flashed heat through her body. "I should have never gone to your seminars. All of this is my fault."

"Taryn, look at me. This isn't your fault. We are going to get out of here alive. I promise."

"Tom went to get you the day Dad died. He nearly snatched you in the driveway, but you were on the phone, and he thought a neighbor with his dog might have seen him in his Lexus." Taryn's eyes widened, watching the doorknob turn.

Tom entered the room alone. He secured the lock from the inside with a key he carried in his front pocket. Taryn hurried to get her red polka dot spiked heels on before she stood up. Women in polka dots, especially on their feet, was one of Tom's kinky fetishes; another was ripping their nipples off.

"So, ladies, how's the little family reunion? Hope you're getting caught up because it's not going to last much longer."

Like a proud cock, Tom puffed his chest while spinning a large knife in his hand. The garish grin on his dark bearded face turned Kristina's stomach. He gripped Taryn by the nape of the neck. There was pleasure in his eyes as he pressed the sharp silver blade under her chin. Kristina gasped and covered her hand over her mouth. She lunged toward Tom.

"No," Taryn strained to warn Kristina to stop.

Tom jabbed the knife in the air toward Kristina like a fencing saber, "En Garde!" Tom laughed. Kristina spun to miss the blade and lost her footing. It knocked the wind from her chest as she hit the carpet.

"Looks like I know whose throat I'll cut first. Kristina, I'll get such pleasure watching your face when I slice right through your sissy's sweet carotids, just like I did to the other sluts." Tom traced the tip of the knife down Taryn's neck and circled each breast. Taryn stood perfectly still without blinking an eye.

"See, Kristina, Taryn doesn't show fear anymore. She plays a game with me, pretending she's not afraid." Tom jerked Taryn's hair harder while he rubbed the blade down her arms. Kristina watched in silent horror. Taryn had complete control of her emotions. It was clear she would rather die than let Tom have power over her.

"At your relationship workshops, Taryn learned she could stand up to Daddy. Isn't that right, little girl? We'll see how strong you are when I slice your nipples off. One. By. One. Swoosh—off it goes." Tom laughed like an evil fiend. Kristina held her breath.

"A lot of women get pleasure from clamped nipples but not you. Oh no, you couldn't be a good girl and let your Master do what makes him happy. I've got news for you, my love, you'll beg me to cut your throat before I'm done with you. But I'll save the rest for a surprise. Kristina, you've been so good at mentoring Taryn that I think it's only fair for you two to have matching dog collars." Tom kissed Taryn's cheek and then shoved her to the floor. Kristina winched and had to turn her head when the disgusting ogre pushed his bare foot into Taryn's petite ribcage. Taryn gritted her teeth but didn't flinch.

"Bitch, put this on your big sister. Tight, the way I taught you to wear it, or I'll do it, and you know I can be such a fucking ass when you don't follow my rules." Tom went to the closet to get two brown leather dog collars with sharp metal spikes. A long, braided rope attached to a silver ring hung down the back. "Whore, put these on: *Now*." Tom threw the collars at Taryn's back.

"Dumbass, get out of there. I need you downstairs." Tom hurried to do exactly what Ginny commanded.

Tom had taken Kristina's watch when he took her clothes, so neither of them knew what time it was. They guessed it had to be close to 7:00 p.m. by now. The Taser gun had a digital clock on it, but with the cameras in the room, they didn't dare take the gun out of Kristina's boot to check the time. Their anxiety mounted with every crack of thunder. The chance of them getting out alive was grim if Ginny didn't leave because of the storm. They prepared their strategy even though the hope of it working dwindled with every flash of lighting.

The central heating kicked up a notch, reminding Kristina of Deedee. She heard her mother's sweet voice in her head. *I like my house nice and toasty*. Her heart sank, and she swallowed hard against the lump in her throat. Thoughts of Timmy and his daughter made her hands shake. She wondered if something happened to her, would DJ know how sorry she was for being hard on him. Picturing DJ's arms around her gave her fleeting comfort. Not trusting men had stopped her from meeting Mr. Right, and now the only thing she had left was trusting that Detective Jakes would find her in time. Kristina knew Jakes was the man she'd always wanted to meet, and now she feared she'd never see him again. The thoughts spinning in Kristina's head about the horrible things Tom said he'd do to them took her to her knees. She fell, paralyzed with fear.

"Kristina, you're okay. I need you. Please, Kristina, don't lose hope. Let's focus on our plan." Taryn helped Kristina back on her feet. For the next twenty minutes, they sat quietly, listening to the storm outside. Again, the lights flickered off. This time, they didn't come back on for several minutes. They stayed close to each other's sides.

Headlights flashed through the windows above their heads. They jumped to their feet. This was their only chance to get out alive.

"Kristina, hurry. Put this collar on. He'll be here in a minute. Hurry, Kristina." Taryn tightened her own collar quickly from experience.

"I can't get it closed. It won't close." Kristina's hands trembled. She couldn't grasp the buckle.

The key turned in the lock of the door. "Here, I've got it." Taryn latched Kristina's collar. Like clockwork, Tom entered the bedroom to have sex with the two of them before he killed them. He carried two heavy green zippered plastic bags, made to store a fake Christmas tree with two red strap handles.

"Nice collar, bitch." Tom yanked the rope attached to Kristina's collar, causing her to choke. "Get used to it, slut. I'm just getting started. Oh, these are for you. Now you have matching body bags too." Tom tossed the plastic bags in the corner of the room.

"So, ladies, it's time that you show Daddy who's the boss here. Right, Taryn? Shall we teach big sissy how we like to make Daddy happy?" Tom took a brown leather flogger hanging from a hook on the back of the closet door.

"Yes, sir." Taryn assumed her position of submission by facing the wall where metal shackles were mounted to hold someone's wrists and ankles. Leather ropes, chains, and several sizes of assorted dildos decorated the wall. Nipple and clitoris clamps were on display in a small metal cage attached to the wall.

Taryn held her hands together high above her head, and she firmly planted her five-inch spiked heels into the thick pile carpet so that she didn't move unless told to. Like a good little submissive, she stared straight ahead, silent, and ready for the beating to start.

Tom lashed the flogger across the back of Taryn's petite frame. Kristina gasped and turned her face, but Taryn stood perfectly still, showing no emotion. Over and over, he hit her. With the thermostat cranked up and his extra body fat, he stopped to kick off his shoes and strip naked, all but a leather G-string cradling his penis like a sock. He stroked himself, getting more aroused. Sweat flung from his overheated body with every lash against Taryn's back.

Taryn knew Tom's exact routine. His obsessive-compulsive behavior never varied, which played better odds that their plan would work. So far, things were right on schedule. Within minutes his flogging became more erratic, less focused. Tom became fully aroused and engrossed with sexual pleasure. Kristina seized the moment to reach into her boot.

Thunder clapped, and the lights went out. The lights flickered on for a split second, then off, then back on. She lost sight of Tom. If she missed him, she'd hit Taryn. Secured with a tight firm grip on the Taser gun, Kristina aimed. She froze, unwilling to risk hitting Taryn.

"*Fuck.*" Kristina knew she'd blown their only hope to survive.

"Go ahead, take the shot, bitch. Kill your sister. I'm going to kill her anyway." Tom assumed the Taser was an actual gun. He had his hands gripped in a chokehold around Taryn's throat, using her as a body shield. The lights going off brought Tom's sexual climax to an abrupt stop. He panted like a dog to catch his breath. Fat boy needed to do more cardio. Kristina kept a firm grip on the gun pointed at Tom in her one hand. With her other, Kristina flashed her fingers by her side like a baseball catcher signaling the pitcher. *One . . . Two . . . Three.* Taryn stomped her spiked heel into the top of Tom's bare foot. "Mother Fu—" Tom lost his grip. Taryn dove like she was sliding into home base. Kristina took the shot.

CHAPTER FIFTY-FIVE

pparently, getting hit in the balls with fifty thousand
volts from a distance of five feet can do some damage to
the genitals. Scumbag Tom was out cold.

"Hurry, get the key out of his pants." Kristina grabbed a
roll of bright pink duct tape out of the closet and taped his
hands behind his back. Tom squirmed with a loud grown.
"Taryn, grab the Taser."

He rolled over on his back and started to sit up. Kristina
planted the heel of her boot in his chest with a swift kick.
"Better keep your ass down." She hog-tied his feet with the
same pink tape.

"Whore, I'm going to kill you," Tom grunted.

"I knew I forgot something . . ." Kristina slapped a beautiful
piece of the bright pink duct tape across his big mouth too.

"Sister, aim low." Kristina stood back.

"Rot in hell, you fucking sonofabitch." Taryn let go on her
ex. The smell of his burning flesh put a surprising and
satisfying grin on their faces. By the look of his charred penis,
he wasn't going anywhere.

"We don't have much time," Kristina said. "I'm sure
Ginny's got her security cameras streaming to her cell phone.
She could be back any minute." Kristina took the Taser from

Taryn. The power light flashed red. There wasn't time to worry if the charge was low. She remembered the zap her old stun gun gave Uncle Ronnie, and she crossed her fingers.

Taryn turned off the light in case Ginny watched on her smartphone. "Don't worry, Kristina, I know this house inside out. Let's go." They grabbed hands, ready to run.

"Headlights. Ginny's back. What'll we do?" Kristina squeezed Taryn's hand, pulled her back into the room, and shut the door.

"Kristina, what are you doing? We need to run. If Ginny catches us, we're dead. She carries a gun."

Taryn listened with her ear to the door. "She's coming. I hear her opening the other bedroom doors. She must think we're hiding in one of the other rooms."

Kristina needed to think fast. "She'll be here soon. Taryn, you stand on that side of the door. I'll stand here, in front of the door. We've used two darts. Angel used one dart in the office. I'm not sure if we've got one more shot with the Taser. Let's pray we do. When she opens the door, throw the light switch. I'll take our last shot, I hope. If this doesn't work, Taryn, you run. Don't worry about me, just get out. I'll be right behind you, I promise."

Taryn steadied herself with her back against the wall and her finger on the light switch. Kristina gripped the Taser gun with both hands and pointed at the door. *One dart, just one dart, that's all we need, just one dart.*

The doorknob turned slowly. Kristina held her breath. The door flung wide open. Taryn flipped the switch . . .

"No, don't shoot." Detective Jakes shouted. Kristina dropped the gun, triggering the last dart into the wall.

DJ grabbed Kristina in his arms. "Thank God."

SWAT stormed the room.

Peter took his turn to kiss Kristina's face profusely, squeezing her in his arms. "KT, what the hell are you wearing?" Peter joked, pushing tears off her cheek with the tips of his fingers.

"It's new. Do you like it? I'm thinking of wearing it to your wedding." She choked back her tears and wiped her nose on Peter's shoulder. Taryn watched in silence.

"Sister, come here. Meet my friends." Kristina put her arms around Taryn's shoulders and kissed her cheek. "Detective Jakes, Peter, this is my sister."

Detective Jakes scooped Taryn into his arms. "I've been a bit worried about you two."

"Thank you. Thank you so much. Kristina never gave up hope. She said I needed to trust you'd find us." Taryn's voice quivered, her body still shaking.

Peter wrapped his arm around Taryn's shoulders, kissing her forehead. "Come on, sweetheart. Let's let our medical team take a look at you."

The paramedics waited outside the doorway in the hall. SWAT and the medics had Tom on a stretcher to take into custody via the emergency room.

"Hey, Peter, sorry bro about earlier. You know, the heat of the moment." Jakes smiled at Peter and snuggled Kristina closer to him.

"We're good, buddy. It's all good," Peter patted Jakes's

shoulder. A police officer wrapped a warm blanket snugly around Taryn on their way out of the room.

"Taryn, wait," Kristina said. "Come home with me. I have an extra bedroom. I don't want you alone."

"Thank you, Kristina. I'm okay. I need to see my best friend. I'm sure she's been going crazy since I went missing. I'll call you tomorrow. Love you, Kristina." Taryn smiled back at Kristina and DJ.

"Love you too, sister. Call me tomorrow," Kristina said. "DJ, what about Ginny?" Kristina wanted to make sure that bitch got what she deserved.

"We got her. She's on her way to the station." DJ gently checked the cut above Kristina's eyebrow.

"Detective Jakes, paramedics are taking Drake Toucuti and George Handy to the ER. They're both in bad shape. Handy needs surgery. He's lost a lot of blood but looks like they'll both pull through. We found Ms. Van Heed's ex-husband chained to a bed, with dehydration, but he seems to be okay otherwise. I'll be downstairs." Detective Kelly smiled at Kristina. "I'm glad you're okay. You had Jakes pretty worried. Do me a favor, take care of him. He's one of the good ones."

"Thanks, Detective. I appreciate your help," DJ said. Detective Kelly nodded with her gorgeous million-dollar smile and headed out the door. "I'll call you next time I'm in Vegas." DJ flashed Kristina his adorable dimples.

"Oh, come on. That's Detective Kelly? Really, DJ." Kristina's eyes bugged out with her mouth wide open, surprised at the sight of the hot detective.

"Kristina, you said you trusted me." DJ pulled her against his body, staring her square in the eyes. With both hands, he had a firm grip on her ass.

"Yeah, I do trust you, but she's friggin' beautiful. Hell, DJ, I'd do her." Kristina smiled with a wink.

"Damn, girl, I like the way you think." DJ snapped the elastic band on her black lace panties. He took a step back to get a good look at her naughty bondage girl attire.

"What the *hell* are you wearing?" DJ unhooked the collar around Kristina's neck.

"Leather and lace, baby. Leather and lace." Kristina couldn't keep her body from shivering. She buried herself into DJ's chest.

"Damn. You're a real badass."

"Aw. You think I'm a badass?" A warm rush calmed Kristina's nerves when she looked at DJ's eyes.

DJ took one of the blankets from a paramedic and draped it over her bare shoulders. "Kristina Truly, I think you're just enough badass to get me in a whole lot of trouble."

Kristina ran her fingers through the back of DJ's hair. "Know who else is a badass? Ms. Prissy."

"She sure is." DJ said taking a deep breath for the first time since this nightmare started.

With both hands on DJ's cheeks, Kristina pulled his face to hers. "Detective Jakes, you know those great martinis you make so well—I'm going to need one, real soon." She kissed his lips with long-anticipated passion.

DJ smiled. "There are a whole lot of people who want to see you, but tonight, you're all mine." He led Kristina by the hand, out of the house, and helped her into his Tahoe. "Two great martinis coming right up, and a large pepperoni pizza, double cheese, extra pineapple, and lots of onions. I'm fringing starving."

"*Damn,* Detective, I like the way you think." Kristina cranked the heater.

DJ punched the gas. "Let's go home."

The Dying Series

If you like Stephanie Bond's fast-paced mysteries,
the wit of Janet Evanovich, and if you like a bit of
grit in a mystery, you'll love this series.
Be the first to read new releases in the Dying Series.
www.sharmynmcgraw.com

Book Two
Dying to Marry
Six Lovely Bridesmaids—and then there was one

Book Three
Dying to Divorce
A good man is hard to find—and harder to hide his body

Book Four
Dying to Love

Thank you so much for reading my novel. Readers are a
writer's dream come true. If you enjoyed *Dying to Date*
and you have a few minutes, please leave a review
wherever you purchased your copy.
I appreciate it very much. Reviews are now more
important than ever for authors.
Please email me with suggestions
Sharmyn@sharmynmcgraw.com

About the Author

Sharmyn McGraw is a native of California and resides in Orange County. She's an internationally recognized patient advocate for those affected by pituitary tumors. After her own brain surgery for Cushing's disease, she found her passion for writing. Growing up with dyslexia, she feared writing so much as a Post-it note; but after her surgery, her passion to help others was bigger than her fear of writing. Sharmyn contributed to television and health journals to shed light on the often-misunderstood pituitary gland. After twenty years in remission, she's having a blast writing about her other passion: fun, sassy mysteries featuring strong, passionate characters.

www.sharmynmcgraw.com